The

• INNOCENTS •

The
• INNOCENTS •

LILI PELOQUIN

razOr
bill

An Imprint of Penguin Group (USA) Inc.

The Innocents

RAZORBILL

Published by the Penguin Group
Penguin Young Readers Group
345 Hudson Street, New York, New York 10014, U.S.A.
Penguin Group (USA) Inc., 375 Hudson Street, New York, New York 10014, U.S.A.
Penguin Group (Canada), 90 Eglinton Avenue East, Suite 700, Toronto, Ontario, Canada
M4P 2Y3 (a division of Pearson Penguin Canada Inc.)
Penguin Books Ltd, 80 Strand, London WC2R 0RL, England
Penguin Ireland, 25 St Stephen's Green, Dublin 2, Ireland (a division of Penguin Books Ltd)
Penguin Group (Australia), 250 Camberwell Road, Camberwell, Victoria 3124, Australia
(a division of Pearson Australia Group Pty Ltd)
Penguin Books India Pvt Ltd, 11 Community Centre, Panchsheel Park,
New Delhi – 110 017, India
Penguin Group (NZ), 67 Apollo Drive, Rosedale, Auckland 0632, New Zealand
(a division of Pearson New Zealand Ltd)
Penguin Books (South Africa) (Pty) Ltd, 24 Sturdee Avenue, Rosebank, Johannesburg
2196, South Africa

Penguin Books Ltd, Registered Offices: 80 Strand, London WC2R 0RL, England

10 9 8 7 6 5 4 3 2 1

Copyright © 2012 Penguin Group (USA) Inc.

ISBN 978-1-59514-582-6

Library of Congress Cataloging-in-Publication Data is available

Printed in the United States of America

To Bill and Margie

July First

Chapter
• ONE •

Her sister's last words hung in the air: "You're just jealous because I belong here and you don't." Alice had goaded her into saying them, had pushed and pushed and pushed, but hearing them still hurt. Or would later. Right now Alice was too numb to feel pain. She was staring at Charlie's face, hot, mad, tear-streaked, and then she was staring at Charlie's back, smooth, tan, naked except for the thinnest of bikini straps and a Band-Aid just above the low-rise denim cutoffs, the flesh-colored adhesive concealing the angel's-wing tattoo. Alice closed her eyes. The sound of long hair whipping around, of bare feet clipping fast down wooden steps. When Alice opened her eyes again, she could still see Charlie's back but not the Band-Aid on it. Charlie was too far away for that, was already halfway down the beach, sand kicking up angrily behind her. She stopped at a towel, a guy and girl—lazy-limbed, drowsy-eyed, enough alike to be brother and sister—lounging on it, smoking cigarettes. Charlie flopped down beside them and started talking, arms waving around wildly. After a bit, they turned to look at Alice, leaning against the railing of the deck. Alice let them look. Then the girl put her hand on Charlie's shoulder, and the guy passed her a flask. They stood, and started walking down the beach. Alice watched. Three backs moving away from her now, not just one. Three backs wanting to be anywhere she wasn't.

A minute later they'd disappeared from view, and Alice wondered if there'd ever been a time when she'd felt so alone. She knew it was weird—beyond weird, sick, really—to blame a dead girl for her troubles, but she couldn't help herself. This was all Camilla's fault. Camilla, no longer living and yet the most alive person she knew. The most powerful, too. Camilla could come between people even if she wasn't in this world anymore. Could do it easy, without even breaking a sweat. A ghost who taunted as much as she haunted. And it was as Alice was thinking these thoughts that she heard it: the high, silvery tinkling. It might have been the wind chimes hanging above the sliding glass door, reacting to a breeze coming off the ocean. Might have been but wasn't, Alice knew. It was Camilla laughing at her from the other side of death, from beyond the grave.

Alice laid a palm flat on either side of her skull, pressed as hard as she could. Blocking her ears, though, didn't block out the sound. Just made it seem like it was coming from inside her head. *She loved her sister; she hated her sister. Her sister hated her; her sister loved her.* Alice turned and fled, running into the house so big that in it she felt like a doll in a house for humans, through the kitchen, and up the twisting staircase to her bedroom. The laughter followed her every step of the way.

Two Weeks Earlier

*A*lice felt her stomach doing this horrible churning flip-flop inside her. Motion sickness. She didn't know if it was from her shiny new stepfather driving his shiny new Mercedes so fast or from his marrying her just-as-shiny-but-not-quite-so-new mother so fast. Sometimes it seemed to Alice as if the relationship had happened in one of those montage things in a movie. It was like they met, fell in love, and got married in a matter of seconds. Go to the bathroom for a quick pee and you missed the whole thing, needed your date to give you a recap. Okay, it was a matter of months, but still. Awfully speedy.

Her stepfather's eyes behind his wafer-thin sunglasses were pointed straight ahead at the road, so she stared at him without fear of being caught. Richard. Richard Flood. Richard Flood *the Third*. Alice had never met anyone before who looked so much like his name sounded. He was tall and lean and perpetually tan. Not the tacky kind of tan you got from a bed or a bottle or from laying out— from *trying*—but the kind you got accidentally, from when you were doing something else, playing tennis or golf or sailing your Alerion Class Sloop (Richard had two of them). His hair was gray in a way that made him appear distinguished rather than old. His face was undeniably handsome, sharp-featured with deep-set blue eyes. There was something cruel about it, though. It was his mouth, Alice decided, the way it turned down at the corners when he was lost in thought.

If Alice didn't quite like Richard, she had to admit that she found him a romantic figure. Not like sexual romantic. Romantic in the old-fashioned sense, meaning mysterious and poetic. His past was so tragic: his first wife, Martha, dying of cancer, then his only child, Camilla, the same age as Alice, dying in a car accident a few months later. Richard was the man who had everything who finally had nothing—nothing truly important, at least—all of it snatched away by the indifferent hand of fate. And, not surprisingly, there was an air of sadness that hung heavy around him. You could feel it, Alice often thought. You could feel the shadows, too, creeping up on him when he wasn't looking. Only her mother seemed able to chase them away. Alice had seen the way his face would suddenly go blank in the middle of a conversation or meal, all expression vanishing from it so that it resembled a mask, something cold and hard and dead, and you knew that behind that mask he was remembering. Then her mother would say something to him, or touch his hand, and he would come back. He'd laugh or shake his head, and all at once he looked human again.

Alice watched the two of them. Richard was steering with one hand, holding her mother's hand with the other. It was still crazy for Alice to think that her funny, spunky mom, who ran around most of the time in jeans and men's shirts with the tails hanging out, hair in a messy ponytail, who claimed to prefer generic Raisin Bran to the real thing, who would only go to see a movie in a theater before six P.M. when matinee prices were still in effect, who voted for Ralph Nader in every presidential election Alice could remember, who helped start the Boston chapter of Food Not Bombs, driving one of the buses down to New Orleans two days after Hurricane Katrina passed and the Red Cross could barely get through, was now a rich man's wife. She was already starting to look the part, Alice noticed uncomfortably: linen suit so simple and understated you just knew it had to cost an arm and a leg, a subtle dab of coral lipstick, hair in a sleek bob. Then it occurred to Alice that maybe her mom had always been this way, only pretended to be the other way because there was no money and she was making the best of a bad situation. Alice didn't know why but this thought disturbed her. It was like she didn't know her own mom, like her mom had been putting on an act her whole life, like her mom really *was* a Margaret, as Richard called her, not a Maggie, as Alice's dad called her.

Her mom had met Richard in April. She was working as a caterer, a part-time job that became full-time when Alice's dad left the family just after Christmas. The party was for the Graduate School of Design at Harvard. Richard was a guest faculty member that semester. She'd just assumed he was a struggling academic with no permanent post and more brains than money when he wandered into the hectic kitchen area, pinot noir dripping down his front. He asked if she had any club soda. Feeling sorry for him, she convinced a male colleague to swap white button-downs. Little did she know that the absentminded professor standing in front of her looking sheepish in his wine-stained undershirt, the one she was scolding for blocking the bus boys' path to the dishwasher, was world famous in his field, having designed several of the most well-known silhouettes in New York's celebrated skyline, not to mention the grandson of one of the richest men in the city's history.

Apparently getting yelled at was new for Richard, and he liked it. Scratch that. And he *loved* it. It had been such a whirlwind romance. He was a guy who knew what he wanted and how to get it. His pursuit of Alice's mom had been swift and relentless. She didn't stand a chance. She was divorced on a Friday, married on a Saturday. Had left behind the falling-down duplex she'd rented for the past seventeen years in a borderline neighborhood in the working-class section of Cambridge, right on the Somerville border, to head, with her two teenage daughters in tow, to a house—one of *three* her new husband owned, the others in Aspen and Palm Beach, plus a co-op apartment on Park Avenue—in the toniest town in Connecticut. Well, on the Connecticut shore, at least.

"Take a picture, it'll last longer," whispered a voice to Alice's left.

Alice, realizing that she'd been staring the whole time, felt her cheeks burning up. She turned. It was Charlie, her younger—younger by one year and one day—sister. Charlie had been listening to her iPod, eyes closed. They were open now, though, and sparkling with mischief. She looked more and more like their mom every day. Same slinky brown, almost-black hair and eyes the color of smoke, same impish grin and curvy body. Alice had always been more like their father, light-haired and light-eyed, skinny build, brooding personality. Also like their dad, Alice was an artist, a different kind of artist, true—

he was a musician, a horn player, jazz mostly; she was a painter, oil and acrylic her specialty—but an artist just the same. Alice only hoped she had better luck than her dad. It had been a tough road for him: playing too many dives for too little money, sidemanning for bands, mainly rock ones, whose music he didn't respect, taking any paying job he could get, which meant he was out of town more than he was in it. It really bothered him that he couldn't support his family even in a modest capacity without Maggie's help. And though he never said it, Alice knew he regarded himself as a failure.

"Here we are," Richard said.

Alice glanced up as they approached a set of massive iron gates. As they passed through it, Alice thought of the other set of massive iron gates they'd recently passed through for the first time together: the set belonging to Richard's beach house.

It was a week and a half ago. They'd arrived at the house late, almost the middle of the night. Richard had insisted on driving straight down from Boston after an evening wedding at City Hall and a fast celebratory dinner following, just the four of them, plus Richard's lawyer and Richard's lawyer's wife. Alice and Charlie had both fallen asleep during the ride, their bodies tangled up in the backseat. Their mom's soft voice had roused them. "Wake up, you two, we're home," she'd said. Still cobwebby with dreams, Alice and Charlie had tumbled out of the backseat, dazedly, disorientedly. Rubbing the sleep from their eyes, they'd looked up. They'd never seen anything like it. Against the black sky Richard's house resembled nothing so much as a castle in a storybook with its turrets and pikes and high stone walls, a place bought by a man with infinite wealth, the kind of money only a king would possess, a place where a beautiful princess might live, locked up and under the spell of a wicked witch. Standing there, heads tilted nearly all the way back, Alice remembered that she and Charlie had instinctively linked hands, lacing their fingers together, as if they were afraid of getting separated, like children in a fairy tale.

The iron gates they were passing through now led to the Serenity Point Country Club, though no sign said so. Alice guessed it was such a big deal you were just supposed to know. Beyond the gates was a long, winding road made of crushed shells, cutting through a sea of emerald grass that stretched all the way out to the actual sea, the setting sun casting a golden light over everything. A golf course was in the distance. So were tennis courts and a croquet lawn, and a large clapboard house, the clubhouse, Alice was betting. There was a crew of groundskeepers, men in Bermuda shorts and polo shirts, swarming the grass with rakes and hoses and trimmers. Alice looked to Maggie, expecting her to ask Richard if the workers were unionized or provided with healthcare, her voice tight with anger.

But when Alice's mom spoke, it was to say in a voice that was anything but angry, that was, in fact, filled with awe, "Oh, Richard, it's so beautiful." Alice was surprised, and then she wasn't. Of course that's what her mom thought, Alice said to herself sourly. Well, lucky Maggie, she'd be seeing a lot of it. Too bad her two daughters had to say the same.

When her mom married Richard, it wasn't just her mom's life that changed. It was Alice's and Charlie's lives, as well. They'd both be heading to Wolcott Academy, an exclusive boarding school— "Aren't they all?" Charlie deadpanned when the news was delivered, making Alice laugh even though she was beyond mad—in Vermont in September. Alice would be entering as a senior. The cliques would already be formed, and breaking into one would be next to impossible. Plus, she already had her friends at Rindge and Latin. She and Angela had been inseparable since the second grade. She had her boyfriend, Patrick, too. They'd been on and off since sophomore year, and even though they were technically still on right now, she knew that wouldn't be for long. Long-distance relationships never worked; all they did was run up your cell phone bill. And then there was her art teacher, Mr. Delgado. It had taken her *years* to get him to notice her, give her special attention. He'd even agreed to help her put together a portfolio for the Art Institute of Boston, where he knew somebody in the admissions department. All that effort for nothing. What a waste. Charlie bitched about the transfer, too, but Alice suspected that it was out of solidarity more than anything else. Charlie wouldn't have any trouble making the adjustment. Her new life would be every bit as good as her old life, better probably. Attracting people was easy for her. It was like it didn't occur to her that it *could* be difficult, so it wasn't. Alice would be the one who wouldn't be able to cut it, to make the grade. She'd be eating her mom and sister's dust by the time the leaves changed color.

But Alice was getting ahead of herself. Before Richard shipped her and Charlie off to boarding school for a miserable fall, he was corralling them into his beach house for a miserable summer. He was insisting that they all live together for the summer "as a family." A family. What a joke. She'd known him for all of three months and had spent zero moments alone with him.

Alice was depressing herself with all this thinking. She turned to look out the window, take in the scenery, blank out her mind.

They were getting close to the clubhouse now. People were lining the road on either side. Expensive-looking people. People with pale clothes and tan skin. People who looked so different from people in Cambridge they might have been a different species. (Was it the city air that made everyone in her hometown appear gray and gritty and sickly, like they were coated in a layer of pollution?) For the millionth time that week, Alice wished that the activities she liked to do put her skin in contact with the sun, didn't all involve staying indoors. She needed protective coloring so that she could blend into this new and hostile environment. It wasn't a matter of vanity; it was a matter of survival. And then Alice noticed something strange: the people were staring at their car. Not every single one of them, but enough. *Why?* she wondered. Sure, a Mercedes G-Class SUV would get you gawked at on certain corners of Mass Ave., but here? Par for the course, she would have assumed.

A guy and girl caught Alice's eye, maybe because they were about her age, and the girl was one of the people staring. Or maybe because they looked like characters in an F. Scott Fitzgerald novel. The guy was wearing a seersucker suit, an *actual* seersucker suit, but it didn't look goofy on him or try-hard or even weird. The cut was stylish and modern, and he wore it with such a dashing, natural air that he pulled it off somehow. The face behind the dark glasses was dissipated, but attractively so. And peeking out of his breast pocket was, if she wasn't mistaken, a flask, the silver cap glinting in the sun. The boys she grew up with would definitely have him pegged as gay. And he could have been. But Alice suspected he wasn't, that, on the contrary, he was a ladies' man of the truly treacherous type. Girl crazy.

Speaking of girls, the one beside him was dressed in less old-fashioned clothes—cocktail dress the same shade of pink as bubble-gum, matching heels—but was good-looking in the same kind of old-fashioned way: high, smooth forehead, mouth that was full yet small, skin so clear and poreless it was like porcelain. The only difference between them was hair color, his dark, hers light. All that tousled blond gorgeousness should have given the girl a generous outlook on the world. Should have, but didn't. When she and Alice touched eyes, she smirked nastily and nudged the guy, pointing to Alice with her chin. For a moment, something like shock froze his features, making his arrogant, cynical face look young and almost innocent. Then the moment passed, so fast Alice wondered if she'd imagined it—did the sun just get in his eyes?—and he pulled the flask out of his pocket, raised it to her in a mock toast.

Humiliated, Alice turned her face away. She wished she'd taken up her mom on that offer to go shopping this afternoon. The fifties-style white organdy dress with the flouncy skirt that she'd bought at her favorite vintage shop in Davis Square had seemed okay back home, cool even, but here it seemed so shabby and street-urchin-y—*vintage*, she thought to herself, a fancy word for *used*—she could scarcely bear to have it touch her skin. Like she was literally wearing rags. To keep the vomit from surging up her throat, she decided to speak. Seizing on the first topic that came to mind, she said, "So, Richard, I know this is a country club, not a yacht club, but do you keep your boats here?"

He didn't say anything. Did he not hear her? she wondered. But how was that possible? His ear was less than two feet away from her mouth.

When it was clear he wasn't going to respond, her mom stepped in, tried to make a save. "Neither of my girls has spent much time on boats. But Charlie loves the water. Just loves it. In fact, I think she might be part fish. She could swim before she could walk. We used to go to Singing Beach in Manchester when the girls were . . ."

As Maggie droned on, Alice stared at the back of Richard's neck. What was his deal? She had such a hard time getting a read on him. He was always polite to her and Charlie, but she sometimes thought he hated them. No, not hated. *Hated* was the wrong word, too passionate, and he regarded them above all else *dis*passionately. As obstacles to be overcome, the things standing between him and what he wanted most—their mother. Occasionally Alice would catch him watching her, an eager, determined look in his eye, and she could practically hear the wheels spinning in his brain: How should she be handled? What would be the best, most effective method? The one that would require the minimum effort and yield the maximum result? (No wonder his architecture firm was so wildly successful— he was such a good and efficient problem solver.) It was like, Alice felt, he was nice to her without actually liking her, which was unsettling, to say the least.

The car had finally reached the parking lot behind the clubhouse. A valet attendant, a young guy with a head of curly dark hair that looked like it had been combed hurriedly, probably with his fingers, came up to the window, knocked on the glass. Richard jumped in his seat a little. And Alice, with something of a shock, realized that he was nervous. Thinking about it, though, she understood she shouldn't have been shocked. He wasn't walking into a new situation the way she and her sister and her mom were, but he almost was. He hadn't been back in Serenity Point since Camilla died. Yes, he'd been in Serenity Point all this past week and a half, but he'd been holed up in his beach house pretty much the entire time. More like holed up in his room. (As he and Maggie loved to remind her and Charlie in this giggly, nauseatingly teenage way, they hadn't gone on a proper honeymoon.) So he hadn't yet reentered Serenity Point society. But that would all change tonight at the annual summer solstice party, the official kickoff of the season.

No wonder he was too distracted to talk about boats. It had only been a little over a year since he'd lost Martha, not even a year since he'd lost Camilla. The wounds were still fresh.

In spite of her personal feelings for Richard, which Alice would characterize as undecided leaning toward negative, she was sorry for him, she really was. But she didn't know how to express her sympathy. The loss he suffered was so great—so devastatingly, monstrously, unimaginably great—that maybe there were no words *to* express her sympathy, and clearly he didn't want her to. It's not as if he'd ever broached the topic with her. No, it was Maggie who had told her and Charlie his sad story, using a hushed voice that warned the girls off asking any questions at the end or holding out hope for further discussion. The subject was introduced, and then, just like that, it was closed. The sick part was, all this silence, the heavy off-limits vibe surrounding Martha's and Camilla's deaths, only made Alice more curious.

Richard handed his keys to the smiling valet, and they all exited the car. They'd just started for the clubhouse when Charlie said, "Oops, I left my bag in the backseat. Don't want to forget that. It has my fake ID in it." Off Richard's look: "Just kidding. Not about having a fake ID, but about using a fake ID. Tonight, anyway."

As Charlie opened the door and leaned in, her short skirt rode up her thighs, slim but rounded and muscular at the same time. Her camisole rode up, too, exposing the angel's wing inked on her lower back. Alice hated that tattoo. Had begged Charlie not to get it on the grounds that it was tacky and low-rent and that she'd regret it later, but Alice couldn't stand to have anyone looking at her sister the way Richard was looking at her now.

Alice wanted to step between them, block Richard's view. It was too late, though.

Richard said to Charlie, his mouth tight, "Did you bring a jacket?"

Charlie looked at him over her shoulder, surprised. "A jacket? No."

Hastily, Maggie slipped out of hers. "Here you go, sweetheart. It'll look cute with the skirt you're wearing."

Charlie, still confused, said, "No thanks, mom."

"Charlotte," Richard said. "I'd like it if you'd put it on."

Recognition dawned on Charlie's face as Richard stared her down. She stared him down right back.

Alice looked on as the silence stretched. There was all this spit in her mouth but she couldn't swallow, could barely breathe. Her sister was the only truly fearless person she knew, which made Alice, weirdly, afraid for her.

Finally Charlie's lips flattened into a smirk. "Well, *Dick*," she said (Charlie hated, *hated*, being called by her given name), "I'd like not to die of heat stroke. It's June, a little too warm for the layered look."

"Just tie it around your waist, honey," Maggie said.

Charlie spun around, ready, Alice could see, to just unload. Then she caught the pleading look in her mom's eye. Her expression softened. She knew as well as Alice did what a hard time their mom had had when their dad left, how tough it had been financially and emotionally. Richard was a godsend. The worry lines had all but disappeared from her mom's face, and when she laughed it was that full-throated laugh that they hadn't heard in so long. Without a word Charlie did as asked.

"We're all ready then," Richard said. And when no one contradicted him: "Good, let's do this."

He started toward the clubhouse, Maggie right alongside him, matching him stride for stride. As soon as he was out of earshot, Charlie cocked her hip and snapped the strap of her thong at him. The valet guy laughed as he got in the car. Charlie, not realizing that she had an audience other than her sister, looked over at him in surprise. She smiled.

"You think he knows where we can buy weed?" she asked as he drove off, expertly negotiating the hairpin turn at the top of the road.

"The night hasn't started and you're already feeling the need to get high?"

"The weed isn't for me. It's for Richard. That guy's wound so tight. He needs to relax. I figured I'd bake some into his morning scones."

"He eats brioche," Alice said, with a laugh. She was so happy to have Charlie with her. There was no way she would have been able to face this party, face any of it—Richard, fembot Maggie, Serenity Point—without her. In fact, that had been the best part of the last ten days, this period of forced isolation: she and Charlie had gotten even closer. They'd always been close, close even for sisters, maybe because they'd shared a bedroom all their lives or maybe because their personalities were so different that they'd never been competitive, engaged in any of that rivalry stuff that Alice knew from friends was so common among siblings. Still, back in Cambridge, each girl had her own social set, her own interests, activities that took up her time and attention. Stuck at Richard's, they were truly stuck, since they had no car. (Richard was strangely touchy about his Mercedes, like possessive of it, and town was miles away and across a bridge, too far to walk. Plus Alice and Charlie didn't want to push him, suspecting that his aversion to teenagers behind the wheel had everything to do with the manner in which his daughter had died. Illogical but understandable.) Consequently, they'd been thrown back on one another for amusement and company, Richard and Maggie being totally wrapped up in each other.

Charlie had said it was like being marooned on a desert island. They'd both complained, but it had been sort of fun, too. They'd spent hours exploring the house, the portraits of generation after generation of stern and stately Floods—male Floods in Civil War uniforms, female Floods in hoop skirts, Flood children in banana curls and lace-up boots—that hung from the walls, spying on their every move. It was a place steeped in the past. But not, Alice and Charlie soon realized, the recent past. They couldn't find a single photo, a single memento, a single strand of hair belonging to Martha or Camilla, and they'd really looked. Well, half-assed looked. Charlie got bored easily, and they had neither the opportunity nor the nerve to venture inside Richard's office or his and Maggie's bedroom. Nevertheless, the lack of Martha and Camilla's presence in the house was so total as to make it glaring. It was like they weren't just absent, they were conspicuously absent, so absent that, weirdly, their absence became a kind of presence.

Charlie snorted. "Of course Richard eats brioche. What an asshole."

"Labor Day," Alice said, in a warning voice.

"Labor Day," Charlie repeated, with a sigh.

Labor Day was the code they'd come up with, the words they'd agreed to use to remind each other and themselves that this situation, no matter how bad it seemed, no matter how unbearable it got, had a definite end date: Labor Day weekend, after which they'd pack up for Wolcott Academy. And after Wolcott Academy, it would be college, their own lives, freedom. If they could make it to Labor Day without screwing things up for their mom, they'd done their daughterly duty.

Alice fixed the collar of Charlie's shirt, then slipped her fingers through Charlie's. And together they walked toward the clubhouse, their mom and stepdad waiting for them at the lip of the door.

*A*s they crossed the threshold, Charlie let go of Alice's hand so she could tug at the hem of her skirt. If a silence could be loud, this one was. Deafening almost. As soon as they stepped inside the clubhouse, all conversation stopped. All activity, too. Everyone seemed to freeze in place. *My skirt's not* that *mini*, Charlie thought. And then she realized that the hush was on account of her stepfather and mom, all eyes in the room turned to the new couple. Was it really so shocking that he'd gotten married again? Charlie wondered. Was he not supposed to? Was his mourning period not long enough or something? Jesus, she said to herself, his wife had died more than a year back—forever ago.

And then the silence was broken when a woman who was too everything, too thin, too tan, too blond, just too *too*, stepped forward. "Rich*aaard*," she said musically, "I heard you were back in town, you bad boy. A whole week. Why haven't you come around to see me? This must be your lovely new wife." She extended an emaciated hand, talon-like and tipped in red, and wrapped it around her mom's. "How do you do? Well, obviously you do very well. Better than very well. Richard's quite the catch. I'm Muffie Buckley. *Such* a pleasure. You must let me introduce you around. I'd, of course, like to keep this strictly *vous et nous*, but I won't be forgiven if I monopolize you. Come on. You too, Richard."

And with that, her mom and Richard were whisked off, disappearing into the crowd, and the party started up again: conversations resuming, champagne reflowing, servers retracing invisible figure-eight-like paths around the room, trays of finger food balanced deftly on the fingertips of their upraised arms. Charlie took the opportunity to scope out the scene, the white tablecloths, the high arched ceilings, the French windows opening out onto a rose garden. If she were in a good mood, which she wasn't particularly, she would call it charming, tasteful, elegant. If she were in a bad mood—which, *ding ding ding ding ding*—that face-off with Richard had upset her more than she'd let on—she would call it stuffy, pretentious, uptight. The guests were mostly her mom and Richard's age. Not all, though. And she zeroed in on the under-twenty-ones. There was a cluster of them in the far corner of the room, and at the center of this cluster was a bombshell-looking blonde, perfect face, perfect body, slim-hipped and long-legged, flanked by two lesser bombshell-looking blondes (less blond, less bomb-y). She'd found her target.

Charlie turned to her sister. Alice was busy staring at some dumb photograph, doing her wallflower act, trying to blend into the scenery. The problem with Alice, Charlie thought and not for the first time, was that she didn't know how pretty she was. Or rather, how pretty she'd become: a full moody mouth, fat-lipped with a sulk to it; clear white skin; a long willowy body. She'd developed a little behind schedule. Was flat-chested and gawky for all of middle school and the first couple years of high school, nose wrong for her face somehow, eyes too big for it, cheeks thin and kind of waxy. It's like her looks came too late to do her any good, after her confidence had been formed, and her identity as a shy bookworm and weirdo artist girl had been established. Charlie was both sympathetic to her plight and impatient with it.

She took off her mom's jacket, tossed it on the back of an empty chair. Then she said, "Come on" to Alice.

"Wait," Alice said. "I want to show you something, a photograph I just saw."

"You can point out its artistic merits to me later."

"No, it's not its artistic merits I want to show you, it's—"

Charlie cut her off: "Later. First we're going to go introduce ourselves."

"To who?"

Charlie looked over at Blonde Bombshell.

Alice followed the line of her sister's gaze. The color drained out of her cheeks. "Wow," she said. "You don't believe in working your way up, do you?"

Charlie shrugged. "They say that if you're the new kid on the playground, you should go up to the biggest bully, the alpha male, punch him right in the mouth."

"Who's they? That's the stupidest thing I've ever heard. And besides, in case you haven't noticed, we're not on a playground, and she's no alpha male."

"She's a queen bee, though, the female equivalent. What's the matter, Allie? Scared?"

"Yes, and if you had any sense, you would be, too."

Charlie sighed. "Look, are you going to come on your own, or do I have to use force?"

When Alice didn't respond, Charlie reached for an abandoned champagne glass on the table beside her, downed its contents in a single gulp. Then she grabbed her sister by the wrist and began dragging her across the room. As she got closer, within feet rather than yards, she saw that the blonde wasn't as good-looking as she'd first thought. Her chin was a hair too long, giving her face a slightly horsey quality, and that gave Charlie a bump of confidence. Alice was wrong about Charlie. Charlie did get scared, and by the same things that scared Alice. The difference between them was, Charlie refused to give in to that fear. She did the opposite, in fact, went after the fear, took it head-on. Which is exactly what she was doing right now.

Charlie had to stand in front of the blonde for several seconds before the blonde deigned to notice her.

"Yes," the blonde finally said, weirdly addressing Alice rather than Charlie. Her voice was everything Charlie expected it to be: cool, disdainful, faintly bored.

"Hi. I wanted to introduce myself. I'm Charlie Flaherty. This is my sister, Alice."

"Cybill Buckley."

Again, the girl—Cybill—addressed Alice rather than Charlie. Another humiliation tactic, Charlie supposed. A twist on the old pretending-the-other-person-didn't-exist routine. She wanted to take Cybill's face in her hand, physically turn it her way. "Nice to meet you, Cybill. We came with Richard Flood."

Cybill furrowed her brow like she was searching her memory bank. "Oh, that's right. You're the substitutes. Mr. Flood got two daughters to take the place of one. Is that in case one of you doesn't work out? He'll have an extra on hand?"

One of the knockoff blondes flanking her tittered appreciatively.

"Can't be too careful," Charlie said cheerfully, smiling like she hadn't registered the insult.

"So, wife number two must be your mother."

Charlie nodded. "Yup. And old muffdiver over there, she must be yours."

A sharp intake of breath from the other knockoff blonde.

Now Charlie had Cybill's full attention. Through clenched, braces-perfect teeth, she said, "My mom's name is Muffie."

Charlie, still smiling, voice still cheerful: "Oh, my bad. I just assumed Muffie was short for something. So, is there anything stronger around here to drink than champagne?"

For a long beat, Cybill just stared at Charlie.

Then knockoff number one said, "There's liquid Drano in the utility closet. Why don't you go chug some?"

Cybill turned to the girl. "Sasha," she said sweetly, "shut the fuck up." Then she turned back to Charlie. "Follow me. Let's see if we can't scare up something with a slightly higher alcohol content. Alice, you come, too. Sasha, Bianca"—the blonde knockoffs perking up at hearing their names—"hold this." She tossed her purse at them. Without waiting to see if either girl caught it, she pivoted on the tip of her pink, extremely high heel—her face might have been a bit of a let down, Charlie thought, but her legs sure weren't—and began walking in the opposite direction.

Charlie turned to her sister and shrugged. "You want to go with her? Could be fun."

Alice looked at Charlie, then she tilted her head to the side and pressed her lips together, jutting the lower one out slightly so that her chin dimpled: sad clown face. Alice and Charlie had been making this face at each other for as long as Charlie could remember, and though neither girl could recall who invented it, it was definitely Alice who had given it its name. The emotion it expressed was both unhappiness and an apology for that unhappiness, like you knew you were supposed to be pleased by something, by some person or situation, but for whatever reason, you weren't, hence, you were a sad clown.

Charlie laughed. "Oh, come on. It's not like we have to take any of this seriously. It's not like this is real life for us."

Alice chewed the inside of her cheek. Looked at her sister, looked away.

"Labor Day, Allie," Charlie said softly.

When Alice nodded glumly back, Charlie tossed her purse to Bianca since Sasha was already holding one. Then she led Alice by the hand over to Cybill, on the other side of the room, waiting for them, and looking none too delighted about it.

Wow, Alice thought, guess Charlie was right about that punch-in-the-mouth thing. Cybill acted like a bitch, and then Charlie acted like an even bigger one. Now Cybill was still acting like a bitch, only not to Charlie and Alice. To Charlie and Alice she was going out of her way to be nice. Nice for her, anyway.

"Not that this is going to mean anything to you," Cybill said, as she weaved her way through the sea of white bucks and pastel plaid bow ties, frosted lipsticks and ballet flats, "but I'm looking for a guy named Jude."

"A dude named Jude," Charlie said. "Okay."

"He always keeps a little something on hand. But if I can't find him, you're just going to have to wait for the party to start killing brain cells."

"We're at the party."

"No, we're at the geezer party. I mean the real party, which begins as soon as this one ends."

With a subtle tilt of her head, Cybill gestured to the couple they were passing on the left. The woman was pretty, underweight, brittle-looking. The man was heavy, but in a way that conveyed prosperity and success, not laziness and loserdom. Like he'd gained the weight not from sitting on the couch drinking beer and watching reruns, but from eating the very best cuts of meat and drinking the very best vintages of wine in the very best restaurants. His red, jowly face and shellacked-looking thatch of reddish-brown hair rang a faint bell. So did his loud, braying voice. He was trying to get the woman to eat a crab cake. "Come on, Bits," he said, holding the fork to her mouth like she was a baby in a highchair, "just take a little bite. One teensy-weensy bite for me."

The woman smiled coyly, shook her head.

"That's lieutenant governor Billy Devlin and his wife, Betsey," Cybill said. "Also known as Jude's mom and dad."

"Oh yeah," Charlie said, her face lighting up in recognition. "From Massachusetts. Our mother campaigned against him. Not that he should take it personally. She hates Republicans on principle."

"You might want to tell her to keep her preference on the down-low around here."

"I'll tell her, but she won't listen."

"Self-preservation isn't really her thing," Alice added.

Charlie laughed, said with affection, "No, it is not. Hey, if we can't find the son, let's hit up the mom. Her pupils are so dilated her eyes are almost all black. Whatever she's on, I want some."

"Valium or Xanax, most likely," Cybill said. "She spent the spring detoxing in a luxury rehab facility in Sonoma Valley."

"Well, looks like she's going to be spending the summer de-detoxing in the Valley of the Dolls."

"Word is Mr. Devlin's been working late a lot. Has been spotted in the company of a pretty intern, too. That's probably what's got her popping pills again."

"He's paying attention to her now."

"Damage control. Can't afford to get her too pissed off. It's her family that has all the money. If she divorces him, he can kiss his political career good-bye." Cybill was speaking to Charlie and Alice in a low, for-their-ears-only voice. Then, in a normal one, she said: "Hi, Mr. Devlin. Hi, Mrs. Devlin. You don't know where I can find Jude, do you?"

Mr. Devlin took the crab-cake-laden fork away from his wife's mouth, popped it in his own. "What's that boy of mine done now?"

"It's not what he's done, it's what I'm going to get him to do."

"So long as it doesn't end up in the papers, it's okay by me. I haven't seen him since we got here."

"Fat lot of help you are."

"Good luck to you girls," Mr. Devlin said cheerfully. Then, when his wife's head was safely turned, he gave them a sort of leering wink. Alice was grossed out, but Cybill and Charlie just laughed, so she guessed it wasn't a big deal.

Cybill and Charlie moved on, resuming the search. Alice followed. Charlie shot her an annoyed look over her shoulder, telling Alice with her eyes that she should walk *with* her and Cybill, not behind. Alice pretended not to notice.

"Who's he?" Charlie said, pointing to an Italian-looking guy, the only man at the party in a dark suit. He had slicked-back hair, was wearing a lot of jewelry. "He looks like a gangster."

"Probably because he is. Bianca's dad. He owns a bunch of restaurants and nightclubs in the tri-state area. I'm sure he's into other stuff, too, but his official title is restaurateur. And behind him is Sasha's mother, Rebecca Menken." Alice saw a thin, severe-looking woman with jet-black hair talking to two men in boat shirts and espadrilles. "Rebecca runs the biggest PR firm in New York. When I graduate from college, I want her to give me a job. That's why I let her sniveling daughter be one of my minions. The men she's with are Sasha's dad, also her business partner, and Sasha's dad's husband. Don't ask."

"I won't," said Charlie agreeably.

"And that over there is the van Strattens and their son, Tommy."

A server stepped into Alice's line of sight, blocking her view. It was several seconds before he moved on. When he did, Alice could scarcely believe her eyes. Standing in between a handsome middle-aged couple was the boy from the photograph, the one she'd tried to show Charlie a few minutes ago, the one she couldn't stop staring at. The boy was a little older now, a little taller, and more filled out. But he had the same soft brown hair, and eyes to match, the same long, clean limbs. In the picture he was on a tennis court. The white collared shirt he was wearing was offset by vertical navy stripes, thick and widely spaced. His right hand hung loose at his side, his fingers gripping the bill of a navy cap. His face was unforgettable somehow. Not because it was handsome—though it was, very—but because of the expression on it. He looked so purely happy, his smile ear-to-ear, practically jumping off his lips. Maybe he was happy because he was being presented with a trophy, large and shining gold in the sun, or maybe he was happy because the girl he had his arm wrapped around, his partner, was so beautiful . . . and so familiar. An actress? Alice had wondered. She was certainly good-looking enough to be an actress. She had the poise of a professional, too, of someone used to having many eyes on her and yet behaving as if she were unobserved, not a trace of shyness or self-consciousness.

Alice was lost in these thoughts when the boy suddenly glanced up. Their gazes met, and the way he reacted, it was as if he'd been looking at a picture of *her* moments before. They stared at each other, stared and stared. He couldn't seem to pull his eyes away from hers anymore than she could pull hers away from his. It felt to Alice like the entire world had ground to a halt. And then his mom laid a hand on his wrist, and with a start he looked down at her.

Alice turned and saw that Cybill and Charlie were several feet ahead, and that Cybill's lips were moving. Not wanting to miss anything, Alice ran to catch up.

". . . and he'll be starting at Harvard in the fall," Cybill concluded.

Charlie craned her neck to take another look. "So, he's the brainy type. Not too hard to look at either."

"He's perfect if you like them perfect. National Merit scholar, was one of the top crew recruits in the country, organized the Oxfam hunger banquet at his school, and look," she said, as he slipped an arm around the older woman's shoulders, "he's even nice to his mom."

"A real Boy Scout."

"A Boy Scout with a jailbird for a dad."

Charlie's eyebrows climbed up her forehead. "Jailbird? You mean that extremely nice-looking, respectable-looking gentleman standing next to him? The one in the Top-Siders and the pink polo?"

"I should have said soon-to-be jailbird. He's a concierge doctor. For now, at least."

"A concierge doctor?" Charlie repeated, confused. "I thought a concierge was the guy in a hotel, the one who, like, asks you if you're having a nice stay."

"Yeah, it is. But it's also a kind of doctor. They're not affiliated with any hospitals, and they run what are called boutique practices. The way it works is that they have private patients who pay them a certain amount of money per year—in Dr. van Stratten's case a lot of money—and then they give these patients their personal cell numbers, pager numbers, all that. So, the patient can reach them at any time, day or night, and they have to come running. They're at the patient's beck and call, basically."

"How do you know all this?"

"He's my mom's doctor, and she calls him constantly. Well, she did call him constantly. She's looking for a new doctor to phone-stalk now, hit up for Ambien prescriptions at weird times."

"Why's he going to go to jail?"

"He's on trial right now for malpractice. A woman's claiming he prescribed the wrong drugs for her husband, made him sicker or something, like almost-dead sick. Word is, he's going to lose. Anyway, he was pretty much the doctor of everybody in town. Now, people are starting to distance themselves."

"Poor Tommy," Alice said, the words out of her mouth before she could stop them, realizing, as soon as they hit the air, how strange they sounded.

Cybill evidently didn't think they sounded strange. She just nodded and sighed and said, "Yeah." Then she said, "Okay, obviously Jude doesn't want to be found, which means he must be doing something truly despicable. It doesn't matter. This'll be over in less than an hour now. Then we can get as fucked up as we want. Might as well get as much of a head start as we can with the champagne."

"Sounds like an excellent plan to me," Charlie said. She took a quick look around to see if any eyes were on her, then grabbed a half-drunk glass off a nearby table.

Cybill stopped her before she put her mouth to the lipstick-y rim. "You don't have to take leftovers, you know. You can get a fresh glass."

"I can?"

"Nobody's parents around here care if they drink, so long as they don't wind up failing out of school or walking around with puke in their hair. You know, embarrassing themselves."

"Wow, okay," Charlie said.

"Shall we go over to the champagne station?"

"Sounds good. Right, Alice?"

Alice said that it did. Then she took one last look at Tommy, his arm wrapped protectively around his mom now, his head bent forward so he could more easily hear what she was saying, and turned around to follow Charlie and Cybill. As she did, she saw something that stopped her cold: it was Richard and *her* mom, Maggie, standing with the Devlins, Richard in conversation with her, Maggie in conversation with him. What surprised Alice wasn't the sight of her mom talking to a Republican politician. Alice would have expected her to seek him out, demand that he justify himself, explain why he'd supported the governor cutting funding for inner-city schools, or why the needle-exchange program in their neighborhood had been shut down last month. No, what surprised Alice was the sight of her mom talking to a Republican politician and *enjoying* herself. And yet that's exactly what she appeared to be doing, laughing, touching his arm, smiling up at him, showing every tooth in her mouth. Maybe, Alice thought uncomfortably, she didn't want to embarrass Richard on his first night back, make a scene. Not making a scene was one thing, but acting so, so . . . kiss-assy was another.

Alice looked over at Charlie to see if Charlie was noticing the same thing she was. But Charlie's attention was on Cybill. Then she turned to Alice. "You coming?" she said, impatiently.

Alice nodded. She couldn't resist a final backward glance, though. Mr. Devlin was now helping her mom remove the toothpick from the watermelon and prosciutto appetizer on her plate, inserting the toothpick in his own mouth, stripping it of stray shreds

of meat with teeth that were very white and very sharp, then dropping it on a passing waiter's tray. Trying to shake the disturbing image, Alice followed Charlie and Cybill over to the bar. The image,
though, wouldn't shake.

Chapter
• FOUR •

*I*t looked like a summer party back home, Alice thought, except it was around a bonfire at the beach, instead of around a cooler in a parking lot or around a keg on someone's parents' bird-shit-covered rooftop: people were laughing and talking, boys were eyeing girls, girls were eyeing boys, joints were being passed around, music was being cranked. Even the drink of choice was the same, vodka and Red Bull, though in Cambridge it was Seagram's and regular Red Bull; here it was Ketel One and sugar-free.

At one point, the outdoor party was bigger than the indoor one had been. Alice didn't know where all the kids had come from. Friends of guests and friends of friends of guests, she supposed. That or they'd marched out of the sea. Cybill, who acted like the unofficial hostess, had introduced her to a bunch of the new people, girls whose names all seemed to be flowers and boys with first names that sounded like last ones. She couldn't keep any of them straight, stopped trying after a while. Now, it was past midnight, and, maybe because the night had started so early, things were starting to die down.

Alice wasn't talking to anyone at the moment, but she didn't feel weird about it. On the contrary, she felt relaxed and at ease, separate from her surroundings yet a part of them, too. Mostly she listened in on the back-from-the-school-year conversations going on all around her, people reconnecting after a ten-month gap, whooping greetings at each other, recalling past adventures, predicting future ones. Charlie would come over every twenty minutes or so to check in on her, make sure she was okay, yell at her for still being on her first drink, then return to what she'd been doing before: making fun of the other girls with Cybill, talking back to the boys, being her usual bright-eyed, sharp-tongued, laughing self.

Sometimes Alice would catch people looking at her. But the looks were curious, not judgmental, *who might you be?* as opposed to *who the fuck are you?* A couple of them even came up to her, tapped her on the shoulder, asked her if she went to St. Augie's or Prentice Hall—everyone here seemed to go to one or the other, no matter that they came from up and down the East Coast—and then lost interest when she said no. Not lost interest in a mean way, more in an apologetic one, moving on with a half smile, a rueful shrug of the shoulders.

Tommy van Stratten had shown up in the last hour, almost when Alice had given up hope. She was watching him without being obvious about it. (At least she *hoped* she wasn't being obvious about it.) He talked to people when they came up to him—and a lot of them did, guys as well as girls—but mostly he seemed content to keep to himself, sitting by the fire sipping a beer, digging his toes into the sand. He'd gotten even handsomer since that photo in the clubhouse had been taken. His face was less round than it was before, more chiseled, his hair shorter, and his body lean rather than slender. The biggest difference, though, was in the aura he gave off. Where was that laughing, happy boy? He seemed so serious now. And sad. *Why sad?* Alice wondered. Because his dad's legal troubles were weighing so heavily on him? Or because he no longer had his arm around that beautiful girl? A few times Alice thought—hoped— he might be sneaking looks at her, too, but then decided it was just absence of mind, him flicking occasional random glances out at the ocean behind her head. The lack of attention he was paying her was disappointing. For a fast second, he'd seemed as taken with her as she had been with him.

Soon the party wasn't just dying, it was dead: the music switched off, the fire mostly burned out, the voices dropping, not just in number but in volume, too, so that the surf was the loudest sound that could be heard.

"Okay," said Cybill after a while, "the fire needs to be put out."

Everyone seemed to agree, but nobody did anything about it, being too drunk and comfortable and generally lazy-feeling, reluc- tant to start the long trudge back to the cars.

And then someone said, "Who's that?"

Alice looked up. A figure was approaching them from down the beach. There was no moon that night, and the fire wasn't throwing off much light anymore, so it was impossible to tell who the figure belonged to, to tell even if it was male or female, young or old. At last, though, it emerged from the darkness and someone—a differ- ent someone—yelled, "Hey, Jude!"

That prompted a chorus of *Hey Jude*s, a few of them even sung to the tune of the Beatles' song.

Alice squinted. It was the guy she'd seen walking with Cybill before the summer solstice party, the one who'd toasted her with his flask. He was still in the seersucker suit and sunglasses. Still had that silver flask sticking out of his breast pocket, too. But judging from the way he was walking, it was quite a bit lighter than it had been earlier in the evening. As he staggered toward Cybill, giving wide birth to the bonfire, his wingtips sinking deep into the sand, Alice was once again struck by how much he and Cybill resembled one another: the clear skin, the face that made Alice think of an old-fashioned doll, his a shade prettier than hers because the long chin looked aristocratic on a guy rather than just too big as it did on a girl. Alice would have them for sister and brother if she didn't know better.

Or not.

When he reached Cybill, he moved in for the embrace. She turned her face to his cheek, like she was going to lightly brush it with her lips, distracted because she was saying something to Charlie, but he surprised her, met her lips with his own. It was a real kiss he was giving her—messy and long and with lots of slippery, thrusting tongue. Cybill neither returned it, nor rejected it, just passively took it. And when it finally ended, there was no expression on her face. She just calmly stepped back, finished the sentence she'd been in the middle of delivering, barely skipping a beat. Alice would have assumed that she was as cool on the inside as she was on the outside, except Alice saw her hand uncurl by her side, saw the crescent-shaped divots in her palm, gouged out by her nails: four little moons of pain, one with a drop of blood trickling out of it.

"Aren't they, like, first cousins or something?" a girl behind Alice whispered. "That's sick!"

Jude turned to the girl, his sunglasses crooked on his face. He took them off, slipped them in his pants pocket, then brought his lips together in a loud, satisfied smack. "Hey, Daisy, if it isn't sick, what's the point? You know what I mean? And, actually, Cybill and I are only second cousins, and once removed at that. So, sadly, it's not as sick as could be hoped for. It's not even illegal in most states."

Instinctively, Alice glanced over at Tommy. His face was turned down toward the sand, but there was anger in the set of his jaw, in the muscle that twitched by his mouth. And when Jude flopped down beside him and he raised his head, Alice saw the gleam of hatred in his eyes.

"Mind if I have a sip of your beer?" Jude said to Tommy.

Tommy stiffly passed him the can, then in a tight voice said, "Have the whole thing. Party's over. I'm going home."

"But the party can't be over. I *am* the party and I just got here."

"Then you got here late." Tommy made to stand but Jude grabbed his arm, pulled him back down.

"I know," said Jude. "Let's play a game. How about, I Never? What do you say, Crash? One round, then I'll go to bed like a good boy, no fussing, no fighting."

Tommy didn't reply, but he didn't try to get up and leave again, either. Tentatively people began moving closer to the fire, dropping cross-legged into the sand.

When everyone was gathered around, Jude clapped his hands, rubbed the palms together gleefully. "Why don't you do the honors, Crash, and go first?"

Tommy didn't say anything, didn't even look up.

"You know how to play, don't you? It's easy. You make a simple but true statement that begins with the words *I never*. For example, you could say, *I never made a girl scream in the good way.* And the people in the circle who have done what you haven't, like me for instance, would take a drink. Get the idea?"

Tommy continued to ignore Jude and glower into the fire.

"Ok, Crash," Jude said amiably, "we'll come back to you after we've warmed up a bit. Don't worry. You'll get the hang of it."

Jude let his eye start traveling around the circle. This guy scared Alice. There was something wild about him, something potentially out of control. And her heart jumped into her throat when his gaze stopped on her, and she saw the focus burning through his blurry-drunk eyes. He took a breath like he was about to speak, but didn't speak. The silence was terrible. And then, at last, he said, "It's the ghost."

Simultaneously relieved and upset—she wasn't *that* pale, was she?—she said, "Actually, I'm, um, Alice." She hated the way her voice sounded: girlish, nervous, eager to please.

"And where are you from, Um Alice?"

Again she flailed around for a response. (Another reason she needed a tan: so she could camouflage her emotions. Blushes were so glaringly visible on pale skin.) Finally Cybill responded for her: "She's from here now. Mr. Flood just married her mom."

Alice's attention was momentarily hijacked when she saw a look of what might have been pain flash in Tommy's eyes. Pain or a trick of light? Before she could determine which, Jude was addressing her again.

"Before we start the game, can I ask you a question?"

She nodded cautiously.

"Is that dress for real?"

"What?"

"I couldn't help noticing that it's white. False advertising or not?" When Alice just stared at him, puzzled, he said gently, "I'm asking you if you're a virgin or not."

She blinked at him as she considered what answer to give. Here was the true one: she and Patrick had come close a couple of times but she'd never been able to quite go through with it, had always made him stop at the last moment. (It wasn't that anything felt wrong with Patrick, not exactly. It was just that it hadn't felt totally right either. To Alice it seemed as if sex with Patrick would be an extension of the fondness she felt for him. And she didn't want to feel fondness when she had sex for the first time; she wanted to feel passion.) Not that she was about to tell Jude the true one. Not that she knew *what* to tell him. It was too late to tell him to go fuck himself, play it like she was outraged and wouldn't justify such an obnoxious query with a response. She had to tell him something, though; time was passing. She opened her mouth, but no sound came out. She heard a few snickers, then a few more. Her blush was so strong now she felt as if her life were in jeopardy, as if her face were about to burst into actual flames.

Then, from the other side of the bonfire, Charlie said, "Sure she's a virgin. She's got to balance me out."

Alice had never been so grateful in her life as when Jude's eyes swung away from her face and over to Charlie's. "And who are you?" he asked politely.

"I'm her sister, Charlie."

"You're depraved enough for the both of you, that's what you're telling me, Charlie?"

"More than enough."

"You earned that tramp stamp, huh?" Alice didn't know how he could see the angel's-wing tattoo unless he had X-ray vision. Charlie's halter was pulled all the way down, plus her back was to him. Had he been watching them earlier? Could he have been at the summer solstice party without them noticing?

If he was trying to embarrass Charlie, it wasn't going to work. Holding his eye, she said, "Every last drop of sleazy ink."

He laughed, was about to say something in response when Tommy stood up. "I've had enough of this shit. You've asked all the questions you're going to ask tonight, Jude."

Jude stuck out his lower lip in a pout. "Oh come on, Crash. Just a few more. I have an inquiring mind."

"Go ahead, ask away," Tommy said. "But it's going to be tough to talk with your teeth down your throat."

The boys stared at each other, eyes hard, muscles tensed. Alice couldn't help but be struck by how good-looking they both were: Jude's features technically better, but too delicate and small-boned for her tastes. She much preferred Tommy's more rugged brand of handsomeness. It was a clean, healthy kind of handsome, the kind of handsome meant for sunshine and outdoors. There was something decadent about Jude's beauty, like he was beautiful almost the way a girl was beautiful. For a moment it looked as if the two were going to come to blows. Then Jude lifted a hang-on finger. A second later, puke exploded from his mouth, narrowly missing Tommy's bare feet, landing on the fire. And a second after that, Jude dropped to the sand, unconscious. It was a miracle: a KO without a single punch being thrown.

After that, the party really did end. Once the bonfire was thoroughly doused, covered in sand and seawater, everyone began the trek up the beach, back to the lot by the clubhouse where the cars were parked. Everyone, that is, except Jude. He got left in the heap he collapsed in, though Cybill did roll him onto his stomach so he wouldn't choke on his own vomit, assuming that there was any vomit left to choke on. She also relieved him of his flask, which apparently wasn't as empty as Alice had guessed because Cybill and Charlie kept passing it back and forth as they walked, doing their level best to shake off the sobriety that Jude and Tommy's near fisticuffs had forced on them.

When they were in sight of the parking lot, Cybill turned to Bianca, that night's designated driver—designated by Cybill, of course—and said, "You and Sasha wait by the car. Charlie, Alice, and I are going to make a quick pit stop."

"Where?" said Charlie. "It's late. Everything's closed."

Cybill flung an arm at the clubhouse, a couple hundred yards away. "I got to go peeps."

"So go peeps in the bushes like a normal person."

"And risk getting poison ivy or Lyme disease? No thanks. It'll just take a second."

Alice quit craning her neck, trying to catch sight of Tommy, see which car he got in, to say to her sister, "We have to go in there, anyway. We left mom's jacket. Remember?"

"Oh yeah," Charlie said.

Cybill grabbed Charlie's hand, Charlie grabbed Alice's, and the three of them made their lurching way to the back door of the clubhouse.

• • •

As Cybill wrapped her hand around the doorknob, she turned to Charlie and Alice and raised her index finger, aiming for her lips but hitting her nose in a sloppy shushing gesture. Her lipstick was smeared, making her mouth look, Alice thought, weirdly childish. Like she was a little girl playing with her mommy's makeup. Cybill twisted the knob and the door fell open. They all tumbled through into the dining room, elbows in one another's ribs, tripping over their own and each other's feet. Lights had been left on, but only a few, giving the room an abandoned, ghostly look. All traces of the earlier festivities were gone, everything perfectly neat and pristine, plates and silverware laid out on the tables for breakfast in the morning. Like the mess had been cleaned up by invisible little elves, Alice, the daughter of a former caterer, noted sourly.

In a loud drunk-whisper, Cybill said, "I have to pee so bad I can't feel my feet anymore."

"I can't believe they leave the clubhouse unlocked at night," Charlie said, her drunk-whisper every bit as loud.

"Lucky for us they do. I lack the necessary motor skills right now to fit a teeny tiny key inside a teeny tiny lock. Besides, they don't leave it unlocked unlocked. The whole club has a massive fence around it, plus a security system and cameras and all that. They just have to leave the clubhouse open at night because of the guest rooms upstairs."

"So it's okay for us to be in here?" Alice said.

Cybill nodded loosely, like her head wasn't screwed tight enough on her neck.

"If we're not trying to fool anyone then why are we talking in library voices?"

"Because we need to be quiet," Cybill said, as she hit a tall lamp with her foot, sending it crashing to the floor. "Oopsie. Like I said, there are guest rooms. Five of them, upstairs."

"But don't all the members of the Serenity Point Country Club, like, live in Serenity Point?"

"God, so many questions," Cybill said crossly. "Yes, they mostly do. The rooms are a courtesy. Or a service. Or whatever. Basically, they're for husbands whose wives have kicked them out for the usual reasons. They stay until they're forgiven or served with divorce papers." She turned to Alice and Charlie. "Okay, you two, stay here. I'll be right back."

"Hey, where are you going?" said Charlie. And then, off the look Cybill shot her: "What? I have an inquiring mind, too."

"The locker rooms are locked up at night so I have to use the"— shuddering—"staff bathroom."

As Cybill weaved off to relieve her bladder, Alice looked at Charlie, rolled her eyes. Charlie gave her a drunken what-are-you-going-to-do? shrug. Alice, shaking her head, righted the lamp and picked up her mom's jacket, which had since been hung neatly on the back of the chair that Charlie had flung it over. Then, without quite realizing she was doing it, she began walking toward the photo she'd been looking at when they first arrived at the clubhouse. It was as if she had no choice in the matter, was being drawn irresistibly forward by a force outside herself, like her limbs were attached to invisible strings. She immediately lost herself in the image. With the tip of her finger, she traced the swell of Tommy's forearm muscle, the muscle in his calf. He looked so happy. She couldn't imagine that the face she'd gazed into tonight could ever look so light, so full of joy.

Who was the girl he was with? she wondered jealously. Once again, she was struck by the girl's beauty. There was something almost black-hole-ish about it; it sucked up everything around it: the fine-cut features, the graceful body, the long blond hair, the white, white skin but white not the way Alice's skin was white—pasty, sallow, shunned by the sun—white the way a pearl was white— shimmering, glowing, luminous. Even the way this girl wore her clothes was compelling: carelessly yet jauntily, thrusting one slim hip forward the way a fashion model would. And then there was the look in her eye, the supreme self-confidence, like she was the center of attention naturally, never having to seek it out, just taking what was hers by right. Alice could have sworn she'd seen the girl before, but where? How? It was unlikely that she'd ever run in the same circles as any of these Serenity Point kids. Maybe the girl looked like someone she knew? She decided to ask Charlie, since pretty much everyone she knew, Charlie knew, too.

"Hey," she said to her sister, lying on the carpet now under one of the tables. "I want you to look at something."

"How about you just describe it to me? You like to paint. Paint me a word picture."

"Get over here."

"The room's kind of spinning right now. I'm afraid to walk."

"So crawl." When Charlie obeyed: "Does this girl look familiar to you? Like someone we know?"

Charlie staggered to her feet. Leaning in and squinting, she said, "Actually, yeah, she does a little bit."

"Thank God. It's been driving me crazy. Who is it that she looks like?"

"You, Allie."

An eerie silence came up around Charlie's words. It was like Alice had known Charlie was going to say them without knowing how she knew. And for an instant, she felt as if she might waken from a dream, only she knew she wasn't dreaming. Finally she managed to say, "That's ridiculous."

"Well, not exactly like you. A little bit, I said. Kind-of-ish, sort-of-ish."

Another beat passed, then Alice, trying to pretend she wasn't unnerved, flapped her hand dismissively. "Oh, what do you know? You can barely stand right now."

"It's true," Charlie admitted. "I barely can."

At that moment, Cybill returned from the bathroom, lipstick freshly applied. "I had to pee so bad I didn't use a seat a protector," she said, as she tugged her tight dress down over her narrow hips. "You don't think I could've caught something, do you?"

"Don't worry," Charlie said. "Poverty's not contagious. Who's the girl?"

Cybill looked where Charlie was pointing. She blinked a couple times, then said, "This is a joke, right?"

"Do you see us laughing?"

Cybill swung her gaze back and forth between the two sisters, her eyes wide and very grave. Then she said in a whisper that wasn't even a whisper, more like a breathing with words in it: "That's Camilla."

The words *that's Camilla* trickled inside Alice's ear and then filled her head, taking up every inch of space, until she could hear nothing else. For the second time in as many minutes, she had that sense of déjà vu, of already knowing something she couldn't possibly have known, of waking up from a dream that wasn't a dream.

Charlie recovered from the shock first, saying, "Camilla? As in Richard's daughter Camilla?"

"You didn't recognize her? But aren't there pictures of her, like, all over the house?"

Charlie and Alice both shook their heads.

"There used to be."

For a while, nobody said anything. Then Alice cleared her throat. "Charlie thinks Camilla and I look alike."

"She does?" Cybill said.

Alice waited for a more vigorous expression of contempt to follow—*You wish you looked like Camilla, in your dreams!*—but instead Cybill said, "Actually, I thought so when I first saw you. But that was from a distance and behind glass, so . . ." She trailed off, shrugged. A second or two later, she picked up again: "But after meeting you, not so much. Your personality is so different from Camilla's. Anyway, looking like her's okay, ending up like her's not."

"Lucky for my sister, and every motorist on the road, she can't drive. Not that Richard seems particularly eager to give her a car."

"I can so drive," Alice said. "I just choose not to do it very often. And at least I have my license."

"Who needs a license when you live in the city?"

"We're not living in the city now."

Cybill looked at Alice and Charlie, confused. "What does driving have to do with anything?"

Charlie gave an uncomfortable laugh. "Well, nothing, technically. But the less time Alice spends in a car, the less likely she'll get in an accident in one."

"Camilla didn't get in an accident."

"I thought she crashed her car?"

"Yeah, exactly. *She* crashed her car. First she crashed it, then she sank it in the Serenity Point Bay."

"What?"

"She drove it right off Greeves Bridge. Like, on purpose. Like, really on purpose. She would've had to have floored the gas pedal to break through the barriers."

"It was a suicide," Charlie said softly.

"That or she was testing to see if her car could fly." Cybill's tone was sarcastic, but the sarcasm was a cover. Alice could hear the quaver in her voice, knew the subject was a painful one for her to talk about. "Has your stepdad been telling you it was an accident? I mean maybe that's what it says on the death certificate, but everyone knows that's bullshit. He just couldn't handle the fact that she was so torn up about her mom that she decided to end her own life. Like, no way would his perfect daughter do such a thing. And technically it could've been an accident but . . ." She trailed off.

"Greeves Bridge," Charlie said. "That's the one that takes you into town, right?"

Cybill nodded. "At first they couldn't even find her body. The currents around here can be really strong, just brutal. She washed up on the shore of a beach in Old Lyme, which is almost twenty miles away, weeks later. Mr. Flood had to drive down to identify her. She was so beaten and battered they had to have a closed-casket funeral. My mom talked to one of the guys in the coroner's office. He said"—here Cybill's voice, already nasally with unshed tears, broke—"she had practically no face left."

A silence developed, the only sound in it Cybill's deep shuddery breaths.

Alice had a feeling she wasn't going to like the answer to the question she was about to ask, but she asked it anyway: "So, Camilla and Tommy, they were a couple?"

Sniffing, Cybill said, "Oh yeah, big time. He was crazy about her. Her death was so, so hard on him. I still don't think he's over it. Or her."

Another long silence developed. This time Cybill was the one who ended it. Wiping the base of her nose with the back of her hand, smearing her lipstick again in the process, she said, "We should probably get going. Sasha and Bianca are waiting in the parking lot, and if I leave them on their own too long they get all disoriented and confused. It's like they need someone to boss them around or they're lost. You two coming?"

Alice made to follow, but was stilled by Charlie's hand.

"Actually, Cybill," Charlie said, "Alice and I are going to walk home. I need to sober up a little before my mom and Richard see me. And I think I remember him saying that the house was a closer walk than a drive."

Cybill nodded. "Much closer. Not even a quarter of a mile down the beach. Speaking of beaches, the club's is pretty nice. Either of you want to do a little sunbathing tomorrow?" She was asking both of them, but really, Alice knew, she was asking Charlie.

"I'm up for it," Charlie said.

And immediately the conversation between her and Cybill turned to one-pieces versus two, suntan lotion versus sunblock, the best time of day to absorb the sun's rays. The back-and-forth went on for five or ten minutes. It was as if, Alice thought, listening to them, they were trying to wash the taste of ashes from their mouths, cleanse their palates of death and disease and disfigurement with girl talk.

Finally Cybill promised to call Charlie when she woke up, which she hoped wouldn't be before noon. The girls exchanged their good-byes, went their separate ways.

*W*hat a night, Charlie thought. A face-off with the town's reigning mean girl, an (almost) brawl between two preppie studs, an accidental death that turned out to be an intentional one. And yet . . . fun. Really fun. And not making-the-best-of-a-crappy-situation fun or a laughing-at-them-not-with-them fun—the kind of fun she'd been expecting to have—but straight-up, in-every-sense-of-the-word fun. She never would have imagined she'd have taken to a bunch of stuck-up rich kids. She did, though. They had style and they knew how to have a good time. Plus, she liked the attitude of their parents: letting their teens drink right out in the open so long as they were cool about it, didn't act like spazzes. No hypocrisy. No unrealistic Goody Two-shoes expectations. It made perfect sense to her. Not to mention, she thought the guys were pretty cute, and they seemed to think she was pretty cute right back.

Speaking of cute guys, she wondered what the story was with Jude. He acted like a creep, and fairly convincingly, but she didn't think he was one. Not really, not deep down. He was smart and he was troubled. Mean also. The jab about her tattoo being a tramp stamp had hurt, even though she was reasonably sure she'd kept the pain from showing. The signals she'd been hoping to send off with it were rebellious and tough, not cheap and easy. Guess Alice had been right about its being a shitty idea. But back to Jude. Charlie was curious about him. She wanted to get to know him better, and she hoped that wouldn't cause a problem with her new alpha-blond BFF. She'd tried to probe Cybill a little on the way back from the bonfire. Cybill's tone when she discussed Jude was casual, flip almost. ("Jude's great, but he's full of shit," she'd said, then swatted the air with a dismissive hand flick.) But something told Charlie that that was just a front, that Cybill's feelings for him ran deep, and that if she, Charlie, was going to proceed, she'd better do so with caution. Not that she was totally sure she wanted to proceed. The fact that Jude was Cybill's second cousin once removed disturbed her, and *disturbed* was the word for it, attracting her every bit as much as it repelled her. She found their behavior sick in a decadent, sophisticated, sexy way—and also sick in a flat-out way. The truth of the matter was, she was shocked by the relationship, which she didn't care to admit, even to herself. She liked to think of herself as unshockable, as too experienced by life to be capable of being shocked, certainly by anything a couple of soft, sheltered, namby-pamby private schoolers might do. But she was.

"Shit," Charlie said, stopping in her tracks. They were walking on a little garden path—pretty, narrow, with carefully random bits of plants and flowers—that ran alongside the golf course, down to the ocean.

Alice looked at her. "What's wrong?"

"Cybill said a quarter of a mile down the beach, but I forgot to ask in which direction. And she and Sasha and Bianca are probably long gone by now."

"Hit the water and take a left," a voice said.

Charlie and Alice spun around. A few feet away from them in the shadows, a guy in jeans and a gray hoodie was tying his sneaker. His foot was propped against the lip of a fountain with a statue in it: a fat naked baby with wings, peeing. It took a second before Charlie recognized him. The valet guy from earlier in the night. He appeared younger out of uniform—her age or maybe a year older, two tops—and handsomer, too, with a pair of bright green eyes to go with that mess of dark curly hair, a slim, tightly coiled body that looked like it could move fast.

"You can't miss it," he said. "Not even if you tried."

"Thanks," said Charlie.

"Always a pleasure to help two damsels in distress," he said with a smile, turning and strolling away.

She watched him as he moved off into the darkness, quick but without seeming to hurry. Charlie watched his back get smaller and smaller, wishing she'd thought to ask his name, until Alice tugged her arm. She turned around and they continued to make their way down to the beach.

Alice and Charlie walked along the beach in silence, each wrapped up in her own thoughts. At last Richard's beach house rose into view. (The valet guy was right: there was certainly no missing it.) They were home, at least in the strictest sense of the word, although

Alice couldn't imagine she'd ever think of this place as home, as it was the opposite of everything she associated with home as a concept: grand, formal, cold.

It wasn't until the girls had let themselves in the front door, walked past their reflections in the cloudy gilt-edged mirror that hung in the entranceway, and were standing at the foot of the staircase, wide and curving with an elaborately carved banister, that Alice finally spoke, her voice echoing in the enormous, empty room.

"Do you think it's weird?" she said.

Charlie looked over at her. "What, that Cybill open-mouth kisses her relatives? And here I thought we were supposed to be the white trash."

"No. Weird that Richard lied to us. Or, I guess, let us believe the wrong thing. Mom told us that Camilla died in a car crash, and he didn't contradict her."

"Well, technically Camilla did die in a car crash."

"Technically Camilla died by drowning, I'll bet." All of a sudden, Alice flashed back to the earlier conversation in the car with Richard, the way he'd gone silent when she asked him about his boat. God, no wonder. Thinking of boats and water probably just made him think of Camilla.

Charlie shrugged tiredly. Then she bent her head forward so that Alice could rub the back of her neck.

Alice's hand began moving automatically. "Anyway," Alice said, "it's a pretty strange thing to lie about, or to lie by omission about. I mean, if you ask me."

"What's so strange about it, Allie? It's obviously an incredibly painful and horrific thing for him. Like, he can't even admit that it actually happened, that she killed herself. So why would he admit it to mom?"

"Do you think she knows the truth? Even if she told us the version he told her?"

"Yeah, I think she put it together."

"What makes you say so?"

"Instinct. Plus, it explains a few things. Like why she's so careful of Richard, so considerate of his feelings. Way more than she ever was of dad's."

Alice's hand stopped. "You noticed that, too?"

Charlie nodded.

"I miss him," Alice said softly.

"I miss him, too," Charlie said, just as softly. "And then"—her voice hardening—"I remember he dumped us, left mom with no money. That helps me miss him a little less."

After a beat of silence, Alice said, "So any guesses as to why she did it? Camilla, I mean."

"No mystery there. You heard what Cybill said. She was upset about her mom."

"And that was enough to drive her to suicide, you think?"

Charlie appeared taken aback. "If our mom was the victim of some horrible disease, dropped down to scarecrow weight, bald and terrified and in pain, you'd probably be in a pretty fucked up state of mind, too."

Alice looked at Charlie, looked away. "Does it make you feel differently about Richard? The fact that Camilla did it on purpose?"

"Differently how?"

"Less sorry, I guess. Not like it's his fault she killed herself, but maybe it is a little bit his fault."

"Actually, it makes me feel more sorry for him. He probably thinks the way you do, that he's to blame. That's, like, a heavy burden to bear."

They fell into another silence, this one considerably longer. It was Charlie who ended it this time. Yawning and stretching in a way that reminded Alice of a cat, she said, "It's been a long night. I'm going to take a nice, hot bubble bath, then go to bed."

"You use that claw-foot tub thing to take baths in?"

"You don't?"

Alice shook her head. "Too fancy for me. I use the shower. The tub makes me self-conscious or something."

"Not me. I'm lapping up this lap-of-luxury thing."

"So you're going to hang out with Cybill tomorrow?"

"That's the plan."

"You like her then?" Alice said.

"Yeah."

"And want to be her friend?"

"Definitely."

"I can't believe you trust that girl."

Charlie grinned. "Oh, I don't. But that's got nothing to do with liking her."

At that moment, Alice's cell phone rang. She fished it out of her bag. Patrick.

"Tell Tricky I said hi," Charlie said, turning, starting sleepily up the steps. "Night."

"Can I come in your room after I'm done talking to him? I'll just stay for a little while, then I'll go to mine. I promise."

Alice had yet to spend the night in her own room. She'd always complained bitterly about sharing a room with Charlie back in Cambridge. But now she was so used to sleeping next to her sister, matching breaths until she dropped off, that she practically couldn't sleep alone. In any case, she didn't want to.

"You know if you come into my room, you'll stay the night. Be a big girl now and sleep in your own bed. And don't bother giving me sad clown face."

"I wasn't going to," Alice muttered. Not true. She was. She'd just been about to, in fact.

"Sweet dreams."

"You too," Alice said, with a sigh.

Alice waited until she heard Charlie's bedroom door close, then looked down at her phone, about to answer it now that she had privacy. But she'd taken too long, and the call had gone to voice mail. Instead of calling back, she dropped her cell in her bag and sat down on the bottom step.

She was tired but keyed up at the same time, her mind racing. It was like finding out that Camilla had died deliberately rather than accidentally excited her, riled her up. She felt it explained something important, only she didn't yet know what that something was. And then, all of a sudden, she did: the peculiar, heavy atmosphere of the house, the air of not-quite-rightness that hung over it, *that*'s what the suicide explained. The place wasn't just sad, it was haunted. Okay, not haunted haunted, like literally haunted. There was no ghostie in a white bedsheet floating around at night, hiding behind doors and jumping out at people, yelling "Boo!" Haunted in a subtle way. But haunted nonetheless. Camilla had died in torment—why else do a *Dukes of Hazzard* off a bridge?—and her restless spirit could still be felt. Alice didn't buy Charlie's reasoning for the suicide. Sure, Camilla's mother's death would have been a horrible blow, devastating. Enough, though, to make a girl that beautiful and talented with a boy as wonderful as Tommy in love with her and a dad as rich and adoring as Richard taking care of her to believe that life was no longer worth living? No way. There was more to this story. Alice could feel it in her bones.

She wandered around the vast downstairs for an hour or so, down halls that seemed never to end, in and out of rooms with ceilings so high it made her head dizzy to look up: the library with the glass-fronted bookcases and Gothic panels, the formal dining room with the giant chandelier that dangled above the table like a bunch of see-through grapes, the sitting room with the velvet chairs and silver urns. Everywhere she went, every room she ducked into, every corner she turned, she was confronted by a Flood, staring down at her from a gilt-framed portrait. The effect was eerie, made her feel oddly self-conscious and exposed, like the house was full of spies, like one of Richard's forebears might rat her out, tell him what she'd been up to. She shook off the feeling as best she could, hunted for old photographs, keepsakes, mementos from the Martha-Camilla days, basically covering the ground she and Charlie had already covered. She found nothing, of course.

Finally, frustrated, and unable to think of an alternative, she headed upstairs to bed. At the top of the staircase, she turned left, opened the door to her room. As she stepped across the threshold, a breeze from the window above her dresser passed over her, making her skin break out in spiky little goose bumps. And she could hear, only just, the wind chimes jangling on the back porch, a faint, strangely muted sound, like a sound heard under water. Listening to it, it occurred to Alice for the first time to wonder: had this room been Camilla's?

*A*lice slept terribly that night, barely at all. And the short time she did manage to nod off for was filled with a strange underwater dream. She was at the bottom of Serenity Point Bay: hazy, refracted light shining down from above, soft sand shifting beneath her feet, and in front of her a mermaid with Charlie's face, then Cybill's face, then Charlie's, then Cybill's, back and forth, over and over. And then, suddenly, there was Camilla, by a coral reef. She was dressed in tennis whites, the same outfit she was wearing in the photo in the clubhouse, her lips curved in the same beguiling smile. Her hair was loose and swirling: a golden cloud floating above her head. A brightly colored fish was beside her ear, whispering into it. She held up a hand and beckoned to Alice. She had a secret to tell. Alice began swimming toward the coral reef, passing mermaid Charlie, her movements languid and slow-motion, the water parting gently for her, as soft and unresisting as air. Camilla was in profile, angled slightly away from her. As Alice got close, though, Camilla turned, and as she did Alice saw that the fish wasn't whispering in her ear. It was eating her face, with teeth that were long and sharp and curved. Half of it was already gone, the skin chewed clean through, the tissue and tendons underneath, too, leaving nothing but gleaming white bone. Alice opened her mouth to scream and water rushed in. She couldn't breathe. Her lungs started to buck and spasm. She awoke clutching her throat, gasping for oxygen.

When she was able, she turned to the clock. If she didn't hurry, she'd be late for breakfast.

Richard was kind of nuts on the subject of breakfast. Everyone had to eat it, together, and in the informal dining room. No skipping or sleeping through, no leaving in the middle. "Most important meal of the day," he liked to say before sitting down, rubbing his palms together vigorously so that they made this annoying, rasping sound.

"It's like," Charlie had whispered to Alice last week when Richard got up from the table to see if the newspaper had arrived, "he's a dad in a fifties sitcom. But a fifties sitcom that's being remade into an eighties slasher movie."

Alice had nodded eagerly. "Right," she said, "so like, he's bland, but bland like a maniac's bland."

"Exactly."

Maggie frowned, shook her head at her laughing daughters.

When he said the words today, though, and Alice glanced over at Charlie to exchange their usual smirk, Charlie didn't glance back. She was too busy covering her egg-white skillet scramble in plugs of ketchup. She looked, Alice thought, un-hungover to an annoying degree, clear-eyed and shiny-haired, full of energy and bounce.

While Alice, who'd barely taken a sip of her drink last night, felt like, in a word, shit.

She picked at the stack of whole-wheat almond pancakes that the cook, Luz, had prepared for her. It was weird for Alice to have people around her who waited on her. It made her feel nervous, not quite right, as if she was violating a fundamental belief she held about the equality of man or something. Like, this wasn't decadent Europe. There was no master/servant dynamic here. At least there shouldn't be. It made her feel unworthy, too (this was at a much deeper level, at an emotional rather than rational level), as if she wasn't fancy enough to warrant this sort of treatment and that having to give it to her was degrading to the people paid to do so. Alice could well remember the agony she'd experienced when she'd first arrived at Richard's, seen her ragamuffin possessions placed around her new room, the knowledge that someone had taken these sad little tatty objects out of a cardboard moving box and thought about where to put them, the best spot, mortifying her. She'd hidden most of them under the bed, out of sight. And she'd requested that the maid, Fernanda, not clean her room. She thought she'd been doing Fernanda a favor, showing Fernanda that she was more democratic in her views, but all she'd done was insult Fernanda. Probably made Fernanda think she had a gross or creepy habit she didn't want found out, too. Like she stashed a huge porn collection beneath her mattress or something.

Alice watched Richard push aside his brioche, cut the yolk out of his sunny-side-up egg, drop it onto her mom's plate without even looking up from the Arts section. (The yolk was the only part of an egg her mom would eat.) And her mother did the crossword puzzle,

alternating sips from her glass—fresh-squeezed grapefruit juice—
with sips from his—fresh-squeezed orange juice—her feet buried in
his lap. Alice marveled at how compatible they appeared to be. How
comfortable with each other, too. It was like they were already an
old married couple. Though not, Alice thought, qualifying in her
head, an old married couple like Maggie and her dad, Phil, had been.
Maggie and Phil had fought, not a lot but some. And while Maggie
had seemed to love Phil she didn't seem to be in love with him in an
active way, had treated him in a more casual and, well, more normal-
type manner. Their relationship definitely wasn't this all-consuming
total mutual delirium thing she had going with Richard. A match
made in heaven, Alice said to herself, sighing inwardly.

When she'd first sat down at the table, Alice had wanted to ask
Richard if she'd been given Camilla's room. Looking at him now,
though, she couldn't figure out a tactful way of phrasing the question. Finally, she let it go. Stopping and thinking about it for a second, she realized that the chances were extremely slim. The house
was enormous, no shortage of unoccupied space. What possible reason would he have for putting her in his dead daughter's room?

"Hey, are you done with those?"

Alice turned to Charlie, pointing with her fork to the barely
touched pancakes. Alice nodded queasily, shoved the plate in her
direction. As Alice watched Charlie pour half the pitcher of syrup
over the short stack, she decided to tell Luz she was switching to
cereal so she'd feel less guilty when her appetite was bad, which it
often was first thing in the morning.

"So, girls," Richard said, laying down his newspaper, "what's
the plan for today?"

Charlie's mouth was full-to-bursting, so Alice answered first. "Maybe read in the morning, sketch in the afternoon."

Richard's already down-turning lips down-turned some more. "You're going to stay cooped up inside all day?"

"Allie likes being cooped up," Charlie said, grinning around her mouthful. "It's kind of her thing."

"Suit yourself. But if you feel like a little exercise and sunshine, there are a lot of places to take a run or walk around here. There's a map at the club that charts out all these great routes, hidden spots, hiking trails. I could show you some after lunch, if you'd like."

But isn't after lunch when you and my mom disappear into your bedroom for an hour or so, come out again all smiley-faced and in different clothes? Alice wanted to say, but didn't. Instead she said, "Thanks. I'm probably going to have a pretty sedentary day, though."

"But I think you'd appreciate these landscapes as an artist. They're very beautiful. You could even bring your pad or your easel or whatever it is you do your"—he paused, and Alice was sure he was about to use the word *coloring*, was bracing herself for it—"work on."

She gave him a tight smile. "I appreciate the thought, but I'm not so much into capturing the natural world. I'm more into portraiture. You know, people's faces, bodies, that kind of stuff." She'd assumed he was only asking to show her mom that he was—quote—making an effort with her—unquote—so she was surprised to see the look of hurt on his face at the turndown. She figured he'd be relieved. He was off the hook, no mopey teenager on his hands.

"And you, Charlie?" he said.

Charlie popped the last bite of syrup-drenched pancake into her mouth. "Shockingly, I'm going to do a little reading today, too. I know, I know, try not to hit your head on the floor when you faint. The thing is, we got our summer reading assignments from Wolcott e-mailed to us last week. Mine is *Tess of the d'Urbervilles.* It's kind of long and I read like a snail. Actually, like a snail who reads really, really slowly. So I figured I'd better get started now."

"Do you need to go the bookstore or library?" Maggie said. "I was going to drive into town today, do some shopping. Maybe we could go together? Not this morning. A little later in the day. Richard and I have a golf lesson together at nine."

"Couples golf? That's so adorable I think I just might throw up."

Maggie playfully threw her balled-up napkin at Charlie.

Charlie, just as playfully, threw it back. "That's all right, I brought a copy of the book from home," she said. Then, hooking a strand of hair behind her ear, "If it's okay with you and Richard, I'm going to sign up for the tennis clinics they're running at the club in the afternoons. I saw a notice about it last night."

Traitor, Alice thought. So Charlie was going to be the good stepdaughter, and she was going to be the difficult one.

"I'm surprised," Maggie said.

"Yeah, I'm surprised, too, Charlie," Alice said, glaring at her sister.

"Surprised," Maggie added, "but happy. Of course it's okay with Richard and me. There's nothing we'd like more."

Ignoring Alice, addressing Maggie only, Charlie said, "I just figured I might want to try out for the team at Wolcott. I probably won't make it. It's got to be a lot better than the team at Rindge and Latin was. Still, there's always JV, right?"

"Absolutely there is. You're athletic like me. You'll get better fast and—"

"Now don't go getting all excited and ruining it for me."

"Okay, okay, I won't," Maggie said, raising her hands in surrender. "But, baby?"

Charlie looked up from her plate.

"I am excited."

Charlie laughed, squeezed her mom's hand. "I know you are," she said, then turned toward the kitchen. "Hey, Luz, could I have another glass of orange juice?"

Alice was in her room, lying across the foot of her bed, a book she wasn't reading, had no intention of reading, open in front of her in case anyone unexpectedly popped in. She was waiting for Charlie, Maggie, and Richard to leave, almost beside herself with eagerness to have the house to herself. So eager, in fact, that she forgot to be mad at Charlie for acting like a turncoat and going to the club, just wanted Charlie to hustle everyone out the door. As soon as she heard the latch click, Alice jumped up, ran to the window. There they were, the three of them, in blindingly white athletic gear, chattering animatedly back and forth, hauling tennis racquets and golf clubs into the back of the Mercedes, looking like a Ralph Lauren ad come to life. Well, except for Charlie's tough-cookie, wrong-side-of-the-tracks angel's-wing tattoo, which flashed every time she bent over or raised her arms—the scene's only spoiler. Alice ignored the pang of jealousy that suddenly rose up in her chest, jammed it down.

Hearing the car's engine start to purr, Alice ran into the hall, glancing over the staircase banister to make sure that Fernanda was still cleaning downstairs. (Fernanda didn't usually make it upstairs until ten thirty, earliest.) Last night's exploring had yielded zip, but she had a feeling that she'd have better luck this morning. Richard's office and his and her mom's bedroom she expected to be veritable treasure troves of Martha and, more importantly, Camilla memorabilia. And with everyone gone, she could explore them to her heart's content.

Alice started with the bedroom, which she'd seen, of course, but managed to avoid ever actually entering. It was a lovely room, with elaborate white cornices and a scrolled ceiling and four tall windows that let in the morning light beautifully. At the center was an enormous bed made of burnished wood, the sheets rumpled in a way that implied sex was recently had. Suppressing a shudder, Alice cut her eyes, turned toward the dresser. A series of framed photographs lined the top, but only of Richard and Maggie, a few of Alice and Charlie. Alice walked over to Richard's closet. When she opened the double doors, her heart sank. It could've belonged to any man: lots of shoes and belts, hanging suits and jackets and shirts and slacks, more ties than any one person would ever need. Alice got more aggressive in her search, looking inside every drawer, every cabinet, under every rug, behind every shelf. Other than a faint medicinal smell, the smell of a sickroom, which was probably only in her imagination—surely Martha would have been cared for in a hospital, with state-of-the-art medical equipment—there wasn't so much as a hint, a speck, a whisper of the former occupants of the house. And she had no better luck with Richard's office, a little messier than the bedroom, but just as impersonal.

An hour after Alice began her search, she ended it. She sat down on the top step of the staircase, wiped the sweat from her forehead, slightly ashamed of the greed of her investigation, more than slightly ashamed that the greed had failed to yield results. It was like, she thought to herself, all evidence that Richard had ever had a wife, other than the present one, or a daughter, other than the two step, had been systematically eliminated. It gave her a sort of spooky feeling. Like she too could vanish from the world without a trace.

Not that Camilla had left no trace. Quite the contrary. People seemed to remember her pretty vividly. She'd killed herself almost a year ago, and they still hadn't moved on. Had Tommy so much as *looked* at another girl since? Alice bet not, not seriously. Even the fact that Richard erased Camilla's presence from his house so completely was in itself a kind of tribute to just how unforgettable she was. Like a single reminder of her would be more than he could bear. Her absence, Alice realized, was as striking as she had been. Who besides her mother and her sister, and maybe Patrick, would remember Alice if she were to die? Her dad sure found it easy to act as if she'd never been born.

Alice felt the tiny hairs on her arms and legs begin to rise. She was creeping herself out with this morbid thinking. Maybe Richard was right. Maybe a little sunshine and exercise would do her some good. She couldn't find the box she'd packed her workout clothes in, so she just threw on a Radiohead T-shirt, a pair of Charlie's short shorts—the only kind Charlie owned—and laced up her Converse. After smearing half a bottle of sunblock on her face, she headed outside.

Chapter
• SEVEN •

The clinic for intermediate players didn't start until one thirty. Charlie had already gone to the club shop, charged a hot-pink sweatband, hot-pink boyshort underwear with little tennis ball–holding pockets—*fancy pants* was the term the sales lady had used, which, *ooookay*—ankle socks with the pom-pom things on the back, a sports bra, two tennis dresses, and a bikini to Richard's account. Now even if she sucked at the game, at least she'd look cute playing it. She'd caged a Band-Aid off the guy behind the concierge desk, too, covered her angel's wing with it, telling herself it was to prevent chafing. (The tag from the skirt she was wearing rubbed slightly against the tattoo, irritating it.) She'd been hoping to run into Cybill, or better yet, Jude, her real reason for accompanying her mom and Richard to the club and ditching her sister. She'd cased the grounds pretty thoroughly, though, and had seen no sign of either one. It was probably still a little early for those two. Not everybody, she knew, was blessed with her immunity to hangovers.

She headed to the café, figuring she'd kill the next couple of hours nursing an iced tea, getting a start on *Tess of the d'Urbervilles*. She opened the door and stepped inside. The café was doing moderate to heavy business. Most of the tables were occupied by post-doubles-match groups of four: women with well-preserved faces, trim bodies—the seriously defined arm and leg muscles, coupled with the perfect makeup jobs and minimal perspiration stains led Charlie to believe that tennis was not their primary form of exercise—hair that was blond-streaked rather than blond, and large but somehow tasteful diamonds dripping from their hands, wrists, and necks. They gossiped as they sipped skim lattes, plucked berries off fruit plates.

Charlie found an empty table near the back by the kitchen door, cracked open her book.

She'd just read the first paragraph—read it twice, though she was going to have to read it a third time if she wanted a chance at actually understanding it—when a voice said, "Guess you found your way home all right."

She looked up. It was the valet guy from last night. Only today he was apparently the waiter guy. He had a little pad sticking out of his pocket, a pencil behind his ear. The tag on his shirt read STAN.

She smiled up at him. "And here I thought you just parked cars."

"I'm a multitalented individual. I park cars when they ask me to park cars, wait tables when they ask me to wait tables." He handed her the menu tucked under his arm.

"At last," she said, putting down *Tess* to take it, "a book I can understand."

He dipped his head to get a peek at the cover. "I'm a *Far from the Madding Crowd* man myself."

"Is that the name of an underground rave or something?"

"It's the name of an early Hardy novel. I liked it better than *Tess*. The heroine's got more snap to her, not such a wet blanket, you know what I mean?"

"No, but I will when I read the CliffsNotes."

"Let me guess, a junior-year transfer to Wolcott Academy."

She looked at him in surprise. "How did you know?"

"I know your year because you're reading *Tess of the d'Urbervilles*, the assigned summer book for Literature and the Human Condition, a course that is usually for juniors, though I took it as a sophomore. And I know you're a transfer because if you were already at Wolcott, I'd have noticed."

"Those are some serious powers of deduction you got there, Stan. You really are multitalented. How do you like Wolcott?"

"It's all right. I'm pretty much in nose-to-the-grindstone mode when I'm there. I came in on a scholarship, and I'm doing my best to go out on one, too."

"Scholarship to where?"

"Yale, if I can swing it. I'm a New Haven boy, so it's always been the goal." He smiled and shook his head, like he was suddenly shy or embarrassed, had revealed too much. "So," he said, a second later when he'd recovered, "you want me to give you the CliffsNotes version of the menu, tell you what's good?"

"Actually, no," she said, handing back the menu to him. "Don't bother. I'm just going to get an iced tea, sit here, and sound out words."

"You're not hungry?"

"Listen, I can move to a different station if you'd like. I know how annoying it is to have one of your tables taken up by a drink-nurser."

He looked amused. "Oh you do, do you?"

"Hey, I put in my time waiting tables. Probably more than you have. Two full summers," she said, and then grinned at the defensive note that had risen in her voice.

He grinned back. "You recently came into good fortune, huh?"

"My mom did, married a fortune. Whether he's good or not, I couldn't tell you. Though"—pointing out the window to Maggie and Richard, full-on making out by the golf carts—"she sure seems to think so."

Stan laughed. As he did, she admired his white teeth and green eyes.

"Anyway," she said, "if you want me to move, I'd be happy to."

"Nah, that's okay. You stay right where you are. Nobody around here eats much, anyway. That was an iced tea you wanted, right . . ." He paused, as if waiting for her to fill in the blank.

"Charlie," she finished.

"How about I make you an Arnold Palmer, Charlie? I've got the lemonade–iced tea ratio down just right."

"Okay. Sounds good."

He nodded, walked away from her with that light, quick step of his. Then a woman at a nearby table called for the check, and he turned around unexpectedly, caught Charlie in mid-stare. They both laughed. Not wanting to get herself in any more trouble, Charlie re-opened her book, took her third crack at that first paragraph.

• • •

Alice's beat-up three-year-old low-top Converse sneakers, as it turns out, didn't offer much in the way of arch or ankle support, and thus weren't ideal for hard-surface training. She quickly veered off the road and onto the sand, removing her sneakers to run along the beach. She couldn't get used to how private these private beaches actually were. So empty they looked post-apocalyptic to her eye. Carson Beach in Southie got so packed in the summer it was tough to find a patch of sand big enough to spread a towel on. Lots of hood-y looking guys with tattoos up and down their arms, girls who smoked and chewed gum at the same time. Sometimes fights would break out and the cops would come. Once someone even found a human bone.

When Alice had started out, she'd had some vague, wishy-washy idea of reaching the Serenity Point lighthouse, which she knew was two and a half miles from Richard's because Charlie ran it every day, and she'd been with Charlie when Charlie made Maggie measure the distance with the odometer in the Mercedes. After a few minutes of huffing and puffing, a stitch pulling painfully at her side, calf muscles burning, she revised her end point: last night's bonfire pit, unambitious but doable, at least.

The morning sun was high and directly in her eyes, so it wasn't until she was practically on top of the pit that she saw the male figure sitting beside it, round-backed and sort of hunched down. As she slowed to a halt, her first thought was that it was Jude, finally roused from his drunken-druggie stupor, hanging his head because it hurt so much. Then she blinked and saw that it wasn't Jude at all. It was Tommy, and he wasn't hanging his head, he was looking down at something in the sand, in between his legs. Squinting, she saw that it was a book of some kind, a notebook maybe. He stopped reading it to flip to a fresh page, then pulled a pencil out of his pocket, began scribbling furiously. He was still wearing his clothes from yesterday, and his hair was flat in spots, spiky in others. Obviously, he'd spent the night on the beach. Guess he hadn't gotten into one of the cars in the club parking lot, after all.

Alice got the feeling that he was doing something private, something he wouldn't wish to be observed doing. She was about to turn around, head back in the direction she came from, when he suddenly lifted his face. They locked gazes. Alice, embarrassed, feeling as if she'd been caught spying, just stood there until he raised his hand in a tentative wave. She waved back, began walking toward him.

As she approached, she saw him slip his pencil back in his pocket, slide the notebook under his thigh and out of sight. "Hi," she said, when she was a foot or two away.

"You're the new girl, right?"

Even though it was more statement than question, she answered it: "Yes."

As they stared at each other, she wondered if he thought she looked like Camilla, too. Then she wondered if that's why she'd loaded up on the sunblock, to keep her skin a milky, Camilla-like white. Or if that's why she'd worn her ponytail high on her head, the way Camilla did in that photograph, not at the nape of her neck, the way she did normally—to heighten the chance resemblance, cause him to associate her with his dead girlfriend. After all, if she did remind him of Camilla, the girl he loved, it would be that much easier to make him fall in love with her.

That she could be that low-down manipulative, even unconsciously, was a disturbing thought, and she did her best to push it out of her mind.

"Doesn't it get cold?" she said.

"What?"

"Out here, at night." Up close, she noticed that the stubble on his jaw was a shade darker than his hair. His face was so handsome. But there was something sad about it, too. It was his eyes, a beautiful soft brown, but the beauty shot through with melancholy.

He shrugged. "My house is right there."

She looked to where he was pointing, and saw a large but not abnormally large—not Richard large, in other words—house a dune or two away.

"It's sort of like camping out in the backyard," Tommy said. "I can go inside, tuck into my nice warm bed anytime I want to. It's just, sometimes I don't want to. Sometimes I like it better out here."

Alice nodded her understanding. "Sometimes I hate people, too."

He laughed, looking different suddenly, younger, less serious.

"Not hate people," Alice quickly amended, realizing how that sounded. "More love alone time. It was hard to get privacy where we lived in Cambridge. Our place was small and kind of cramped for four people, and I shared a room with my sister. When it got to be too much, I'd climb out onto the roof. I would do it even in the winter when it was freezing cold. I'd just bundle up, bring a blanket. Anything to be by myself, you know?"

"Yeah, I do. There just are times you need to be alone with your thoughts."

She dropped down beside him in the sand. When she did, she saw that it wasn't his thoughts he'd been alone with last night; it was the view. In the distance, but dead ahead, front and center, was the Greeves Bridge, the spot where Camilla had chosen to end her young life. Alice flashed back to a book she'd read in American Lit last year, *The Great Gatsby*, and the green light shining at the end of Daisy Buchanan's dock, the one Gatsby would spend hours staring at across the bay.

They sat there in silence for a while, listened to the sound of the waves, the scattered seagull cries, the occasional crack of a golf ball.

After a bit, Tommy said, "You play golf?"

Alice shook her head. Then it occurred to her that he might have been about to ask her to go golfing with him, and she began kicking herself for her answer. She was about to revise it when he said, with a sigh, "Me either. It's the world's most boring game, as far as I'm concerned. My dad loves it, though. He can't get enough of it."

Unable to think of anything else to say, she said, "My stepdad's teaching my mom."

"Poor her." Tommy stood up, brushed the sand off the seat of his khakis. "I think I'm going to head home, catch a couple hours' sleep. I'll see you around."

As he started off toward his house, Alice called out to him: "Hey, you forgot this."

He turned around. She held up the notebook. His face reddened as he jogged back to retrieve it. Running his finger along the spine, biting his bottom lip with two very slightly—and very adorably—crisscrossed front teeth, he said, "I know it's pretty girly, having a diary, which is why I call it a journal, more masculine-sounding. But my English teacher told me that if I'm serious about wanting to be a writer, I should write every day. It seemed like keeping a journal would be a good way of making sure I stuck to that resolution."

"I don't think it's girly."

He nodded, as if he appreciated her saying that, but avoided meeting her eye. Then he turned and started walking again. She watched him until he disappeared inside his house, the screen door swinging shut behind him.

Charlie had been a little worried that she'd be too intermediate for an intermediate clinic, or not intermediate enough. But that wasn't the case. She was just the right amount of intermediate. It'd been fun. And she could already feel the improvement in her game. She'd even taken a practice set off Sasha, who was on the team at St. Augie's. Charlie dropped her racquet on top of her bag, picked up her crappy cell, a strip of masking tape holding the battery in, to see if Cybill had returned the text she'd sent before stepping on the court. Nope. Nothing. She hadn't imagined Cybill asking her to go to the beach today, had she?

As Charlie was showering in the locker room, she decided to go to the beach anyway. Maybe Cybill was already there, had left her cell at home or hadn't programmed Charlie's number right in her phone or something. In any case, Charlie had bought a bikini and she planned to wear it. After drying off, applying the complimentary lotion, she changed into it. She shoved her new purchases, racquet bag, and dirty clothes in a locker. Then she caged a second Band-Aid off the concierge guy—the tag in the bikini was in the same place as the tag in the tennis skirt—grabbed a fluffy white club robe, and headed down to the water. As she passed the café, Stan leaned out the window.

"Saw you slugging away out there," he said. "Maria Sharapova better watch her back."

Charlie laughed and waved, but kept walking. As soon as her toes touched the sand, she spotted Jude and Cybill. The beach was uncrowded, a few stray forms here and there, and they were an eye-catching duo: slim and tanned, side by side on a single towel, one head dark, one light, identical pairs of sunglasses perched on identical long, straight noses and raised to the late afternoon sun. Before approaching them, Charlie slipped out of her robe, stuffed it in her shoulder bag. As she got closer, she saw that Cybill was wearing a bikini, too, canary yellow, cut high in the leg. Charlie was pleased to see that while Cybill looked good, she looked better. (Cybill's lanky, slim body was made to be in clothes; Charlie's shorter, curvier body was made to be out of them.) She was less pleased to see that Jude was wearing an oxford shirt over his trunks.

When she reached their towel, Cybill said, "Who's blocking my sun?" She lifted her sunglasses. Seeing it was Charlie, she let them drop again. "Oh," she said, "hey."

"Hey. Did you get my text?"

"I didn't check my phone."

"I thought we were supposed to get together."

Cybill stifled a yawn with the back of her hand, before saying, "Were we?"

"Yeah, we were. We made the plans last night."

"I drank a lot."

Charlie was getting blown off. That much was obvious. She knew she should drop it, move on. Alice was right about Cybill. She was probably right about Jude, too. But she was mad now, pissed at the bored-sounding bullshit that was coming out of Cybill's mouth. And maybe a little hurt as well. "You think that's polite behavior?" she said, letting a little aggression enter her voice. "Making plans and then forgetting about them? No apology?"

"Don't pay attention to her, Charlie," Jude said. "She's acting like a bitch, but it's not her fault. She has a hangover, and the best cure for a hangover is a Bloody Mary, and I remembered the tomato juice but I forgot the vodka."

Charlie smiled down at him. "How's a Bloody Mary a cure for a hangover?"

"Science."

"Science?"

"Yeah, science. Think about it. The vodka lets your body deal with new alcohol instead of old, and then the tomato juice is full of fortifying vitamins and antioxidants and all that crap. See," he said, grinning, pleased with himself. "Science."

Without a word, Charlie turned, started walking. She heard Jude call out her name. Not Cybill, though.

Charlie casually made her way toward one of the few other sets of bathers on the beach, a middle-aged husband and wife lying next to each other on club towels. In between them was a fancy-looking picnic basket, as big as a suitcase and wide open. The couple appeared to be sleeping, though their sunglasses were blocking their eyes, making it difficult to be sure. When she was in front of them, Charlie leaned over to scratch her ankle, casual as could be. The man's thighs were furry but his shins, she noticed, were hairless, rubbed bald, no doubt, from years of wearing socks under his business suits. The skin on the woman's face was tight, but Charlie could see a network of fine scars along the underside of her jaw and neck. Charlie only had a second to look in the basket. She reached for a bottle of clear liquid, lifted it out, hoping for the best. It could've been gin. It could've been sparkling water. It wasn't, though. Stolichnaya, chilled, the cap still sealed.

She dropped it in the sand beside Cybill.

"Russian vodka, my favorite," Jude said, looking at the bottle appreciatively. Then, looking at Charlie, even more appreciatively, "Beautiful and bad, also my favorite." And then, as if giving her a reward, he began unbuttoning his shirt. His body, Charlie noted with satisfaction, wasn't bad, wasn't bad at all. In fact, it was good, flat-out: a lean stomach, well-defined pectorals, a sexy little tuft of dark hair on his breastbone.

"You seem pretty spry for a guy who passed out a few inches from his own puke," she observed.

He grinned. "My recuperative powers are formidable. Cybill can testify to that."

"She can't if she doesn't know what *recuperative* means," Cybill said.

"I'm not totally sure what *recuperative* means either, Cybill," Charlie said, her eyes on Jude's, "but I think—and I could be wrong here—but I think he wants you to tell me that even though he drinks to the point of falling down, he can still get up. So to speak."

Jude cocked a finger at her like a gun, pulled the trigger. "Bingo. Get up and stay up. Stay up all night. Though that testimony I asked Cybill to give, it wouldn't be based on firsthand knowledge, naturally."

"Oh, very naturally," Charlie said.

"She's my confidante. I tell her about most of my conquests."

"Only most?"

"One or two I keep to myself."

"Sure. You've got to, right? I mean, if you want to hold on to that all-important air of mystery."

Again he cocked his finger at her, pulled the trigger.

Charlie was playing along with him, talking cool and relaxed, echoing his mocking tone, acting like she knew things, when she was actually growing more confused by the second. Was he saying that he and Cybill did sleep together or that they didn't sleep together? Or was he saying that they did sleep together but, for appearances' sake, pretended that they didn't? That it was an open secret, to be understood but not spoken of? Charlie realized she was supposed to be savvy enough to read between the lines, but the truth was, she wasn't and couldn't, not with any real confidence.

"I'm going to go take a quick swim so I can make myself thirsty," he said, and began walking down to the water.

Charlie watched him.

"Why don't you sit?" Cybill said, indicating the spot Jude had just abandoned.

Guess she was back in Cybill's good graces, and all it took was a little petty thievery, Charlie thought to herself as she dropped down to the towel. Still, the truth was, she was glad to be there.

Cybill turned to her. "Look, all that talk about his recuperative powers—"

"Don't worry. I didn't take it seriously," Charlie said quickly, though, of course, she wasn't sure if she did or didn't. But maybe she was sure now? Maybe Cybill was telling her subtly but definitively that they weren't sleeping together?

"No, I was just going to say, he didn't have much to recuperate from. Not last night, anyway. Almost as soon as Sasha dropped me off at my house, he knocked on my window. Wanted to know what I'd done with his flask."

Charlie laughed. "Good to know he has his priorities straight."

"Yeah, he spent the night in a nice soft comfy bed. If he'd spent the night on cold, throw-uppy sand, believe me, his mood would be much worse today."

Spent the night in a nice soft comfy bed with you? Charlie wanted to ask, but didn't. Didn't because she felt Cybill wanted her to ask, and if she did ask, she'd lose something, concede some advantage.

Cybill kept talking: "His mom really should've had her tubes tied before she had Jude, not waited till after. She and Mr. Devlin were just not cut out to be parents. They left for Boston right after the party last night. Jude's alone in that big old house—well, alone except for the staff—ninety percent of the time. It's not right. Hey, Charlie, would you mind rubbing a little oil on my back? I want to make sure my tan is even all over."

As Charlie pushed the long blond ponytail out of the way, worked the Korres Walnut & Coconut Suntan Oil into the sharp shoulder blades, she wondered if Cybill was befriending her because she wanted to be friends, or if Cybill was befriending her because she wanted to neutralize a threat. Whatever Cybill's reason was, she was glad. She wouldn't want to have a girl like Cybill for an enemy.

On Friday night, Richard and Maggie hosted a small dinner party. It was for Jock Pollard Jr., the man who ran the Boston Art Institute, the biggest and best museum in the city, and his wife, Susanna. Plans were afoot to build a new wing, and Richard was vying for the high-profile job. After the wedding, he'd taken a two-week "honeymoon" vacation, which ended a few days ago. Alice had assumed that meant he'd be back in New York during the week, only in Serenity Point on weekends. But, of course, Richard didn't trudge off to an office every day, like some common nine-to-five drone. No, he worked out of the office upstairs, and then only in the mornings. (He was between projects right now, so his duties were light. Plus, he had plenty of minions to delegate to.) Basically, he was, to Alice's utter, utter dismay, around as much now as he had been on vacation, a largely silent but intensely judgmental presence, one that cast a long, dark shadow across the house.

This dinner, from what she could gather, was a sort of informal job interview, like an audition to get an audition, a high-pressure situation for both Richard and Maggie. She and Charlie were expected to attend, to be charming but not attention-grabbing, to be pretty but not sexy, to be articulate but not chatty, to, in other words, reflect as well on Richard and Maggie as the Chippendale dining chairs did, or the Tiffany lamps, or the crystal chandelier, or any of the tasteful knickknacks scattered about the room.

It was a long meal, a lot of courses. While the adults talked shop, or museum, or whatever it is they were going on about, Alice put on the bland smile she wore like a mask and did what she wanted behind it: thought her thoughts, watched her sister sending text messages under the table from the new iPhone Richard had bought her, marveled at how skilled her mom was at being a powerful man's mate. Quite the geisha girl—geisha woman, whatever—her mom had turned out to be, so good at anticipating her man's wants and needs. Richard never had to ask her for anything because she'd already given it to him, topped off his wine glass as soon as he drank from it, kept the wife occupied and amused so he could focus all his energies on the husband, even set him up to tell his best stories and jokes. Occasionally, Alice would tune in to the conversation. Just, you know, in case someone said something to her, asked her a question. (She didn't want to be *completely* at sea.) This time when she tuned in it was to Richard, in mid-pitch:

"Of course, Jock, you can always go the safe route, give the commission to Carlo Gianelli. His work is excellent—classic, serene . . . unthreatening. But he's done museum additions in Los Angeles, San Francisco, Manhattan, Miami, and, most recently, Dallas. All the museums are going to start to look to alike."

"I agree," said Mr. Pollard, a very small man and completely bald. "His style is a little subdued. But surely tranquility isn't a bad thing in a place in which people are meant to view and appreciate great works of art. I'm not asking him to redesign Gillette Stadium, after all."

"No, but the new wing is to be called the Modern Wing, yes?"

"Yes," conceded Jock. "So?"

"So *modern* implies new and exciting, not staid and same old, same old. You want a space that reflects the content, is in harmony with it, a cohesive vision. And frankly you want a space in opposition to its surroundings. Boston is already fuddy-duddy enough. The city's got to be sick of playing second-best to New York. What am I talking about? Second best? It's barely in the running anymore."

"Setting does affect response," Maggie said, as if sensing Richard was going too far, offending his guest, wanting to steer him back on track. "When Richard and I saw the Modern Wing of the Art Institute of Chicago, it completely changed how I viewed the—"

"But you and Richard have never been to Chicago," Alice said, the words slipping out of her mouth almost before she realized it.

Maggie turned and stared at her. Immediately Alice understood she shouldn't have interrupted, should've waited till she and her mom were alone to say something. There was a long silence. So long Charlie even looked up from her iPhone.

Blushing a deep scarlet, Maggie said, "You're right, sweetheart. I must've . . . I must've seen it with your father. My goodness, how embarrassing." She covered her face with her palm.

Susanna Pollard, who was very pretty and much, much younger (and much, much taller) than her ancient, tiny husband, laughed. "It does get hard to keep the spouses straight. Jock here is constantly calling me Meredith. Now, Jock, I forget. Was Meredith wife number three or wife number four?"

"Technically, three," Mr. Pollard said, "though she was my fourth marriage. I married Yasmin twice." He waggled his eyebrows when he said *Yasmin*, which Alice guessed meant she was especially sexy. Gross.

"See what I mean?" Mrs. Pollard said, with a smile. "When people ask which number Mrs. Pollard I am, I always say the last." She turned to Alice and Charlie. "Girls, if you're smart, you'll marry once and marry right. It makes life so much less confusing."

Everyone laughed, except Alice. And then Richard, without so much as glancing her way, went back to subtly running down Carlo Gianelli, not so subtly promoting himself. Mr. Pollard, Alice noticed, seemed to be growing increasingly receptive to his argument. A few minutes later, coffee and tea were served, and Maggie told Alice and Charlie that they were free to leave the table. She didn't have to tell them twice.

"What was that?" Alice whispered to Charlie, as they stepped out of the dining room and into the hall.

"You saw? God, hawk-eye."

Alice put a hand on Charlie's arm. "Wait, I don't think we're talking about the same thing. What are you talking about? Saw what?"

Charlie took a quick look around, then lifted her shirt, revealing a bottle of red wine stuck in the waistband of her skirt. "And here I thought I'd been so stealth." She pouched out her lower lip: sad clown.

Alice rolled her eyes. "The wine's not what I was talking about, though you should put it back. I was talking about mom's lie about going to Chicago with dad."

"What makes you think that was a lie?"

"When did mom and dad ever go to Chicago?"

A pause while Charlie searched her memory.

"See," said Alice, "you can't think of a time."

"They did have a life together before we were on scene."

"Give me your phone. You know, the new one, the one you let Richard buy for you."

"Hey, he offered to buy you one, too. It's not my fault you wouldn't get off your high horse and say yes. And why do you want to borrow mine? Who're you going to call? Not Patrick. He's been calling you and calling you. I haven't seen you pick up once."

"Just shut up and give it to me. I'd use mine but yours has Internet on it." After thirty seconds or so of tapping the screen, Alice held up the phone triumphantly. "There," she said, pointing to the screen. "Look. I knew it."

"And what am I looking at?" Charlie said, in a bored voice.

"The Wikipedia page of the Art Institute of Chicago."

"And what is it on this Wikipedia page that you find so fascinating?"

"That Modern Wing at the Art Institute of Chicago that mom was talking about? It really is modern."

Charlie, interested in spite of herself, said, "How modern?"

"Not even two years old."

Charlie was quiet for a second, then said, "That doesn't mean anything. Dad gigs all over the place. I'm sure he's been to Chicago in the last two years. In fact, I'm sure he's been more than once."

"So what if he has? Since when does mom go with dad on gigs? Hardly ever. And definitely not to Chicago. And definitely not in the last two years."

Charlie's voice rose, "So what are you saying? That mom and Richard got together before they said they did?"

"It makes sense, doesn't it? They seem to know each other really well, like way too well for the amount of time they've supposedly spent together."

Alice watched her sister absorb the implications of what she was saying, then watched her sister try to shake those implications off. "Whatever. You're too obsessed with detail."

"And you're too oblivious to detail," Alice shot back.

Charlie let out a long-suffering sigh. "You maybe, possibly, but not definitely caught mom in an itsy-bitsy, teeny-weeny fib. Big. Deal."

"So it doesn't bother you that mom deceived dad, was with another guy while she was still with him? That she's a cheater?"

"*May* have deceived dad. *May* be a cheater." At that moment, Charlie's phone buzzed: a text message alert. Looking down at the screen, she said, excited but trying to play it cool, "Cybill and Jude are at the front door."

"God, it didn't take you three long to become attached at the hip. What are they doing here?"

"I invited them. I figured we could go out back to the deck. Mom and Richard won't care. The house is so big they'll barely know we're here. Why don't you come?" After a beat, she said, "Labor Day, Allie."

"You're overusing that Labor Day thing," Alice grumbled. "It's going to lose its power before June's over, definitely before the Fourth of July."

"Such a grouch." Charlie took a strand of Alice's hair, stretched it against Alice's arm to see how long it was. It reached the crook part. "Come on, hang out a little bit. You might even have fun."

Alice didn't want to hang out, but even less did she want to go up to her room and brood about her mom and Richard, or feel guilty for not calling Patrick back, so she nodded. Let Charlie lead her by the hand past the tall, spotty mirror in the entranceway to the front door.

Alice couldn't take the scene on the deck for more than an hour. Really, she couldn't take it for more than a half hour, but Jude had broken out a joint and she didn't want him to think that she was leaving because she was scandalized by his oh-so-risqué behavior, so she gritted her teeth, readjusted her weight in the chair, knowing she'd have to stick around for another thirty minutes now. Out of the corner of her eye, she watched him. He was bringing the joint to his lips, soft and pink and in the shape of a bow. There was something corrupt about his looks. There was something corrupt about *him*. Alice could see that he was interested in Charlie. *Amused* might be a better word, might more accurately convey the superiority of his attitude, its air of aristocratic condescension. Like he thought Charlie was sexy and charming, a pretty diversion, but his feelings for her didn't run any deeper than that. Charlie was sure all caught up in him, though, which was just the way he wanted it, as caught up in him as Cybill was. (Both girls played it cool, pretending that their interest in him was casual, but sharp glances here and there betrayed their true feelings.) Alice bet that sex wasn't even what he was after. Not sex for its own sake. No, he was the type that was far more excited by the game than the conquest. Manipulating people, bending them to his will—that was what really turned him on. A bad-news guy, no question.

The energy between him, Cybill, and Charlie was certainly weird. It was like the erotic vibrations were shooting off every which way, in every which direction, far too many for Alice to keep track of. Sometimes it seemed like the two girls were fighting over him. Sometimes it seemed like Charlie and Cybill were in league with each other against him. Sometimes it seemed like he and Cybill were in league with each other against Charlie. Alice suspected he wanted to pull her in the mix, too, turn this *ménage à trois* into a *ménage à quatre*. No thanks. Anytime she caught him looking at her, she returned his gaze, keeping her eyes steady and expressionless. He was always the first to look away. Good. She didn't like games, not his games at least, and no way was she going to let him trick her into playing. How, she wondered, did someone so young get so jaded? How, she also wondered, did she ever allow herself to be intimidated by this jerk?

Alice was snapped out of her reverie by the sound of her name. She looked up. It was Cybill, holding out Jude's flask to her. "You thirsty?"

Alice waved away the offer, remembering, but only barely, to smile so she wouldn't seem rude.

"Charlie, I know *you're* thirsty."

As Charlie laughed and leaned forward to accept the flask, the back of her shirt lifted, and Alice saw that her angel's wing was covered by a Hello Kitty Band-Aid. She had been so mad at Charlie when she got the tattoo. She was even more mad at Charlie now, seeing her hide the tattoo she'd wanted so badly, ashamed of it because Jude judged it shameful. It was hard for Alice to believe that her strong, tough, take-no-shit sister was letting herself be influenced by this smirky rich kid. It was like Charlie was so used to boys turning themselves inside out to get her attention, she couldn't resist the one boy who kept a little distance. What a cliché. But Alice didn't feel as if she could say anything to Charlie about the situation or warn her off Jude, as much as she wanted to. Not now. Not after she'd just unloaded her suspicions about Maggie and Richard onto Charlie and found her so resistant. Charlie would simply write her off as paranoid, quit listening to anything she said.

If Alice had to bite her tongue, then she couldn't hang around any longer and watch Charlie falling for Jude's manipulative push-pull bullshit, or she'd bite her tongue clean off at the root. She stood up from her chair, nearly bumping her head on the sand-dollar wind chimes hanging above the back door.

"I'm going to take a walk on the beach," she said. "My legs are falling asleep from all this sitting. You guys have fun."

Everyone made disappointed noises, but nobody, she noticed, seemed sad to see her go.

It was cooler along the water than it had been on the deck, windier, too. The ocean seemed a little wild tonight, the waves moving in choppy, uneven lines, frothy on top, cracking against the shore. Alice wasn't walking in any direction in particular but soon found herself on the stretch of beach in front of the club. She looked up. Next to the bonfire pit was Tommy van Stratten. And seeing him sitting there, as still as a piece of driftwood, knees pulled into his chest, notebook open in the sand beside him, gazing out at the Greeves Bridge in the distance, the only thing that surprised her was that she wasn't surprised at all. She'd known he'd be here, she realized. That's why she'd come.

She hadn't seen Tommy since that morning a couple days back. Not in person, anyway. She'd gone to the club with Charlie a few times, gotten lost in that photo of him and Camilla hanging in the dining room, his face so young and open and carefree, hers so beautiful and self-possessed and mysterious. Still, Alice had a rough idea of how he was doing: not so hot. The verdict had come in on the malpractice suit, and, as predicted, it wasn't favorable to Tommy's dad. He wasn't going to be facing jail time, but his medical license had been revoked. He could never work as a doctor again. What's more, the patient's wife was also seeking damages, so Dr. van Stratten would likely be on the hook for a lot of money. And Charlie had told her that word around the club was that when Mrs. van Stratten found out that her husband was being forced to declare bankruptcy, she'd said she'd had it, was filing for divorce.

Tommy seemed no more surprised to see Alice than she was to see him, like his unconscious had set this encounter up with her unconscious, like they'd made a date to meet in their dreams. She pushed the notebook out of the way with her foot, dropped down beside him. Starting out with small talk, the polite ritual of question-and-response, seemed pointless—as if, somehow, they were already beyond that. And something about the lateness of the hour, the darkness covering them, made her normal shyness vanish. Her normal reserve, too.

"I heard," she said simply. "I'm sorry."

"Thanks." There was a long silence before he said, "I'm actually sort of glad it's happened."

"You are?"

"Not glad glad, obviously. It's just, we've known it's been coming, have been waiting for the shit to hit the fan for so long now."

She nodded. "Yeah, the waiting can get super wearing."

"Can it ever."

"And at least now it's over and done."

He laughed, but it was a laugh that didn't express happiness—the opposite, actually. She looked at him. His face was so handsome in the moonlight, she thought, all sharp bones and hollow cheeks, strong square jaw, liquid brown eyes. Saliva shone silver on his lower lip. "Nothing's ever over and done, Alice. I used to believe things ended. Now I know they don't. They don't end even in . . ."

He was about to say *death*, Alice was sure of it, thinking of Camilla and his love for her, still alive and strong after she no longer was. But he stopped himself at the last second, trailed off.

Why did she do it? Alice wanted to ask him. All she'd have to do is say the word *why* and he'd know exactly what she meant, no puzzled looks or cocked heads, no misunderstandings of any kind, she could feel it. Just as she was about to, though, she shivered, once, a mixture of fear and excitement rippling through her body.

Thinking she was cold, Tommy immediately unzipped his windbreaker, draped it over her. It was slipping off one shoulder, and as she reached up to catch it, her hand brushed his, and then he was sliding his fingers through hers. She turned her face up, and for a long moment he looked down at her, his mouth so close to hers that she was breathing his breaths. But the moment passed, and he didn't kiss her as she was hoping. Instead he pulled her to him, against his side. And they sat like that, her head on his shoulder, his arm wrapped around her waist, until the sky lightened and night turned to day.

Chapter
• **NINE** •

W hen Charlie woke up the next morning, she stayed in bed
for a long time, trying to decide something. (Richard and
Maggie were taking the Pollards out for an early round of couples'
golf, so the mandatory family breakfast sentence was temporarily
suspended.) She had a tennis date with Jude in half an hour. Or
did she? That's what she was trying to determine. He'd thrown
out the invitation casually, and late into the night, when he, she,
and Cybill were drunk from the wine, high from the pot. "We
should play tomorrow," he'd said. "I had a match scheduled with
this guy, Chip, at ten, but he sent me a text a few hours ago,
canceling. Be a shame to let the court go to waste." She'd controlled her excitement—the joint helped—shrugged casually, said,
"Sure." Neither of them, though, had mentioned it when she'd
walked him and Cybill to the door. Could be he forgot he made
the offer as soon as it passed his lips. And she didn't want to show
up to be stood up, reveal that she took him seriously, cared more
than he did. Although, she didn't want to miss the chance to be

alone with him either, part of a couple for once instead of part of a threesome.

Fuck it, she said to herself, jumping out of bed, pulling off her T-shirt. She'd head on over to the club. It was where she spent most of her mornings, anyway. And if Jude was a no-show, so what? She'd practice serves or get in a workout with the ball machine. She walked over to her closet to make sure that Fernanda had washed her favorite tennis skirt—she had—then beelined for the bathroom to take a shower. She'd have to make it a snappy one if she didn't want to be late.

Charlie kept her head down as she exited the clubhouse, concentrating on straightening the strings of her tennis racquet, adjusting the placement of her vibration dampener. She told herself she'd get a hopper of balls from one of the pros, do serve drills if it turned out she was solo. She didn't lift her head until she'd reached the chain-link fence surrounding the courts. When she spotted Jude on the other side, she felt pure joy rising up in her, traveling from her stomach to her throat, bursting out of her mouth in a jaw-cracking smile. And she realized that she'd only been fooling herself with the hard-boiled talk, that she'd have been bitterly disappointed if he'd blown her off, that no way would she have spent the next hour practicing her serve.

The joy was undercut when she saw what he was doing: flirting with the college-age girl pro standing at the fence behind him. Jesus, Charlie thought, as she watched the girl laughing at something Jude said, how hard up do you have to be to accept the attention of a high school guy when you're already, like, what, twenty? Not, Charlie admitted to herself, that this girl looked like she was hurting for male attention. She was a slim brunette with a face that was cute if you didn't mind snub noses. Still, though, she should stay out of the nursery.

Charlie slipped the cover off her racquet and tossed it on the bench, then walked over to Jude and the girl.

When he saw her, he smiled big, and she understood that he'd suffered none of the insecurities she'd suffered, had known all along that she'd show, that she wouldn't forget. "Charlie," he said, waving her over, not in the least embarrassed, of course, to be caught hitting on one girl while waiting for another, "this is Lucy. She went to Saint Augie's with me. Was a senior when I was a freshman."

Charlie looked at him. "But I thought you go to Prentice Hall?"

"I do. But that's only because they kicked me out of Saint Augie's. Lucy was the best-looking girl in the senior class, no contest. Lucy, this is Charlie."

Charlie waved to Lucy through the chain-link fence. They exchanged a few pleasantries. Charlie asked her how she liked playing for Amherst, taking pains to be extra friendly and polite. (Nothing, she knew, betrayed jealousy quicker than a lack of manners.) Finally, Lucy told them both to have a good match, then sauntered off to the doubles class she was teaching a few courts over. Jude made a point of watching her go.

"You ready?" Charlie said to him, when Lucy was out of sight.

He turned to her. "Wait, aren't we going to warm up first?"

"Nope."

"Skip the foreplay?" He shrugged, grinned. "Well, okay, baby, but just this once."

"Do you want to serve or receive?" she said, keeping her voice cool, all business.

"Normally I'd let you receive because that's just the kind of guy I am. But my arm's kind of cold, so I'm going to have you serve first."

As Charlie jogged to the other side of the court, she decided that she didn't just want to beat Jude; she wanted to destroy him. Leave him broken and humiliated, begging for mercy. And when she tossed the ball in the air for her first serve, she really went after it, tried to hit the cover off. The ball went into the net, but the aggression still felt good. And, as she stepped to the line for serve number two, she saw Jude take a giant step backward. Good, he was scared.

They were evenly matched, neither one ever more than a game or two ahead of the other. Jude took the first set in a tiebreaker, 10-8. Then Charlie rallied back from a 5-3 deficit to capture the second set 7-5. At times, Charlie got the feeling that Jude was holding back, keeping things close when he could have broken the match wide open, surged ahead, dinking the ball over the net instead of hitting the clean winner deep in the corner for the pleasure of watching her run. She got the feeling that he was toying with her, in other words. Whatever. If he wanted to underestimate her as an opponent, that was his business. Or rather, his loss. She'd make sure of that.

Charlie served for the match at 5-4 in the third set. A point away from the win, she hit a weak backhand slice up the line. Instead of blasting the ball crosscourt, Jude opted for one of his patented feathery drop shots. Charlie sprinted forward, managing to get the ball over the net, but barely. Again, instead of going for the outright winner, Jude decided to get cute some more, throwing up a high topspin lob that the wind blew short into the service box. Charlie waited for the ball to bounce up to the perfect height, making small adjustment steps with her feet just the way she'd been taught, then smashed her racquet head into it as hard as she could. She aimed for the center of Jude's chest. She would have hit it, too, had he not ducked at the last second (the fastest he moved all day). She threw up her arms in triumph.

If Charlie had been hoping for tears, she didn't get them. She didn't even get a flash of annoyance or bad temper, which she would have settled for, gladly. Instead Jude hopped over the net and laughingly congratulated her on a match well played. She couldn't help but notice that he was roughly half as sweaty as she was, making her feel foolish for trying so hard, for getting so worked up about a dumb game that obviously meant nothing. She'd been tricked, she realized, duped into showing how much she cared. A winner, and yet, somehow, in a more important way, a loser, too.

Jude took Charlie to the café for a victory lunch. She was looking forward to spending time with him in a way that didn't involve standing seventy-eight feet apart and slugging a little yellow ball back and forth. Consequently, she was less than delighted when she saw Cybill sitting at a table by the bay window, staring down at her iPhone, looking fresh and clean and pretty in a pink cap-sleeved polo shirt and a pleated white miniskirt that showed off her long, high-crossed legs. Charlie felt like more of a disheveled mess than ever.

"I texted her to meet us here when we switched sides on that last changeover," Jude said, whispering into her ear and placing a hand lightly on the small of her back. "I knew she'd be at the club. Can't have her feeling left out now, can we?"

"Nope," Charlie said back, forcing herself to smile. "Good idea."

"You cut yourself?"

She looked at him, confused. "What?"

He touched the Band-Aid on her back, just above the waistband of her skirt.

She flinched. "Oh, no, that's a mosquito bite. It's kind of inflamed so . . ." She trailed off.

"Ah," he said, in a way that she knew meant he didn't believe her.

Looking away, she said, "We better not keep Cybill waiting."

Cybill glanced up from her iPhone as they approached, wrinkled her nose in distaste. "Wow, Charlie, you take your tennis seriously. You won, I hope."

"She did," Jude said, bending over to kiss Cybill's cool blond cheek, taking the chair across from her. "Shows no mercy, this one."

"Spares no effort either, from the looks of her. I'd have thought you went swimming with your clothes on, Charlie, not played a few measly sets of tennis."

"Nice table," said Jude.

"I took it for the stellar view. But the service so far has been less than stellar."

"Maybe that's because your whole party wasn't here yet," he suggested.

"Or maybe it's because the service here is for shit."

Stan chose that moment to saunter up to the table in his club uniform. "Hey, Charlie," he said, grinning. "How's Tess doing?"

Cybill shot her a sidelong look, like, *you know this person?*

"I couldn't tell you. We haven't been spending much time together these days," Charlie said, trying to sound relaxed but her words coming out tight-voiced.

"Do you have menus for us or something?" Cybill said. "I've been sitting here for, like, ever."

"Actually, miss, I'm not your waiter, but I can go get—"

"You are *a* waiter, though, right?"

The grin vanished from Stan's face. He got a so-that's-how-it's-going-to-be look in his eye. There was a pause; then he said, "I am, yeah." He passed out the menus under his arm. When Charlie took hers, she didn't have the nerve to look up at him. "We've got a couple of specials today. Would you like to hear about them?"

Cybill snorted. "Not really. If they were so special, they'd be on the menu every day."

"Waters would be great," Jude said. "Charlie and I just spent the last hour giving each other quite a workout. Didn't we, Charlie?"

Why was he saying this? Charlie wondered. *To taunt Stan?*

Stan returned Jude's eye contact. Then, his voice light, said, "It's important to replenish those bodily fluids."

"Yeah, waters really would be great," Cybill added. "The whole time I've been sitting here no one's offered me a glass. You waiter guys do depend on tips, don't you?"

Charlie could feel Stan's eyes on her, but she kept her gaze fixed firmly on the napkin in her lap, ashamed of herself for not speaking up. Not enough ashamed, though, to actually speak up

"Yes, we waiter guys do depend on tips," he said coolly. "I'll be right back with those waters."

As he walked off to the kitchen, Jude said to Cybill, "Jesus, you want to be a little less of a raging bitch to the help?"

"Sorry, I just hate it when they get so friendly, acting like we're all equals here, pulling that kumbaya bullshit. It's like, no, you're serving me. We are not on par."

"He goes to Wolcott, you know," Charlie said quietly.

Cybill rolled her eyes. "Oh yeah? On whose dime? Not his own, obviously."

"Just take it down a notch or two," Jude said. "I'm thinking of ordering the clam chowder and I'd rather it didn't come with a side of loogie or sperm." Jude turned to Charlie. "You know, if that guy's bothering you, or making you feel uncomfortable in any way, just tell me. I'll have him fired. Cybill's right. He's out of line. The staff's really not supposed to fraternize with the guests."

But it's okay when Lucy, the sexy tennis pro, does it. Why? Because she graduated from your prep school and paid full tuition for the privilege? Because her parents are both members? Because she's obviously taken the job more for fun and to work on her tan than because she needs the actual cash? Charlie didn't say any of this, though. Just thought it. She shook her head.

"You're too nice, Charlie," Cybill said.

Jude leaned in close to Charlie. "And I suppose it wouldn't be right to punish a guy for having good taste."

Charlie gave a tight smile, then opened her menu, hid her face behind it. She didn't think she could feel like a bigger loser than she did after beating Jude on the court this morning. She was wrong. This victory lunch had the victory match beat. Hands down.

• • •

It was back to the club for dinner that night, a family affair. It was meant to be a celebration. The old guy with all the wives had called Richard that afternoon to tell him he was giving him the commission for the museum—or, as Charlie liked to call it, the *snoozeum*—job. It was a formalish occasion, so they were eating in the dining room rather than in the café. Charlie was praying that Stan wouldn't be on duty this evening. He was, naturally, but at least he wasn't assigned to their table.

She cut the steak she ordered into bites, but didn't eat them. She was too preoccupied to be hungry. Not only was she trying to avoid stumbling into accidental eye contact with Stan, she was also waiting for the perfect moment to bring up the party in New York City that Jude and Cybill were driving down to in under an hour, a party that she, well, not desperately—okay, pretty desperately—wanted to go to. (It wasn't the idea of going to the party itself that had her so hot and bothered; it was the idea that if she *didn't* go, Jude and Cybill would be alone together.) When the non-Stan waiter brought out the coffee and dishes of coconut sorbet that Richard and Alice had ordered for dessert, Charlie gathered together her nerve and broached the subject. "So, mom," she said, bisecting a stray bread crumb on the tablecloth with the edge of her thumbnail, "there's this party tonight . . ."

Maggie smiled indulgently. (Maggie was in a seriously good mood this evening, Charlie noticed, very pleased with herself. She seemed to think she was as responsible for winning the commission as Richard, which, Charlie supposed, maybe she was.) "That's fine," Maggie said. "It's a weeknight, but it's summer vacation. You can go. Have fun. Just no drinking and driving. And be home by twelve."

"I was thinking maybe you'd let me stay out a little bit later tonight."

"How much later?"

"Well, actually, twelve's fine. Just twelve noon, not twelve midnight."

"What?"

Talking fast, Charlie said, "The party's in New York, you know, Manhattan. Jude and Cybill are leaving for it in a little bit, and I said I'd ask if I could go."

Maggie set down her coffee cup so hard it clattered in the saucer. "No."

"Mom, why?"

"You're asking, I'm answering. You absolutely cannot go."

"Oh, Margaret," said Richard, "let her. It's still early and it's only a two-hour drive to the city. She'll be back by tomorrow."

Maggie shot Richard a rare—rare to the point of never—buttout look, then whipped back around to face her youngest daughter. "You think I'm going to let you drive down to New York City and spend the night with that wild Devlin boy who has no parents?"

"Jude has parents."

"Well, you wouldn't know it because they're never around. He's raising himself, from what I can see. Wealthy but deprived. The father's so busy lieutenant-governing Massachusetts or whatever it is he does, he lets his teenage kid run completely wild."

Charlie was surprised at her mom's vehemence. She sounded like the old Maggie, Cambridge Maggie. Serenity Point Maggie was much more permissive, much more laid back, too blissed out with Richard to be bothered sticking her nose in her daughters' business.

"I'm not spending the night with him," Charlie mumbled. "I'd just be staying with him at some apartment in the city his parents own. And Cybill will be there."

"Well, excellent, then he'll have company since you won't be."

"But, mom—"

"Alice, what's your opinion of this Jude person? You know him."

Alice quit staring at that old photo on the wall of Tommy van Stratten—Jesus, obsess much?—to stare at her mother.

"Well," said Maggie, impatient, "what is it?"

Alice opened her mouth, but then closed it again. She looked like a guppy. Finally she dropped her gaze to her sorbet dish, shrugged.

"That's what I thought," Maggie said, a gleam of triumph in her eyes.

Charlie stood up from the table quickly, letting her napkin fall to the floor. "I need some fresh air," she said. On the way out, she squeezed Richard's hand, to let him know she appreciated his support, and pointedly did not look at Alice to let her know what she thought of her traitorous ways. As she opened the door, she was annoyed to see the waiter pick up the napkin, neatly fold it, and return it to the side of her plate. Some dramatic exit.

Charlie leaned on the railing of the clubhouse porch, let the breeze coming off the ocean cool her hot face. Knowing that Cybill would have Jude all to herself tonight was filling her with more anxiety than she could handle. She knew her feelings were ridiculous, totally unjustifiable. It's not as if she spent every waking moment with either one of them. They could easily be getting together behind her back. In fact, she suspected they were. Still, suspecting and knowing were two entirely different things. And knowing for sure they were going to be alone together for the next twelve to eighteen hours, a bed in the near vicinity, was making her nuts, just itchy with nerves and dread.

What a bitch her mother was being. And Alice, that little priss. Little phony, too. She'd crept in the house at dawn this morning. Charlie had seen her through the window when she woke up with dry mouth, went to the bathroom for a glass of water. Richard was proving to be all right, though, a little stiff maybe but basically a decent guy. He got it, at least. Knew what it took to make it socially in Serenity Point. Her mom didn't have to know what it took because Richard had already made it for her. And Alice was happy to be an outsider, preferred it that way.

A voice cut into her thoughts: "Nice view."

She turned, saw Stan on the dark end of the porch. He slipped something into his back pocket—a paperback, it looked like—strolled over to her. "Yeah, it is," she said. "Not that I was looking."

"What are you doing out here then?"

"Cooling off. I got into a fight with my mom."

"How come?"

"Because, well, because she's an asshole, basically."

Stan let out a low chuckle. It drifted off into the night. They listened to it go.

"She's not really an asshole," Charlie amended, after a bit. "She's just acting like one. Bossing me around."

"Yeah, moms'll do that. You shouldn't let it get to you so much."

Normally this kind of advice would have annoyed Charlie no

end. Like, gee, why didn't I think of that? Not this time, for some reason. "Speaking of acting like an asshole," she said, "I'm sorry for earlier today."

"It wasn't you. It was the people you were with."

"I was an asshole for letting them."

He didn't disagree with this statement. The silence between them lengthened and filled with night sounds, sounds Charlie normally didn't notice but now were suddenly all she could hear: the creak of insects, the distant pounding of the surf, the low whistle of wind moving through trees. Over the flat expanse of golf course, she could see the ocean glowing brightly under the moon.

"So what were you reading?" Charlie said after a while.

Stan pulled the book out of his pocket, handed it to her.

"Mikhail Bulgakov, *The Master and Margarita*, " Charlie said, reading off the cover. "Is that German?"

"Nope, Russian. Like me."

"You're Russian?"

"My name is Stanislav. What else would I be?"

"I thought Stan was short for Stanley. Were you born in Russia?"

"I was, in Moscow. But my family came to America when I was three, so I don't remember it."

A second silence, even longer than the first. "Is the book any good?" Charlie finally said.

"Yeah. I'll lend it to you when you're finished with *Tess*. It'll wash the taste of Thomas Hardy out of your mouth, if nothing else."

"Got to get the taste in my mouth before I can wash it out."

He slid the book back in his pocket. "So, you ready to put on your nice face, go back inside?"

She nodded. "Thanks to you I can probably make it through the rest of dessert without bitch-slapping my mom."

He laughed. "Glad I could help."

They walked through the door together, then headed in opposite directions: he toward the kitchen, she toward the dining room.

Chapter
• TEN •

*A*lice was the recipient of one very cold shoulder at breakfast the next morning. Charlie wasn't giving her the full-on silent treatment, but close: single-word answers and minimal eye contact, all the while lavishing attention on everyone else at the table to really drive the point home. Not a big believer in the subtle approach, her sister. Alice guessed that Charlie was mad because she didn't stick up for Jude at dinner last night with Maggie. The truth was, Alice thought she was being nice by keeping her mouth shut, that she was doing Charlie a favor. She didn't run Jude down, which was what she'd wanted to do, and which is what she would've done if she'd actually answered. No, she'd stayed discreetly silent. Well, that's what she got for being considerate.

"Hey, mom," Alice said, "are you going into town today?"

Her mom put down her slice of cantaloupe, touched her fingertips to her napkin. "Why? What do you need?"

"Nothing, really. I was just thinking of going to the bookstore. I finished *The Omnivore's Dilemma* yesterday."

"Is that what you were reading for school?"

"No. For pleasure."

Charlie snorted at that one, momentarily forgetting to feign deafness anytime Alice spoke.

Ignoring her sister, Alice said, "My assigned reading is *The Magus*, which I saw on one of the shelves in the library. So there's no need for me to pick up that. Anyway, I'm on kind of a nonfiction kick these days."

"I have no plans to go into town today," Maggie said. "But you know who does?"

Alice felt a flicker of dread as she lifted one shoulder in a shrug.

Richard looked at her over the top of his paper. "I was planning on driving in at around eleven thirty, picking up the jacket they're altering for me at the tailor's. I can wait a little if you won't be ready by then."

"She'll be ready," Maggie said. "Won't you, sweetheart?'"

If Richard's eyes weren't right on her face at that moment, Alice would have glared at her mother. As it was, she didn't dare. Just nodded, went back to her Grape-Nuts.

Alice lingered around the dining room after everyone else had wandered off. She helped Luz clear the table. Luz was a short woman in her mid-sixties. She was almost perfectly round, as wide as she was tall, with a cap of spiky salt-and-pepper hair and a cheerful, grandmotherly face. She hummed while she worked and liked to talk about her grandkids.

As Luz stood over the kitchen garbage can, a stack of dirty dishes and bowls at her elbow, Alice leaned against the counter. With as much casualness as she could muster, she said, "So how long have you worked for my stepdad, Luz? A long time?"

"Oh, no. I'm almost as new as you are. Mr. Flood hired me and Fernanda a couple of weeks before you and your mom and your sister moved in. We reopened the house for him. Got things ready."

"Oh," said Alice, disappointed.

"Will you hand me that spatula, sweetheart? This oatmeal seems to want to stick to the bowl." As Alice obliged, Luz said, "You know, that's not completely true."

"What's not?"

"That I'm as new to the house as you are. I'd been here a few times before. Back when the first Mrs. Flood was here." Luz looked up at Alice, flushing slightly, as though fearing she was being tactless or insensitive. "But only two or three times. She used to throw parties. Big ones. They needed extra staff."

"So you knew the family?"

Luz raised her right hand, held the tips of her thumb and index finger very close together to indicate just how small her knowledge was.

"What was Camilla like? Was she beautiful?" There. Alice had said the name out loud. Camilla. It was a huge relief, like some giant pressure inside her had been eased.

"Yes," Luz said, then glanced over her shoulder as if to make sure no one else was listening. "A very beautiful girl. So full of life. Oh, and that smile of hers. As soon as you saw it, you just had to smile back, no matter what kind of mood you were in."

"That's what I've heard."

"And good at so many things. She got a perfect score on her SATs. I know because she tutored a niece of mine. She used to volunteer at the YMCA. At Meals on Wheels, too. Oh, my niece loved her, just worshipped the ground she walked on. Thought she was the smartest, prettiest, nicest girl. It was all she would talk about when she got home."

Alice took in what Luz was saying hungrily, greedily, like an eavesdropper crouched outside a cracked window. It didn't matter that what she was hearing was painful, was making Tommy seem further and further out of reach. She had to listen, couldn't get enough.

Luz continued: "And I'd see Camilla's name in the paper all the time. She seemed to win every tennis match she played. Could sail as good as your stepdad could, too. Boy, was he crazy about her. Thought the sun rose and set with her. Like I said, I only knew the family a little bit, but I felt so bad for him, didn't know how he was going to make it after, well"—her voice dropping to a whisper—"what happened."

"Yeah," Alice said quietly.

Luz took off her yellow latex cleaning glove so she could pat Alice's hand awkwardly. "I hear you're very talented yourself, Alice. You draw, is that right? I always wished I could do that. Very relaxing, I'd think. And so nice to have something at the end, something to hang on the wall."

Alice made murmurs of agreement, but she found Luz's words depressing. What a talent. Transferring things that existed in the real world onto a flat piece of paper. Camilla's talents sounded so much more exciting, so much more dynamic.

As Alice left Luz, wandered back upstairs to her room, she

thought about Camilla. Camilla who possessed a beauty that couldn't be forgotten, an intelligence that was as generous as it was penetrating, and a smile so high-voltage it could light up a room. Good at everything she turned her hand to and yet patient with those less gifted. Somewhere in the house her laughter still lingered. There were rooms that contained objects she had touched, patches of floor that her feet had walked across, mirrors that had held her image. She was more present dead than Alice was alive.

Who's really the ghost here? Alice wondered.

Alice slid the metal tongue into the metal buckle, then leaned back in her seat. Richard inserted they key in the ignition, turned it. He pressed the button to lower his window, then paused, looked at her.

"I won't if you don't want me to," he said.

"No, I don't mind."

"Are you sure? I could put on the air conditioner just as easily."

"Seriously, it's fine. I'm not fussy about temperature."

He gave her a tight smile and nodded.

Alice looked out the window as they started down the long driveway. Though she was dreading this little outing, she was hoping it wouldn't be a complete waste of time. Last night she'd received an e-mail from her best friend, Angela, who was big into Occupy Boston, the Boston faction of Occupy Wall Street. A group was going to be gathering in Dewey Square on Tuesday to demonstrate. Alice had been following the movement in the news for what seemed like forever now and was itching to get involved. This struck her as an ideal opportunity, made that much more ideal by Patrick's guaranteed absence. (According to Angela, he'd be in New Hampshire visiting his cousin through the weekend, which meant she'd only have to duck his calls.) Not that she never wanted to see or talk to him again. She just wanted to wait until she knew where she stood with Tommy before having a conversation with her kind-of, sort-of, not-really-boyfriend boyfriend.

Alice was worried that her mom would say no to the trip since there was a strong possibility she would get arrested. Not that getting arrested for a political protest would have upset the old Maggie, Cambridge Maggie. On the contrary, Cambridge Maggie would have regarded it as a rite of passage, proof of political commitment. But Serenity Point Maggie appeared to have been built without a social conscience. Alice was thinking, however, that Richard might be a valuable ally if approached right. After all, he'd supported the idea of Charlie's going to New York for the night, and that was just for some dumb party. And it sounded to Alice as if Camilla had been pretty heavy into community service, so he'd get it.

"Hey, Richard," Alice said, turning in her seat to face him. When she saw she had his attention, she lowered her eyelashes like they were curtains then looked at him from up under them the way she'd seen Charlie do.

"Yes, Alice?"

"I was thinking about asking mom if I could go to Cambridge for a day or two this week."

He smiled at her. "Oh yeah? What for? To visit friends?"

"Sort of."

His smile got bigger. "Or to visit a boyfriend? Your mom told me about Patrick."

Annoyed that her mom discussed her personal life with Richard, but trying to ignore the annoyance, she said, "Actually, I wanted to go for Occupy Boston."

All of a sudden, Richard's expression clouded. "And why would you want to get involved with a loser cause like that?"

Shocked, Alice said, "You think fighting against corporate greed and corruption and for social and economic equality is a loser cause?"

"I don't think it. I know it. It's sour grapes. Hippie, commie sour grapes."

"I think that you might be simplifying things a little bit and—"

Richard rolled right over her: "No, I'm not simplifying. It *is* simple. It's the ones who can't hack it railing against the ones who can. It's the weak trying to bring down the strong. You know what it takes to earn a good living in this world?"

Alice folded her arms tightly against her abdomen. "Why don't you tell me?"

"Brains, talent, and will."

"If you want to know what God thinks of money, just look at the people He gave it to."

Richard snorted out a laugh. "Clever."

"I'll tell Dorothy Parker you said so."

"And what's that slogan of those Occupy Wall Streeters?" Richard made his voice puffed up and blowhard-y: "*We are the 99 percent*?" Back to his normal voice: "Well, I can talk percentages, too. Who pays 38 percent of federal income taxes? That 1 percent they hate so much. This country would go under without us. We *are* this country."

Alice didn't respond because she was afraid if she did, she might cry. They drove the last mile in silence. Out of the corner of her eye,

Alice looked at her stepfather, at his handsome, inscrutable face and his steel-gray hair, at the muscle twitching in his clenched jaw. What was his problem? What was so different about her joining a group that rallied against the overprivileged and Camilla's volunteering her time at the YMCA to help the underprivileged? Why did he care so much about her political views? If she believed the influence of corporate money was too powerful and needed to be checked? Did he feel she was attacking him by going to Occupy Boston? That attending the protest was her way of protesting him? He definitely seemed to be taking this whole excursion extremely personally. (He didn't even *work* in the financial sector.) He was so much more easygoing with Charlie.

Alice had thought for a while that his preference for her sister was all in her head, but now she was sure it wasn't. Was it because Charlie was naturally livelier and higher-spirited, like their mom? Was it because she fit so seamlessly into Serenity Point, already indispensable to her circle of friends? Or was it because she, Alice, recalled Camilla in all the wrong ways? A similar—though lesser—version of his dead daughter, simultaneously too much like her and not enough? Reminding him of Camilla, only to remind him of all he'd lost when she died?

At last, they reached town. As soon as Richard parked the car, Alice got out of it, sick of the silent comparisons: *Why can't you look more like Camilla? Act more like Camilla? Be more like Camilla.* "See you at home," she said.

He called her name a couple of times, but she didn't turn around. Just kept walking, the tears she'd managed to hold back now streaming out of her eyes, practically blinding her.

Chapter
• ELEVEN •

*C*harlie had *Tess of the d'Urbervilles* open in her hands, but she wasn't reading a word. She was too distracted to concentrate, was too distracted to do anything but kick the heel of the leg thrown over the arm of the wicker deck chair she was sprawled across. She was waiting to hear from Cybill. Cybill and Jude should've been back from New York hours ago. But so far, not a word. Not a single, solitary peep. And then, a peep. Or, more accurately, a *beep*: Charlie's new iPhone, the one Richard had just bought her, telling her she had a new text message. It was from Cybill.

> Hey u. At beach with Jude. Trying to sweat out last night's
> booze. Sweat out other stuff too. Join us???

Charlie forced herself not to get up from her chair, stared at that same page of *Tess* for another twenty minutes before allowing herself to text back a B RITE THERE so as to avoid seeming overeager. As she ran upstairs to change into her bikini, ready herself for the beach, she thought about Alice, wished she could take her sister with her. But Alice hadn't come back from town with Richard, which meant she was probably planning on mooning around the bookstore for the rest of the afternoon. And besides, Charlie was officially still mad at her. She planned to punish her for at least another day or two. The thing about Alice was that while she often acted as if she was socially oblivious, she wasn't. On the contrary, she was extremely sharp about people and situations. Her instincts were excellent. And right now, Charlie could use some of that sharpness and some of those instincts. She wanted to ask Alice whether or not she thought Jude and Cybill were hooking up. So far she hadn't had the guts. It was like she didn't want to know for sure, and if Alice gave her opinion, she'd know. (Okay, not know know, but pretty much know.) Now, it was no longer a matter of wanting or not wanting. It was no longer a matter of choice.

She *needed* to know.

Well, Charlie thought with a sigh, her needs would just have to hold their horses until Alice came back. She tossed her book, sunglasses, and iPhone into her beach bag, left a sundress and pair of capri pants out on the bed for Fernanda to take to the dry cleaners, then ran downstairs and out the door.

Cybill and Jude were at their usual spot on the club's private beach. "Charlieeeee," Cybill said in that way of hers, talking through her teeth as though she were too rich or too bored to actually open her mouth. She and Jude looked a little hungover maybe, wincing at the brightness of the sun and slightly puffy around the eyes, but otherwise normal. In fact, the whole afternoon Charlie spent with them was normal—tomato juice, vodka, Korres Walnut & Coconut Suntan Oil—except that she didn't react to it in her normal way. For the first time, she didn't have fun with them. It was like she was too annoyed to have a good time. And it wasn't Jude who was annoying her—it was Cybill.

Cybill kept talking about the night before in this cryptic language that only Jude could understand, cracking jokes meant only for his ears. Basically, she was speaking to him in code. At first Charlie tried to be a good sport and enter into the spirit of the hilarity, get her bearings. Like when she asked Cybill to explain the story behind "things are getting interesting," a phrase Cybill repeated to Jude throughout the afternoon, always to great effect. "There was this billboard above the Lincoln Tunnel for this low-rent champagne-y, cognac-y type drink and—" was as far as Cybill got before dissolving into a fit of giggles. After a while, Charlie stopped asking. She knew Cybill was just trying to make her feel excluded, and it was working.

After Cybill made her third reference of the hour to Hostess cherry pies, Charlie shed her sunglasses—the identical style and brand as Cybill's and Jude's, bought for her by Richard the same day he bought her the iPhone—and stood.

"I'm going to take a dip," she said.

As she dove into the green face of a tall wave, she decided she was going to make her move tonight. Screw Cybill.

It was time to advance the plot with Jude.

At ten that evening, Charlie, pleading a minor headache, trudged upstairs to bed. She waited in her dark room until she heard the doors to Maggie and Richard's room close, the door to Alice's room close, and then waited for nearly an hour on top of that (Alice never went to sleep straightaway, always read first) before sneaking down the stairs and out the back door, tennis gear in hand. It was a warm night, the air hot and heavy. And the moon hung low in the sky, full and fat, a bright, buttery yellow. She walked to Jude's house, about a quarter of a mile down the beach in the opposite direction of the club. Not that she remembered walking. She was too anxious and excited and panicked and eager for her brain to function properly. But she knew she must've because suddenly she found herself there.

Why am I so nervous? she wondered, wiping her sweaty palms on her knees. It's not like she was a virgin. Far from it. Well, actually not that far. Still, it wasn't like she had *no* experience. But Jude had obviously had so much, and with sophisticated girls who went to boarding school, not townie guys who lived in their parents' basement. Ugh. She had to stop thinking like this. But she couldn't. The thoughts were coming at her fast and furious and relentless, like bullets from a machine gun, *rat tat tat tat tat*. And then she stepped on a piece of broken seashell. The shard sliced into the flesh of her big toe. The pain it caused her, though, was weirdly welcome, offering her a strange kind of relief—sharp and bracing. It calmed her mind, let her focus on the task at hand.

As she crouched down to pour water from her Evian bottle over the bloody toe, wrap it in one of the many Band-Aids she was carrying around in her bag, she was relieved to see that the light was on in Jude's first-floor bedroom, the window thrown wide open. She crept up to it. She heard a voice inside talking, and her stomach dropped to her ankles because at first she thought that meant he wasn't alone, that Cybill was with him. But she listened for a while, and his voice was the only voice. He was on the telephone, she realized.

"He said no? But did you tell him it was me?" he was saying. There was a pleading note in his voice that Charlie had never heard before, and wouldn't even have thought that cool, bored, contemptuous voice was capable of making. "Yes, I understand it's late, but it's not that late. Just tell him I really need to talk to him."

Silence while he listened to the person on the other end of the line.

"What do you mean, he won't take my call?" Jude faltered on the word *mean* in a way that let Charlie know tears were on the way. But instead of crying, he got angry. "Remind him I'm his son, the only one he has. Can you do that for me? Yeah, I'll wait."

Again, silence as he listened.

Sounding frustrated now, he said, "No, don't wake my mom. She has a hard enough time falling asleep as it is. Okay, fine, yeah, sure, my dad and I will talk tomorrow, no problem. Tell him it's a bit much, though, not returning my calls for five days straight. Kind of an asshole move, tell him. I get that he's a busy guy, too busy to be a father, but this is getting fucking ridiculous."

A third silence.

"Yeah, you give him that message word for word. And be sure not to leave out the *asshole* or the *fucking*, you suck-ass, brownnosing piece of shit. . . . Yeah, yeah, you have a good night, too, *Todd*."

The sound of the phone being slammed into the receiver, and then silence.

Charlie pulled out the tennis ball that she'd sliced open, stuck a note inside—*Rematch. Midnight. Winner takes all*—from her bag, rolled it around her palm. Her timing, it seemed, couldn't have been worse. Hard to imagine Jude would be in the mood for a romantic interlude after that scene with his dad's staff member or whoever that Todd guy was. Then she reflected on the situation a bit more. Realized that maybe her timing wasn't as bad as she'd first thought. After all, Jude was vulnerable right now, cracks finally showing in his too-cool facade. Could be he was ready to loosen his grip on that ironic edge of his. Could be he was ready to let somebody in.

Her, if she played her cards right.

She decided to take the chance. After counting to a hundred slowly in her head so he wouldn't know she'd overheard anything private, she snuck a quick peek in the window. Jude was lying motionless on his bed, staring up at the ceiling, flask open and balanced on his stomach. She lobbed the ball through the opening, listened for the sound of it landing, then ran back down to the beach.

Charlie walked fast. Not fast enough, though, to beat Jude. By the time she hopped the club fence, crossed the enormous golf course, he was already on the lit-up court, twirling his racquet. He must've driven, she thought as she approached the net, forcing herself to slow down, to walk not run.

"You got my message," she said, regretting the words as soon as they were out of her mouth. Obviously he got her message.

But he didn't seem to notice the dumbness of her observation. "You could've just texted me, you know."

"Where's the fun in that?"

"I guess there isn't any." He dropped the ball, caught it when it bounced back up.

"Well, there you go," she said. She tried to arrange her body in a way that felt natural but she was stiff-jointed, and every one of her limbs was sticking out at a sharp, tense angle. And in that moment she realized that even though she had Jude right where she wanted him, everything going according to plan, that she'd never be able to pull it off, was in way over her head. Black panic started to overtake her.

Jude looked down at his feet, then back at her face, bounced the ball a couple more times. "So, how long were you standing outside my window?" he asked, with a laugh he cut off almost as soon as it began.

And hearing it, she understood he was nervous. (That's what all the ball bouncing was about, to show he was at ease, but he wasn't, not even close.) She understood *why* he was nervous, too: he was afraid she'd witnessed him in a vulnerable state. Charlie had been so nervous herself all night, so filled with uncertainty and dread, it hadn't occurred to her that he might be as well, even if for an entirely different reason. And knowing he was made her relax, every bit of tension suddenly draining out of her body. "Not long," she said, holding his eye.

He continued to bounce the ball in that casual/not-casual way. "How long's not long?"

"However long it takes to run up to a window, throw a ball, run away from a window. Two seconds? Three maybe?"

He nodded, but then turned his face away, so she couldn't tell if he believed her or not. He must've, though, because when he turned back thirty seconds later, a smile had formed on his lips—half-cocky, half-lazy, all Jude. "Winner takes all, the note said. High stakes."

"The highest," she agreed.

"Spin to decide who serves first?"

"No. I'll do the deciding. You serve first."

Without waiting for his reaction, Charlie turned around. She unsheathed her racquet, tossed the cover, then strolled back to the baseline. Crouching down, she got into ready position. Jude started his service motion. The ball came at her. She let it pass by without even attempting a swing. "Whoops," she said.

He looked at her, confused.

She moved from the deuce side to the ad. Again the ball came at her. Again she let it pass without attempting a swing. "Should we do this another forty or fifty times?" she said. "Or are you starting to get the picture?"

"I think I might be."

"I could go through the hit-and-miss motions, but I'd rather not."

Nodding, beginning to walk from his side of the court to hers, Jude said, "Yeah, too warm a night for that."

"Exactly. And I don't want to get all hot and sweaty. Not playing tennis, anyway."

"That would make you the loser in this competition then."

"Yes."

"And me the winner."

"Yes."

"So I take all."

"Those were the terms."

He was close to her now, very close, their bodies nearly touching, and she could feel the heat of him through his T-shirt and shorts, the swirl of his breath in her ear when he said, "Then I think it only right that you should take it"—pausing, grinning—"off."

An excited giggle was starting to make her lips tremble, so she clamped them down. Everything was going the way she'd imagined. She almost couldn't believe how exactly. And she'd mapped out the disrobing process in her head in advance, had choreographed it, basically. The order in which she'd remove clothing items, how she'd avoid awkwardness when it came to unhooking her bra (she'd purposely worn a black lacy push-up that lifted and separated, not a horrible sports bra that flattened her breasts, turned them into a single fleshy pancake).

As she reached for the zipper on the side of her skirt, though, Jude stopped her, placing the frame of his racquet on the back of her hand. "No, not your clothes. I want you to take off your Band-Aid."

"My Band-Aid?" she repeated.

"Yeah. I want you to show me what's underneath."

"You've seen what's underneath."

"And it's not a mosquito bite. I want to see again."

"Why?" The word came out a whisper.

Before he could respond to the question, she shook her head, rescinding it. She'd set the rules. Now she had to obey them. After all, he'd already exposed himself to her tonight, even if without knowing. She owed it to him to return the favor, to make herself vulnerable. Besides, she'd been prepared to get completely naked.

What he was asking for should be a piece of cake in comparison. She grasped the edge of the Band-Aid with her pinched-together thumb and index finger. One fast motion, she told herself. As she started to pull, though, a jolt of fear ran along her spine, an electrical charge that made her fingers withdraw, curl self-protectively into her palm. She tried, but she couldn't uncurl them. A silence developed, grew so deep she could hear the wet, clammy thud of her heart in it.

And then Jude said softly, "I'll do it."

He laid his racquet on the ground and put his arms around her almost in an embrace, but looser. His hand slipped under the back of her shirt, his fingers locating the spot just above the waistband of her skirt. He removed the adhesive slowly, his eyes on hers the whole time. She winced, but not at the pain. In fact, the air felt good on the always-covered patch of skin. So did his fingers, moving lightly over it, then clinging to it, applying different pressures, changing angles, deftly, skillfully, tenderly. He didn't even seem to want to look at it, which should have relieved her, since it was the thought of the tattoo being viewed, and by him in particular, not touched, that made her stomach twist, the back of her neck start to sweat.

And yet, and yet, Charlie was afraid she was going to burst into tears. Shame, disappointment, humiliation, relief—she didn't know which one it was, but it was rising in her like a wave, tightening her throat, making speech impossible. She did her best to fight off the tide of emotion, to push it back, jam it down. And she managed. Almost. All that came out of her was a single tear, spilling over the brim of her eye.

Jude leaned forward and kissed it off her cheek. She fell into him, burying her face in his chest.

Chapter
• TWELVE •

he following afternoon, Alice was at the club. She was waiting for Charlie to finish her clinic, then the two of them were
going to head into town to see the new Ryan Gosling movie, maybe
go for Thai food after that. A slinky black Town Car had swung by the
house for Richard and Maggie an hour ago. They were being driven
to Boston, the guests of honor at a dinner the Pollards were hosting
to introduce them to the museum's biggest donors. Alice was glad
that she and Charlie were spending the evening together. It seemed
like forever since they'd done anything, just the two of them.

As whenever she was in the club, Alice found herself drawn help-
lessly to the dining room, to the photo hanging on the east-facing
wall. She didn't know how long she'd been standing there, staring,
but it must have been for a while, because before she knew it Charlie
was beside her.

"Who is it you're looking at in this picture?" Charlie said. "I used
to think it was Tommy, but Tommy's on the rowing machine in the
gym right now. You could be ogling him live and in the very buff flesh

if you wanted. So Camilla must be the one." Raising an eyebrow, she said, "Obsessing over a girl who's dead and semi-related to you. Now that's twisted, like three perversions rolled into one."

"She doesn't look like the type who'd kill herself, does she?"

Charlie sighed. "We've been over this already. Life had just flipped her off big time. Her head was all messed up. Plus, she might have been having a really bad hair day." Off the look Alice shot her: "I'm kidding, obviously. Lighten up. Seriously, she might have been unbalanced to begin with. You know, like chemically. And what happened to her mom pushed her over the edge."

"You think that was it?" Alice said. "A chemical imbalance?"

Charlie shrugged. "I'm just throwing it out there as a possibility."

"But she sounded so high-functioning. A whiz kid at school, Mother Theresa-ing in her spare time, not to mention the active social life, serious boyfriend, and all that."

Charlie nodded. "Yeah, and upstairs there are a bunch of plaques and trophies with her name on them. She must've been some tennis player. She was winning the women's singles events here back when she was, like, eleven. So her highs were really high, but maybe her lows were really low."

"Does Cybill ever talk about her?"

"No."

"No as in *not often* or no as in *never*?"

"The second one. I mean, apart from that first night. And you were there for that."

"Well," Alice said, turning to Charlie, "don't you think her silence says something?"

"Yeah, that she doesn't want to talk about it." Charlie's eyes widened, a thought suddenly occurring to her: "Hey, how did you get Richard to cough up the keys to the Mercedes? He's weirdly possessive of that car of his. I mean, for a guy who could buy a fleet of them without making a dent in his wallet."

"I don't think his possessiveness has anything to do with money."

"No, I know," Charlie said, with a sigh. "He's nervous about teenage girls getting behind the wheel."

They were both quiet for a few beats. Then Alice said, "Mom did it for me. I figured she'd have better luck. Probably had to swear that we'd use the car to go to a movie, nothing else, no detours or stop-offs." Glancing down at the clock on her cell phone, she added, "Speaking of which, it starts in fifteen minutes. We should get going."

Charlie took a step, winced.

"What's wrong?"

"Nothing. I cut my toe on something last night. It's a little sore today. Plus, I didn't sleep so great."

"God, you're a mess."

"I know," Charlie said, letting her forehead drop, resting it on Alice's shoulder. "I hope Ryan Gosling takes off his shirt a lot. Like, *a lot* a lot."

Alice ran her fingers back and forth across the nape of Charlie's neck a few times before fishing the Mercedes keys out of her pocket. "Yeah, you and me both," she said, an arm around her sister's shoulders, guiding her out of the club.

It was still light out when Alice and Charlie left the movie house. They'd shared a tub of popcorn, so they weren't hungry. Not meal hungry, at least. They got ice cream cones instead and strolled along the pretty town streets, looking in shop windows, bumping shoulders. As they were cutting through the small park at the center of Serenity Point Square, they passed a tiny old woman on a bench, sitting with a heavyset woman in a nurse's uniform reading a magazine.

The old woman was looking at her, so Alice turned to smile.

"Camilla!" the old woman shouted suddenly. "Camilla, it's you!"

Alice and Charlie stopped and stared as the old woman staggered to her feet, lurched toward them. To Alice's horror, the old woman grabbed her arm, the gnarled fingers with the long, yellowy nails surprisingly—shockingly—strong, digging into her flesh like claws. Alice's ice cream cone fell to the ground.

"Camilla, where have you been?" the old woman said, fixing Alice with a bright blue eye. The other was milky white, crusted at the corner, unseeing, obviously.

Alice, trying to hide her revulsion, speaking gently, said, "I'm not Camilla. Camilla's gone. I'm Alice."

"I wait for you every week, Camilla."

"I'm Alice," she said again, a little more forcefully this time.

"The other girl never remembers that I hate stewed carrots. She always brings me stewed carrots. Stewed carrots make me gag." The old woman was so excited, her dentures were becoming loose, dripping thick, gooey strands of saliva onto Alice's arm. "Why does she do that, Camilla?"

"I'm Alice," Alice said, almost pleading now.

"You never brought me stewed carrots, Camilla. You always remembered that I couldn't eat them, brought me creamed corn instead." Tears were leaking now from the old woman's one good eye, disappearing into the deep wrinkles on her cheeks. "Why don't you come see me anymore? Did I do something wrong?" On the word *wrong*, her teeth slid all the way out of her mouth, landing with a soft *plop* in the chocolate ice cream melting on the pavement. "I'm so fond of you, Camilla. Can't you please start visiting me again?"

Alice tried to free her arm, but the old woman's grip only tightened. Panicked, Alice turned to Charlie. "I don't know what she's talking about."

"Of course you don't. She's fucking nuts." Charlie yelled out to the nurse: "Hey, if you don't get your patient off my sister, I will. And I won't be gentle."

Slowly the nurse put down her magazine, rolled to her feet. "What's got into you, Mrs. Graves? You leave these girls alone. Come on, now. Let's go back home. I'll make you a nice cup of tapioca pudding. How does that sound?"

All of a sudden, the old woman's one eye narrowed shrewdly. "You're not Camilla," she said, shaking Alice's arm. "You're nothing like Camilla. Why are you pretending to be her? Where is she? What have you done with her?"

All at once, the strength drained out of the old woman's grasp, and Alice was able to pull away.

"Camilla," the old woman moaned, collapsing against the side of her nurse, her body wracked with sobs.

The old woman didn't look scary anymore, like some cackling evil crone out of a B horror movie; she just looked small and confused and very, very elderly, half-blind, her toothless mouth caving in on itself. "I'm sorry," Alice kept murmuring over and over. "I'm sorry."

"What do you have to be sorry for?" Charlie said. "It's not your fault she's lost her marbles." She grabbed Alice's hand, tugged. "Let's get the hell out of here before she gets her teeth back in."

"God," Alice said when she and Charlie at last emerged on the other side of the park. "That poor woman. But kind of spooky, right?"

"*Kind of* spooky? Full on heebie-jeebieville, I'd say."

"She must've been from the Meals on Wheels program that Camilla did volunteer work for."

"See, that's why I never do anything selfless. Bites you in the ass. With its gummy, old-person mouth." Charlie shivered delicately. "Hey, did we park on this street or one over?"

"One over."

A minute later, Charlie was chattering away, the traumatic event in the park all but forgotten. Alice, though, could still hear the sounds of the old woman's weeping. Didn't stop hearing them until she got into the Mercedes, crossed the Greeves Bridge, leaving town behind.

It was still early when the two girls returned to the beach house. Not wanting to end the night just yet, they climbed into Charlie's bed, bringing her laptop with them. They'd been working their way through *Buffy the Vampire Slayer* back in Cambridge and were halfway through season three. They picked up where they left off, starting the next episode on Hulu. Charlie was out before the credits even rolled. Alice hit the pause button, moved the computer to the desk. Then she pulled the blanket up to Charlie's chin and crept back to her own room.

As she lay on top of her bed, not daring to slip under the covers, waiting for the clock to strike midnight, she had trouble keeping her eyelids from closing. It was like tiny weights had been sewn into them. She'd been sleeping so little lately, sneaking out to join Tommy at the bonfire pit on the beach for the last couple of nights, staying with him until the sun came up. She'd get in a nap before breakfast—and nap was the word for it, losing consciousness for two hours, three at the most—and the lack of rest was beginning to catch up with her. Not that she cared if it did. No way was she going to stop meeting him for so boring a reason as clinical exhaustion. These clandestine encounters were better than any dream she could be having. Sometimes she thought they *were* a dream she was having.

When she and Tommy got together, they didn't talk, not really, not after that first night. Truthfully, they didn't do much of anything. They just sat, often holding hands. These rendezvous felt romantic to Alice, though they weren't sexual—Tommy had never even tried to kiss her—so she didn't know if she was fooling herself about the romantic part or not. Her feelings for him were definitely romantic. And sometimes she thought his for her were, too—the way he'd look at her, his eyes soft on her face. But other times he seemed so distant, like he was worlds away, no reaching him or calling him back.

That was how it was tonight, right now. They were huddled together. She was sort of tucked into him, fitted in between his legs, her back against his chest. She craned her neck so she'd have a view of his face, saw that faraway expression on it, and her heart swelled painfully in her chest. A small sigh escaped his lips. She bet he didn't even know he'd made the sound. But she knew he'd made it, and she knew why he'd made it, too: out of longing, or rather, frustrated longing. He was wishing that it was Camilla he was holding in his arms, wishing it was Camilla's blond hair that his chin was resting in, wishing it was Camilla's scent that his nostrils were filling with. And knowing what he was thinking was causing Alice's heart to swell past the point of pain, swell to the point where she was afraid it might actually burst, kill her. Unable to control herself anymore, she said to him, "Just say it. Just say what's really wrong."

He looked down at her. "Wrong? What are you talking about?"

"I know you have lots of worries these days. Your dad losing his medical license, money problems because of the bankruptcy, him and your mom splitting, and—"

"They're not splitting."

Alice stared at him, confused. "What? But I thought you told me they were getting a divorce?"

"They are. They're not splitting, though. Not really. My mom didn't even want to file. My dad made her do it before he started the Chapter Thirteen proceedings. That way she can keep some of the assets she brought into the marriage. Her parents left her a bunch of money and—" Interrupting himself. "Whatever. You don't need to hear all this. It's a whole complicated legal thing. The long and the short of it is, they're still together, even though I think she should get as far away from him as she can."

"And your family's not broke?"

"We're looked down on, laughed at, the people who were begging my dad to take them on as patients six months ago now cross to the other side of the street when he walks by. And we aren't rich anymore, at least not by Serenity Point standards, but we're definitely not broke. Which is convenient because"—smiling—"Harvard is seriously expensive."

"That's good," Alice said, not bothering to smile back. "Still, though, I think something's troubling you. Something apart from your family situation, I mean."

He looked at her, waiting for her to continue.

She took a deep breath, let the breath out, then said it: "Camilla." It's like she'd broken down her internal resistance to speaking the name out loud when she spoke it out loud to Luz, and now she wanted to speak it out loud again. It pained her to do so, but, at a deeper level, it soothed her, too.

"Camilla?" he repeated.

Her heart pounding at her own daring, Alice said, "She's dead and you're still in love with her."

The expression on his face was odd, half-angry, half she didn't know what. "That's not true."

"It is true," Alice said, nearly in tears. "Why else would you act the way you act, sit here every night staring out at"—unable to say the words, so flinging her arm in the direction of Greeves Bridge—"that? You think of nothing but her. And the only reason I get to be here with you is because I remind you of her. And not even that very much."

Tommy was quiet for a long time. The skin on his face looked too tight, and his eyes were strained and miserable. When he finally spoke, he spoke slowly, obviously choosing his words very, very carefully. "I do think about Camilla a lot, you're right. But that's because I feel guilty about her, not because I love her. I don't. Not anymore. The truth is, I'm not sure if I ever did."

"Of course you did," Alice said, almost indignant. "She was your best childhood friend and then your girlfriend. You were made for each other. Cybill told me. And the way your face looked in that picture . . ."

His brow crimped in confusion. "What picture?"

"The one hanging in the dining room of the club." She tried to jog his memory when he continued to regard her blankly: "You and Camilla had just won some kind of tennis match? You were being handed a trophy? You had on a stripey shirt and your arm was around her?"

Tommy's tense face relaxed into a smile as the memory broke through the surface. "Oh yeah. The junior mixed-doubles championship. We won because of her. She was a much better player than I was, completely carried me. That was a fun day," he said, and then, abruptly, the smile was gone, replaced by a scowl. "It was also a long time ago. Things change."

"I know you probably think it's weird that I'm asking you about her. That *I'm* weird. That I'm curious or morbid, or whatever. But I can't help myself. I'm just at such a disadvantage here. A living girl I could compete with. At least try to. How am I supposed to fight a dead one?"

For a while Tommy was silent. And then he rubbed his face roughly with the heels of his hands. Sighing, he said, "Maybe you're right. Maybe I did love her once. But I hated her every bit as much. And it got so ugly at the end, I guess it colored the time before in my mind. And as for that other thing you said, that you're only here with me because you remind me of her. You couldn't be more wrong. Okay, yes, I first noticed you because you looked so much like her, but I wanted to be around you because of how different from her you are."

Now it was Alice's turn to go silent for a while. And then she said, "You said it got ugly at the end. Ugly in what way?"

"Camilla wasn't what you thought she was, Alice. She wasn't what anyone thought she was. Straight-A student, nationally ranked tennis player, volunteer at the YMCA and Meals on Wheels program. Or she was that, but that was only half the story. She also had a dark side. Not that you'd have known it if you'd met her." His voice growing bitter, "You'd have probably been taken in like the rest, thought she was the best-looking, smartest, kindest, most generous person you'd ever had the privilege to meet. She was so good at sizing people up, telling them what they wanted to hear, showing them what they wanted to see."

After a beat, Alice said, "How dark was this dark side?"

"Dark. She always had it. It was there when we were kids. She was the first person I knew smoking pot, getting drunk. And she lost her virginity young, like scary young. To a nineteen-year-old."

"God."

"I felt so bad for her when she told me about it. I wanted to kill him, but he was already long gone by then."

"Who was he?"

"Some guy who worked on her dad's boat for a couple weeks. Not from around here. Went to UCLA or USC, one of those California schools. For years I had these extremely vivid fantasies of tracking him down, bashing his head in with an oar. Later, I started to think that he was probably her victim. Like, she seduced him, lied about her age before they had sex, then afterward confessed the truth, laughed and laughed when he freaked out." Tommy was quiet for a minute or so, picturing the scenario he'd conjured in his mind. When he spoke again, his voice was calmer, quieter: "So this dark side of Camilla's that, like I said, was always there, got darker as we got older. Bigger, too. Then her mom died, and it just took over, blotted out the light side entirely. Soon there was no place for me."

"What do you mean?"

"I mean, I was part of the light side, so I was getting blotted out, too."

"I don't understand," Alice said. "Blotted out how?"

"She was cheating on me at the end. Probably with a bunch of guys, but only one I knew for sure." His face darkened, and he looked down at his hands. "Since we didn't go to school together, it was hard for me to keep total track."

"You didn't?"

"No, she went to St. Augustine's, which is in Greenwich. Not far. Technically she was a boarder, but she came here almost every weekend. And my family lives here year-round, so we saw each other plenty."

"Anyway, that's why I finally broke up with her, a week before she—" breaking off, like he couldn't say the words.

"Killed herself?" Alice said, gently.

"I overlooked so much and for so long because I knew how wrecked she was over her mom's death. Then I reached a point where I couldn't overlook anymore."

"Who was she cheating on you with?"

"Jude Devlin."

"Jude?" Alice said, surprised, more than surprised—shocked. "Why him?"

"Because he's a bottom-feeder. She was weak at the time, he preyed on that weakness. Believe me, it's not something I'm proud of, not something I want people knowing, that she chose that scumbag over me. Luckily, they were quiet about it. I didn't even hear rumors about them. She's the one who told me."

"It's just, I wouldn't have guessed they had much in common."

Tommy shrugged. "They did drugs together. That gave them enough in common, I guess. He was probably into kink, too. I was definitely too meat-and-potatoes for her that way. She was dropping these little hints about wanting to—" He cut himself off, shook his head. "I'm sure you can guess what the little hints were about."

Shocked on the inside, calm on the out, Alice lied and murmured that she could.

"Plus, she thought the way I spent my time was dumb. Revoltingly wholesome, she said. I was always playing sports, or studying, or hanging out with my family. She did all those things, too. But they were her cover, what she did to keep her perfectionist dad off her back, give him the things he wanted so he'd give her the space to do the things *she* wanted."

"And what things did she want to do?"

"Nighttime things, she called them."

"Nighttime things?"

"All-nighttime things would have been a more accurate term for them. Like, she never went to sleep."

"She must've slept sometime."

"Well, yeah, obviously she slept sometime. But not much. She slept less and had more energy than any person I've ever met. I tried, but I just flat-out couldn't keep up with her. Not for long. Not without my rowing and my schoolwork going down the toilet."

Alice considered for a bit. "Maybe it was the drugs she was doing with Jude. Certain ones can give you superhuman stamina." A sheepish smile breaking across her face. "Or so I've read."

Tommy nodded. "I'm sure they helped. Or, I guess, didn't help. Also not helping was Jude. He was bad for her, encouraged all her worst tendencies, her worst impulses."

"I'm sure that's why she was with him. If she wanted a nice guy, she would have stayed with you." After a pause. "Why does he call you Crash?"

Tommy looked at her sharply. "What?"

"Jude. Why does he call you Crash?"

Looking away from her, eyes on the sand, he said, "I was driving my dad's golf cart a couple years ago. I meant to press the brake pedal, pressed the gas pedal instead, knocked over a few trash cans. It's a stupid nickname. He's stupid."

After delivering this verdict, Tommy fell into a brooding silence.

Alice broke it. "Look, I understand why you feel guilty, Tommy. I do. But why do you feel *so* guilty? What more could you have done? If someone keeps pushing you away, eventually you have to stay away. I mean, right?"

When she looked to him for an answer, she saw that he was shaking his head at her. And coating his eyes was a sheen of moisture, either from emotion or from the wind, which had just picked up. "Listen, I appreciate you saying that. But there are things you don't know. Things you couldn't possibly under—"

Before he could get the rest of the sentence out, she leaned forward, stopping his mouth by kissing it. The kiss was fast. Barely a kiss. A graze, really.

He stared at her, surprised by what she'd done. Not as surprised, though, as she was.

Embarrassed, she started to apologize. The words passed directly from her mouth into his, never hitting the air, because he was kissing her now. It was a careful kiss, not greedy, almost questioning. She could feel his lips trembling under hers.

It was dawn when Alice began creeping up the steps to the deck at the back of Richard's beach house, shoes in hand. Her fingers were wrapped around the knob of the door that led to the kitchen when she heard something: the sound of tires on gravel, then a car door opening and slamming shut, then her mom and Richard's voices chorusing out a good night. Alice froze. They must've decided not to make a night of it in Boston after all, to come directly home at the end of the Pollards' dinner party. Even though she was bone-tired, Alice forced herself to duck out of sight. She waited fifteen minutes to tick by on her cell phone clock, listening to the gentle tinkle of the sand-dollar wind chimes above her head, watching the pink-orange sun climb slowly up out of the ocean, before letting herself in, quietly ascending the servant's staircase at the back of the house.

She went on highest tippy-toe, treading extra lightly as she passed her mom and Richard's bedroom. Though the door was closed, she could hear them talking inside, their voices perfectly understandable if a little muffled. She wasn't trying to listen, but it was like looking at letters: your brain automatically put them together into words even if reading wasn't your intention. What she accidentally heard made her stop dead in her tracks.

It was her mom speaking, her voice sleepy but happy, so that Alice knew the night had been a success. "Don't you remember?" Maggie was saying. "We ran into him at that poky little inn in Nantucket over that Christmas Stroll Weekend. What's it called? The Jared Something House?"

"The Jared Coffin House," Richard replied, a clattering noise as one of his shoes, then the other, fell to the floor. Alice didn't need to see the scene to picture it: him sitting on the edge of the bed in his tux, jacket off, tie hanging loose around his neck, her mom unscrewing the backs of her earrings at the dressing table.

"That's right," Maggie said, "the Jared Coffin House."

"We ran into him? I don't remember."

"Lucky for us he didn't either, because you introduced me to him as your sister."

"No," Richard said, sounding amused yet not quite believing, as if the antics of his former self both delighted and appalled him. "I did? Really?"

"Yeah, I guess you thought the only woman you could have your arm around other than Martha was your sister."

"But I don't have a sister."

"Fortunately for us, Peter Cohen doesn't know that. Also, he only thinks about himself, so his memory for other people isn't so awfully good. Otherwise we'd have some explaining to do."

Richard laughed. "Come here, sis," he said.

The dry, shuffly sound of bare feet crossing a hardwood floor, then the wet, smacking sound of two mouths kissing. For a moment or two, Alice listened in fascination and disgust. Then she turned, continued on her way back to her room. Alhough she didn't bother to be quiet anymore; she doubted either her mom or Richard heard her.

Alice had a full two and a half hours before breakfast was served. Longer, probably, considering how doubtful it was that her mom and Richard would actually be making an appearance at the table this morning. She wasn't able to take advantage of the extra time, though, cop a few much-needed Zs. She wasn't able to cop even a Z. She was too wired for sleep, her mind going a million miles a minute. Just before her alarm was set to sound off, she hit the switch. Then she streaked across the hall and into her sister's room, jumped into the bed.

Charlie turned to her sleepily, cracked one eye. "Hey," she said. "What are you doing here?"

"Are you awake?"

"Not by choice."

"You have to be up, anyway. Breakfast is in ten minutes. We need to talk."

Charlie groaned. "This second?"

"Yeah, this second." Alice shook Charlie's arm when she saw Charlie had let her lids drop again. "Hey, don't go back to sleep, hey! There's something I need to tell you."

"If it's not about what happened on the *Buffy* episode I missed last night, I don't want to hear it."

"It's about mom and Richard. I heard them talking in their bedroom."

"And how did you do that? Put a drinking glass to the wall, press your ear to it?"

"Just, listen, okay?" Alice said. Then she gave a full recounting of the conversation, repeated it word for word. Or as close to word for word as memory would allow.

By the time she'd finished, Charlie was sitting up, her back against the headboard. She didn't look sleepy anymore. "This just happened?"

"No, not just. A little bit ago. Around dawn."

"What were you doing lurking in the hall at dawn?" Charlie said, the look in her eyes somewhere between intrigued and suspicious.

A pause while Alice considered whether or not she should tell her sister about Tommy. It wasn't that she felt she'd done anything wrong or had anything to hide. It's just that she didn't know exactly what was going on between the two of them, where they stood. Also, Charlie, she knew, tended to get easily sidetracked, couldn't really process more than one thing at a time. If she introduced the topic of Tommy, the topic of Richard and Maggie would go out the window, so she decided to leave Tommy for another day. "Nothing. I couldn't sleep. I heard voices," she said, which was more or less the truth. And then when Charlie continued to stay quiet, stare moodily at nothing, she prompted her with a "So?"

"So?" Charlie repeated. "So what?"

"You're kidding, right? You need me to explain the significance of their dialogue? Okay, fine. It proves mom and Richard were having an affair. This isn't like the slip-up mom made at that dinner with the Pollards a couple days ago, the thing about the Modern Wing at the Art Institute of Chicago. This isn't a maybe-they-did-maybe-they-didn't, open-to-interpretation, easily-explained-away-type deal. This is cut and dried, incontrovertible, undeniable evidence. Mom and Richard haven't taken a trip to Nantucket since we've known they've been together. Nor has a Christmas occurred since we've known they've been together. Ergo, they were together before we knew they were together. Ergo, mom was unfaithful to dad."

Alice looked to Charlie for her reaction. There wasn't much of one.

"Yeah," said Charlie, "but it's not like what you overheard changes anything. What we pretty much knew for sure, we now definitely know for sure."

"Pretty much knew for sure? You didn't act too sure when I pointed out the Chicago discrepancy thing to you at the time. In fact, you acted like I was being crazy, grasping at straws. Told me I was too obsessed with details, if I remember correctly."

Charlie shrugged.

Alice was shocked at her sister's blasé attitude. It was like the calmer and cooler Charlie appeared, the more out-of-control upset Alice could feel herself getting. "Well," she said, "it changes things for me. I'm going to call dad."

Charlie tossed off the covers, stepped out of the bed, not in any particular hurry. She must've gotten up, changed after Alice tucked her in last night. She was wearing a black T-shirt that ended above her navel, a pair of bikini underpants that dipped almost to her pubic bone. The Band-Aid covering her tattoo was peeling off her back, and Alice saw that she had a tan line in the shape of it.

"Well, good luck getting a hold of him," Charlie said sourly, as she bent over to pick up a pair of jeans off the floor. "He's touring with that pianoless quartet in Japan." She dropped her voice a few notes in imitation of their dad's: "A country that actually appreciates jazz." Back to her own voice: "His cell won't work."

"Then I'll leave a message with his answering service."

"He switched services, remember?"

"Oh yeah. Okay, then I'm going to send him an e-mail."

Charlie plucked her iPhone out of the pocket of her jeans. Letting them fall back to the floor, she said, "That's a smart move since he checks his e-mail, oh, about once every other month." She then strolled over to the open window on the other side of the room, curled her body up on the sill. Tapping the screen of her cell, she quickly became engrossed in what she saw there.

Alice watched her. In profile, she looked older than Alice wanted her to look. Also, harder. And there was something about the way she sat, one leg propped up, the underside of her thigh taut and muscular from all the tennis, the foot at the end of the other leg bobbing, the toenail polish on it, cherry-red and chipped, that bothered Alice as well. It was too sexual, somehow. Too experienced.

Looking away, Alice said, "Have you completely stopped caring about him? He's been wronged here. Like, in a pretty big way."

Charlie glanced up from her phone. "What? No, of course I haven't stopped caring about him. But he basically dumped us. And it's not like we were the ones who screwed around on him. So exactly how much of my sympathy does he have dibs on? And, besides, why drag him into this? What's done is done. Can't you just let things alone for once? You got this information in a not-above-board way. It's, like, not information you should have. Really, this is none of our business."

"You don't think our family life is our business?"

"Not the parental-sex-life part of it, no."

Alice stared at Charlie for a long second. Understanding suddenly flared in her brain. "You're not saying that because you believe it."

Charlie laughed. "Oh really, Oprah? Then tell me, why am I saying it?"

"You're saying it because it's in your best interest to say it. You don't want to lose what you get from your association with Richard."

"My association with Richard?" Charlie said, mocking Alice's formal word choice. "And what exactly am I getting from my association with Richard?"

"A fancy life, fancy house, access to fancy people."

"So what if I don't want to lose these things? That makes me a bad person?"

"Yeah, actually, it kind of does. It's corrupt."

"Oh grow up, Allie."

"No, it is. I mean to care about stuff more than you care about people. More than you care about me or dad or even mom."

"That's ridiculous. I just don't see what the point is in stirring up a whole shit storm about something that's already over and done with. It's not like knowing that mom fell out of love with dad and in love with Richard a couple months earlier than she said she did is going to change anything, is going to make her fall back in love with dad, or make her love Richard any less."

Alice was quiet. *Is Charlie right here?* she wondered. *Am I sticking my nose where it doesn't belong? Making trouble to no real end? After all, spilled milk is spilled milk, isn't it?*

Charlie, as if sensing the trajectory of Alice's thoughts, pressed her advantage. In a softer voice, she said, "I mean, right, Allie?"

"No," Alice admitted grudgingly, "I guess not."

"So let's just stay out of it, try not think about it. Mom's behavior is kind of gross, I agree. But, also, it is what it is."

Alice snorted. "Deep."

Charlie, leaving her phone on the windowsill, walked back over to the bed, knelt beside Alice. "Come on," she said, tugging gently on Alice's ponytail, "we better not be late for breakfast. Nothing's worse than getting yelled at by a pair of breakers of the—wait, which commandment is adultery?"

"Seventh, I think."

"Breakers of the seventh commandment for a minor time infraction."

"Actually, I'm pretty sure they're going to sleep in this morning." Alice gave her sister an abashed smile. "Sorry, I guess I should've let you do the same."

"That's okay. I'm more hungry than sleepy now. Let's go down, anyway."

Alice nodded, followed her sister out of the room. All of a sudden, she felt very, very tired.

Chapter
• THIRTEEN •

*T*hat night the club was hosting an event that Richard was insisting the whole family attend: the Clambake Luau. It wasn't really a clambake, Alice saw once she stepped inside the clubhouse. Nor was it a luau, whatever that was. It was really just a regular party, only with more seafood and candles on the tables made of halved coconut shells and the staff wearing floral short-sleeve button-downs instead of their usual polos. People were dressed to the nines, to the eights, at least—it was still summer in a beach town—and milling around the foyer area and dining room, drinking and eating, one eye on the person they were talking to, the other on the door to see who walked through. There was an open bar and a long table with chilled shrimp and crab legs and oysters on it, an indoor grill where a chef was cooking fresh lobsters to order. One of the club's employees, that cute valet-waiter guy, was handing out leis to guests as they entered.

Alice spotted Tommy right away. (It was like she was equipped with an extra sense where he was concerned, could feel his presence in a roomful of people, hone in on it immediately.) He was in the far cor-ner with his parents. As always, he was extremely attentive to his pretty, nervous-looking mom, his arm, sinewy and golden-brown, wrapped around her shoulders like he was propping her up, giving her strength. His dad stood next to him, stiff-necked, a drink in his hand. Nobody was talking to them; nobody was even going near them. It was as if they were radioactive or something. And Alice wondered what point Dr. van Stratten was trying to prove by showing up, making his fam-ily show up with him: That he'd been stripped of his right to prac-tice medicine and barely escaped a prison sentence, but that he wasn't ashamed? That he was down but not out? That there was no getting rid of him so the people of Serenity Point better get used to it?

Alice was anxious about seeing Tommy in a public setting. Their relationship so far had been conducted almost entirely in private, just the two of them in their own little world, no outside inter-ference or influence. She wasn't sure how he'd behave toward her tonight. Would he pretend they barely knew each other, were the most casual of acquaintances? It wouldn't be that strange if he did, she told herself. If anything, it would show his discretion, prove that he was as protective of her reputation as his own. After all, it could be viewed as a little weird, a little creepy, that he was involved with the stepdaughter of the man whose daughter he'd been dating when she'd ended her life. And it wasn't as if they were boyfriend and girlfriend, Alice reminded herself. They'd only kissed. An intense kiss, definitely, but nevertheless, just a kiss. Still, Alice knew that no matter how much she reasoned with herself, came up with justifica-tions and rationalizations for why he might ignore her, if he did it would crush her. All she needed was something small, some tiny little thing that acknowledged the specialness of their relationship and connection. And then Tommy looked up from his conversation with his mom, and Alice's heart caught in her throat as their eyes touched. He smiled at her, raised his index finger, and crooked it in a mini wave. Relief surged through her body as she crooked her index finger in a mini wave back. She could breathe now. Could at last shift her focus away from him on to the party at large.

Alice did a quick scan of the crowd. Her mom, she saw, had been waylaid by Cybill's mother, Muffie, drawn into a circle of emaciated blond women, Muffie the blondest and most emaciated of all. Richard, though, was still on the move, striding across the room. Finally he stopped in front of Tommy's dad, gave the disgraced doctor a friendly clap on the shoulder, kissed Tommy's mom on the cheek, shook Tommy's hand. He asked Dr. van Stratten about his golf handicap and, when Dr. van Stratten proved too stuttery-stunned to mount much of a reply, started talking about his own. Everyone in the room was watching the exchange while pretending not to. After a bit, a couple of the men broke free of their conversations, wandered over to the newly formed group, greeted Dr. van Stratten, if not as warmly as Richard had, at least politely. Women soon followed, congregating around Mrs. van Stratten. Richard, Alice realized, had single-handedly saved Dr. and Mrs. van Stratten from complete social pariahdom. She found herself experiencing her first positive feelings toward her stepfather in days, since their ill-fated trip into town.

Alice's eyes resumed their scan. Where was Charlie? She'd peeled off from Alice as soon as they'd set foot in the clubhouse. Had gone off in search of Jude and Cybill, no doubt. Had found them, too. At least, had found Cybill. The two girls were sitting on one of the old leather couches by the bridge table, talking. Jude was on the other side of the room, leaning against the bar. He was wearing his seersucker suit, silver flask playing peekaboo in the breast pocket, sunglasses clamped to his face even though the sun had long since set, making a play for Lucy, the pretty college-age tennis pro, in a blatant way. And she wasn't discouraging him. On the contrary, she seemed amused by his behavior, maybe even charmed by it. Charlie, though, not so much. She was seething. Not that anyone would be able to tell, but Alice could: the narrowness of her eyes, the tightness of her lips, a darker shade than usual—new lipstick?—the way her nose appeared slightly sharper than normal. Though she was carrying on a conversation with Cybill, and in a pretty convincing fashion, all her attention, Alice knew, was concentrated on Jude.

It shocked Alice, upset her, too, to realize that Charlie's feelings for Jude had grown serious, that the relationship was no longer just a bit of flirtatious fun. Like Charlie was into him only because he was different from the guys she'd known in the past, because he represented a challenge. As Charlie looked at Jude, her eyes, Alice could see, were full of emotion. *How did this happen so fast?* Alice wondered. *More to the point, how did she not see it coming, do more to prevent it?* Alice wished she could warn Charlie off Jude if it wasn't already too late, tell her about his on-the-sly relationship with Camilla, how soon it was after the two became involved that Camilla drove off Greeves Bridge. But it wasn't her secret to reveal. It was Tommy's, and she didn't have his permission. She had the opposite, in fact. He'd explicitly told her that he didn't want people knowing Camilla was with Jude while Camilla was still with him. And if she couldn't tell Charlie what she'd learned from Tommy, she knew she might as well not open her mouth at all. Her influence with her sister was already seriously on the wane. Charlie thought she was all gloom and doom, seeing menace everywhere because of her suspicions about her mom and Richard. Suspicions, incidentally, that had proved fully justified. Didn't matter, though. Alice understood that if she went on a tear about Jude too, without proof, Charlie would dismiss her completely. Charlie was just looking for an excuse to write her off as a no-fun, killjoy, conspiracy-theory nutcase, so she couldn't give her one. No, Alice would just have to bite her tongue until she could go to Charlie with something solid, something that couldn't be brushed off.

Out of the corner of her eye, Alice saw a flash of movement: Jude, on the go. He was leading Lucy by the elbow out of the main party, to the back porch. He was saying something to her that was making her laugh, his lips at the rim of her ear. As the door closed behind them, Charlie stood up abruptly from the couch, leaving Cybill staring at her, confused, in mid-sentence. For a tense moment, Alice thought she was going to go after Jude and Lucy, make a scene. Breathed a sigh of relief when she didn't. Instead she spun around, walked across the room to that valet-waiter guy—STAN, his name tag said—struck up a conversation.

Alice's relief was short-lived. Charlie, she quickly saw, was making a scene in a different way. She wasn't talking with Stan. She was hitting on him. Aggressively. At first he seemed pleased by the attention, delighted, in fact, but was fast growing uncomfortable. She was standing too close to him, trying to pull him onto the dance floor, though there was no music playing. (And it wasn't lipstick that had darkened her lips, Alice realized, it was wine.) Alice even heard Charlie make a *get leid* joke about the flowered necklaces he was handing out. People were starting to look, not Maggie and Richard, who fortunately both had their backs to Charlie, but other people: Sasha and Bianca, tittering by the bar; Mrs. van Stratten over her son's shoulder, her face as blank as always, but her eyes wide; and, most alarmingly of all, a middle-aged man with a hairline mustache and a clipboard, Stan's boss. Alice was just about to go up to Charlie, try to lure her into coming outside—not out back, where Jude and Lucy were, but out front, where, she hoped, no one was—when Cybill did it for her, taking Charlie by the hand, dragging her off. Alice considered following to see if she could help, then rejected the idea: her presence might only rile Charlie up.

Alice was standing by the food station, stiffly casual, eyes flicking over to the front door every few seconds, waiting for Charlie and Cybill to return from wherever it was they'd disappeared to, when Tommy came up to her, though it didn't look like that's what he was doing. It looked like he was picking up a little plate of spicy mayonnaise for himself at the dipping-sauce table behind her. The way they were standing, she facing forward, he facing backward, reminded her of the way two police cruisers sometimes parked: next to each other but turned in opposite directions, driver's-side windows lined up so that the officers inside could talk.

"Am I going to see you later tonight?" he said. His voice was low, intimate.

"Why not? I can sleep when I'm dead, right?" She winced before the words were even out of her mouth. "Sorry," she said. "Yes, you will."

He laughed. "Jesus, I don't seem that sensitive, do I?"

"It's probably me just being sensitive to you being sensitive. A whole vicious-circle thing."

He laughed again, then leaned over her like he was reaching for the soy sauce, lightly tracing his index finger along her forearm, from the inside of her elbow all the way down to her wrist. She felt the tiny hairs on her arm rise.

"You having an okay time?" he said.

"It's a little weird being in the same room with you and not being able to talk to you, but yeah, otherwise I'm having a fine time."

"We're talking now."

"You know what I mean."

"It's not like you're my secret shame, Alice."

"Well, okay, but you're mine."

He smiled, but then his expression got serious. She loved his eyes, soft and dark and watchful. "All we're doing is holding off on the official-declaration thing for a bit. It's not that I don't want people knowing we're together. It's just that I feel like I've been in the public eye a lot lately, you know, because of my family. There's been all this scrutiny. I want to have something that's private, that's mine and only mine, just for a little while. That's okay with you, right?"

"Yeah, it is," Alice said, though she was not entirely sure if she meant it. Almost involuntarily she turned her eyes to the photo of him and Camilla hanging on the wall. It didn't look like he had any trouble showing Camilla how he felt about her, or showing the world how he felt about her.

"You sure?" Tommy said.

Alice pried her gaze off the photo and brought it back to his face. She nodded bravely.

"Tommy," Dr. van Stratten called out across the room. "Hey, Tommy. Come here. There's someone I want you to meet."

"Be right there," Tommy said to his dad in a loud voice. Then, to Alice in a soft one, "It's the daughter of a guy he wants a job from. Runs some hedge fund in Stamford. My dad's hoping he'll hire him to do research on the pharmaceutical industry, like as an analyst or consultant. The daughter's going to be a freshman at Harvard next year. I'm thinking thick glasses, greasy hair, maybe a facial tic or two."

From your lips to God's ears, Alice said, though only to herself.

"I'm supposed to be nice to her," he said, with a sigh. "At least until my dad gets the offer."

Trying to be supportive, Alice said, "That's great he's trying to turn over a new leaf, get into a different line of work or whatever."

Tommy grinned. "Yeah, making the leap from doctor to pimp." He turned to her. "Well, how do I look?"

She ran her eyes over his face and body. "I'd pay to have sex with you."

He laughed, then squeezed her hand discreetly, before crossing the room.

An hour or so later, Alice was leaning against a pillar at the back of the dining room, in the shadows of a tall, leafy plant, watching Tommy listen intently to something the Harvard girl—a pretty redhead, not remotely bespectacled, greasy, or tic-afflicted—was saying. She was watching so hard she didn't realize someone was standing beside her. She turned. It was Cybill, engrossed in a heartache-y scene of her own, arms crossed tightly across her chest so that it appeared as if she was hugging herself, and almost to the point of pain. Alice tracked her gaze, followed it out the window, over to Jude. He was on the porch, on his hands and knees, trying to get to his feet. He was by himself now. No college-girl tennis pro around. He was so drunk or high, he was like one of those cartoon characters stuck in glue, couldn't pull himself up off the ground.

"He didn't used to be like this," Cybill said, softly, almost to herself.

At last Jude gave up the struggle, stopped scrambling, and just collapsed, lay there on his back, limbs splayed, mouth open, a bit of drool trickling out the side. His sunglasses had fallen off his pretty doll's face and onto his chest, looking to Alice's eye like a small black bra. "Oh yeah?" Alice said. "He seems to me like the kind of guy who was born wild."

"Wild, yes. But not out of control."

"When did it change?"

"A year ago."

"A year ago," Alice repeated, her brain starting to buzz, make connections.

Cybill blinked, like she suddenly realized that she was talking in a personal way to someone she barely knew, and wasn't even sure she liked. Her voice got louder, harder, more flip: an in-public voice. "Yeah, a year ago. You know, when his dad got elected to office. Mr. Devlin stopped being around, Jude started acting out. Cries for attention and all that. Typical kid-of-a-famous-person behavior."

"His dad got elected two years ago."

Cybill rolled her eyes. "Okay, two years ago. Whatever. Minor computational error. God, I didn't realize you were president of the math club."

"No, I don't think you did make a computational error. It was a year ago that he changed. Right around the time he got involved with Camilla. Isn't that right?" When Cybill failed to respond: "Isn't it?"

Cybill looked at Alice, and Alice could see she was trying to decide something. Finally she nodded.

"So all this bad behavior is the product of guilt? Is that what you're telling me?" Looking at this girl beside her, this girl who was her sister's friend but really, Alice sensed, her sister's enemy, she felt herself harden. And her voice, which had started out sympathetic, rapidly turned faux sympathetic, sarcastic. "Does he feel bad for fucking Camilla up more than she was already fucked up? Inching her that much closer to the edge? Maybe giving her a little push? Is his conscience hounding him? Just won't let up? Driving him to drink and drugs?"

"Uh, you've got it backward. She was the one doing the fucking up."

Alice snorted. "That's not what I heard."

Cybill, eyes flashing with anger, said, "You *heard*? I was *there*. I've loved Jude since we were kids, since we were babies. And I was Camilla's best friend, remember? I knew her better than anybody"—voice dropping to a whisper—"and I didn't know her that well, as it turns out."

"So who did?"

"I don't think anybody. Camilla was"—pausing, searching for the right word—"complicated. She had secrets."

"What kind of secrets?"

Cybill lifted her shoulders in a shrug. "That's why they're called secrets. I guess she had to have them. Her dad watched her pretty close, was kind of a hawk-eye."

"Her mom, too?"

"No, Mrs. Flood was sweet. Plus, she was too busy obsessing over Mr. Flood to obsess over Camilla. Then she got cancer, was too sick to obsess over anything." Cybill was quiet for a moment, biting her thumbnail. "Anyway, before Jude got mixed up with Camilla, he was just a fun-loving guy. Wild like we said, yeah, and loved attention, but sweet-natured, basically, didn't mean any harm. Wanted to have a good time, that's all. Drank, but no more than anyone else. Kind of a pothead, but not a drug person. Was into girls, but not all manipulative and game-play-y about it. He was, like, innocent. He—"

Cybill broke off, something catching her eye. She turned to look out the window. Alice followed suit, saw Dr. and Mrs. van Stratten stepping onto the porch. Mrs. van Stratten almost tripped over Jude's leg. Jude stirred, opened a single bloodshot eye. When he saw who was standing above him, he rolled over onto his stomach. His hands were under his body, and his elbows were moving like he was fumbling with something. His belt buckle, as it turned out. A second later, his bare ass was staring up at the appalled couple. They quickly stepped over him, went on their way.

"Not so innocent anymore," Alice observed.

Cybill looked upset, but she laughed. "No, he isn't. You can thank Camilla for that one. It's like she poisoned him or twisted him or something. I don't think she meant to, but she did. He was different after they were together. Darker. Crueler." She fell silent for a bit, then said, "Your sister, she thinks she's in a love triangle with Jude and me. But she's not. She's in a love triangle with Jude and Camilla. She wishes she was competing against just me. *I* wish she was competing against just me. She'd win and she'd be good for Jude. Fresh blood, fresh energy, fresh start."

"But there's no way, right?" Alice said softly.

Cybill shook her head sadly. "He's as hung up on Camilla now as he was when she was alive. Nobody beats Camilla. She's stronger than anybody, above ground or below it."

Alice was quiet for a beat or two, then said, "Everyone says how strong she was, but strong people generally don't commit suicide."

Cybill turned on Alice fiercely. "You didn't see what happened to her mom. How ugly it got, how nasty. Mrs. Flood had been diagnosed with breast cancer when Camilla and I were in middle school. She was sick for a while, but she got better and the cancer went into remission. For a couple years she was healthy, doing well. And then it came back the winter of Camilla's and my sophomore year. Stage four, had already spread to her liver. It was incurable but it was supposed to be manageable if properly treated. And for two or three months she seemed like she was improving, so much so that they sent her home from the hospital. Then she got worse, fast. I mean, really fast. It was like she fell off a cliff or something. She was dead within days, not weeks. God, that was a horrible spring."

"She died in the house?"

Cybill nodded. The two girls looked at each other for a while, not speaking, thinking, digesting.

Finally Alice said, "Where's Charlie?"

"Sasha found a joint she forgot she had rolling around the bottom of her purse. A bunch of them went down to the beach to get high. I wasn't in the mood."

Alice nodded. She was about to ask Cybill more about Camilla's relationship with Richard, but at that moment, another couple appeared on the porch, a man and woman Alice didn't recognize. They saw Jude on the ground, pants halfway down his thighs, lips mashed against one of the dirty wooden planks. They stared down at him for a second before shaking their heads in disgust, walking around him, the man kicking Jude's foot out of the way harder than strictly necessary.

Cybill winced in sympathy. Said, as Jude turned onto his back, "Great, now he's going to get splinters in his ass," and laughed a sad little laugh. And for the first time, Alice found herself liking Cybill.

"Here," Cybill said, handing Alice her drink with a sigh.

As Alice took it, Cybill walked through the back door, out onto the porch. She crouched down, pulled Jude's pants up over his skinny hips, then began slapping him on the cheek, lightly at first then not so lightly. He squeezed his eyes tight before cracking them open.

"You," he said, moaning groggily. "Why can't you leave me alone? I want to get away from you, but you won't let me. Why won't you let me?"

His head was sort of lolling on his neck, like it was too heavy for him to hold up, so he probably meant to look at Cybill as he spoke those words. But it wasn't Cybill he was looking at. It was Alice, standing in the window, a few feet away.

Spooked, she stepped back, out of sight. Hiding in the shadows, she resolved to leave the party. What she'd do, she decided, was go find her sister, down on the beach with Sasha. Then they'd walk directly from the water back to Richard's, that is, if Charlie would listen to reason, could be persuaded to listen to reason. (Charlie had seemed so agitated an hour ago, so *un*reasonable.) Alice suspected she would. Pot usually had a mellowing effect on her personality.

Alice had just left Cybill's drink on a nearby table, turned to head for the front door, when she walked straight into Sasha.

"Oh, Sasha," she said, "hey. I was just about to go looking for you."

"You were?" Sasha said, surprised.

"Well, sort of. I was just about to go looking for Charlie and I heard she was with you."

"Who told you that?"

"Cybill. Like, a minute ago. She said you two were on the beach."

"She meant Bianca. She gets us confused. In Cybill's mind, we're interchangeable. But we're actually two distinct people."

Sasha sounded perfectly good-natured as she said these words, not the slightest bit bitter or upset, so Alice laughed, not least because she'd always thought of Sasha and Bianca as interchangeable, too. "So," Alice said, "Charlie and Bianca are down on the beach then?"

Sasha made a toking gesture with her fingers. "Last I heard." Her face was separated from prettiness by an all-important degree or two, but it was a nice face: big eyes full of mischief and a quick smile. "What about Cybill?" she said. "Where did she wander off to?"

"She's taking care of Jude outside."

Sasha rolled her eyes. "She's a funny one, that girl. Spends almost all her time with guys but they don't do that much for her."

"She seems pretty enthusiastic about them to me."

Sasha's voice taking on a hushed, confidential tone, "She was with this guy Massie for half of her sophomore year and she told me that every time they were together, she didn't, like, *feel* anything."

"Really? Nothing?"

"That's what she said."

After a thoughtful pause, Alice said, "Well, could be this Massie guy was just really not good at it."

Sasha sighed, nodded. "Yeah, probably. High school boys. Okay, I'm going to go look for her. She might need me. You know, to hold her lip gloss tube or, like, unwrap a tampon for her."

Alice laughed for the second time. The two girls waved good-bye, went off to find their respective people.

Before Alice found Charlie, Richard and Maggie found Alice. Turns out, they were still beat from the Pollards' dinner party and wanted to make an early exit. Alice sent Charlie a couple of texts, asking if she was ready to call it a night. The texts went unanswered.

Richard, Maggie, and Alice walked to the parking lot behind the clubhouse—no valet tonight; apparently the Clambake Luau didn't qualify as a party party—Richard in the center, one arm slung around Maggie's shoulders, the other around Alice's, calling them "my girls." Alice was surprised by his affectionate treatment of her for two reasons: one, because he was usually so formal with her, never touched her in a casual or familiar way, and two, because they'd avoided each other ever since that disastrous car trip into town a few days ago, had barely exchanged a word. Maybe he was embarrassed by how he'd acted, attacking her and her politics like he was a crazy person. Alice suspected that he might have been since he obviously hadn't told Maggie about the fight. Neither had she, for that matter. Maybe this was his way of apologizing without saying the actual words *I'm sorry*. Well, she wasn't one to hold a grudge, especially not after she'd seen what he'd done for Dr. van Stratten, the rescue he'd performed.

As they approached the car, Richard automatically headed for the driver's side. Maggie put a hand to his chest, stopping him. "Richard, I think you should let me drive."

He looked at her. "What? Why?"

"You had a couple glasses of wine."

Ah, Alice said to herself, *he'd been drinking*. That explained the out-of-nowhere affection. Well, supposedly your real feelings come out when you're drunk, so maybe he truly was sorry for how he'd behaved.

"Yes, I did," Richard said to Maggie. "A couple, as in two."

"Well, that's one too many."

"Okay, okay," he said good-naturedly, raising his arms above his head so she could frisk him. As she reached into his trouser pockets, pulled out the keys, he leaned in unexpectedly, gave her a fast kiss. She laughed, opened the passenger door for him. He obediently went inside.

From the backseat, Alice watched Maggie and Richard. They were in love and very happy together, that much was obvious. And she tried to leave it at that. She wanted to leave it at that, almost more than anything she wanted to leave it at that, but she couldn't. Her brain wouldn't let her. And as they started down the crushed-shell road that led in and out of the club, it occurred to her for the first time to wonder *when* exactly her mom and Richard had become a couple. Before they said they had, obviously, that much was established, but how much before? It suddenly struck Alice that she'd focused solely on her dad as the betrayed party, had forgotten that Martha might have been betrayed as well. What was she saying? Might have been, *was.* Flashing back to the conversation she'd overheard in the hall that morning, Alice realized that Martha would've had to have still been in the picture when Maggie and Richard got involved. Otherwise why would Richard have told that Peter Cohen guy that Maggie was his sister when he ran into him at Christmas Stroll in Nantucket? If he was worried about protecting Maggie and her marriage, he could've just said she was his girlfriend then given her a fake name. Nothing wrong with a widower taking a consenting lady friend on a romantic getaway. But, no, he claimed she was a family member to explain why he was physically affectionate with her. Which means he was worried about protecting his own marriage as well. Which means there was a marriage to protect.

Which means Martha was alive at the time.

Alive—but sick with cancer. How sick would depend on which Christmas season Richard and Maggie had spent together in Nantucket. Best-case scenario it was three Christmases ago, when Martha was in remission. Worst-case scenario it was two Christmases ago, when Martha found out the cancer was back, and for the long haul. Thinking these thoughts, Alice was starting to feel a little sick herself. She looked out the window. As she did, she saw a sign for

Serenity Point Hospital flash by. Another thing Cybill had said came back to her: Martha dying in the house mere days after she'd left the hospital where she'd been enjoying a period of recovery. How odd. And yet how fortunate for Richard. With his first wife dead and gone, he got everything—the woman he loved, the daughter he adored (no way could he have predicted that her mother's death would drive Camilla to suicide), the houses, the money, and all without scandal or a negative impact on his big-time career. No muss, no fuss. So convenient.

Too convenient? Alice wondered. She'd had glimpses of Richard's temper just the other day, could see how controlling he could get, could feel his need to bend her will to his own. And she wasn't even his flesh and blood. She was just the nearly grown daughter of his new wife, someone who reflected on him barely at all. From what Tommy and Cybill said about his relationship with Camilla, it sounded as if he could get really bad, just relentless, like he watched Camilla's every move, tried to oversee each aspect of her life so that she had to turn secretive to survive, to keep anything for herself. No question, Richard was a seriously determined guy, and incredibly domineering. Alice could imagine him killing someone who got in his way, stood between him and what he wanted and felt he was entitled to. Sure she could. Didn't even take that much effort.

Alice would look into the matter tomorrow. Not on the home computer, though. Too risky. What if Richard was somehow monitoring it, checking out the sites she visited? Tommy said that Camilla felt the need to have a cover. It was unlikely she'd have gone to the trouble of creating a public identity to mask the private without good reason. No, Alice would do her research at the library, away from watchful eyes. She'd head over in the morning, after break-fast.

An hour later, Charlie was walking back from the beach to the club. She'd have rather gone straight home, but she'd stupidly checked her bag with her wallet in it, and now she had to retrieve it. She felt like shit, just awful, worse even than earlier. She'd hoped smoking weed with Bianca and Bianca's friends from St. Augie's would help, would lift her out of her mood. It didn't. It just sank her further into it and made her disoriented on top of depressed. She couldn't believe the way Jude had acted at the party, going off with that Lucy girl, and in front of everyone. After last night on the tennis court, she'd imagined things would be different between them. They hadn't had sex, but what they'd done felt even more intimate. And she'd thought—no, she didn't want to say what she'd thought. Not even to herself. It was too hokey. Too embarrassing.

Equally embarrassing was the memory of how she'd reacted to the way he'd acted, throwing herself at Stan the way she did, scaring him, weirding him out, possibly jeopardizing his job. What was wrong with her? Why was her behavior so spastic? She just hoped he was on cleanup duty in the kitchen or had already clocked out for the night so she wouldn't have to face him. At least her mom and Richard wouldn't be there. Alice had sent her a text a while ago telling her that they were leaving early, asking her if she wanted to come. A text that, by the way, she hadn't bothered to respond to. Of course she hadn't. When she was acting like a self-destructive idiot—and not just self-destructive, other-destructive, too, even worse—who thought only of herself and her own needs, she went all the way with it. No half measures for her.

When she got close to the clubhouse, she ducked behind a pillar, peered into the giant bay window. The luau appeared to still be going on, but was definitely in the wind-down phase, only a few stray couples left, the employees subtly starting to tidy up. No sign of Stan, thank God. Charlie went around to the back, creeping up to the porch door. As she reached for the latch, she heard something crunch under her foot. She looked down. A pair of sunglasses. Jude's, if she wasn't mistaken, one of the lenses shattered thanks to the heel of her wedge shoe. The glasses had probably flown off his face when he was having wild sex with Lucy in the bushes. Charlie picked the glasses up by the ear-hook part, flung them as far as she could.

She pressed down on the latch, opened the door, entered. Eyes pointed straight ahead, feet moving fast, she made it to the foyer area without seeing a soul. No one was manning the coat-check station. Charlie took a quick look around, then ducked inside, found her bag. After hooking the strap over her shoulder and dropping a couple dollars in the tip jar, she walked out the door, this time the front one.

Charlie made her way back down to the beach, taking a different route than before, relieved that she'd recovered her bag sans any embarrassing run-ins, her pulse returning to normal, breath evening out, becoming less quick, less shallow. She was safe. Then she looked up. Realized she'd spoken too soon. There he was, the very person she wanted least to see, smoking a cigarette by the statue of that peeing baby, wearing sneakers, jeans, a gray hoodie. His face was angled away from her, pointing down and to the right. And there was a possibility that she could escape without being spotted if she moved fast, got a little lucky. But as she was about to turn, she stopped herself. No, she couldn't slink off like a coward. She had to face him, give him the chance to tell her to go fuck herself if he wanted to. She forced herself to keep walking, stay the course. Ten seconds later, she was standing in front of him.

"Hi, Stan," she said. Up close she saw a small Wolcott Academy insignia on the breast of the sweatshirt.

He glanced up at her, continued smoking. He didn't look surprised to see her, or unhappy to see her. He didn't look anything to see her. His eyes were blank. "Hey," he said.

"So you're not perfect," she said, indicating the cigarette between his fingers, smiling. "Nice to see you've got a bad habit or two."

Not returning her smile, "I've got more than one or two."

"I owe you an apology. Again."

"Okay."

Charlie licked her lips, nervous. "So, here it is. I'm sorry." When he didn't say anything back, she forged on, "I hope I didn't get you in too much trouble with your boss."

"Nope. I only got a warning."

"What does a warning mean?"

"Nothing. Unless I get a second warning, in which case I'm fired." His voice as he said these words was cool and neutral, not hot and mad.

"I could talk to him," Charlie said, "explain the situation. Tell him that it was me, not you."

"I'd appreciate it if you wouldn't."

She nodded. Stan was acting polite but too polite, polite in a way that kept her at arm's length. She'd rather he yell.

A long silence developed during which it grew clear that he had nothing more to say to her, probably wanted nothing more to do with her. Not that she blamed him. With a sigh, she said, "Okay, well, I really am sorry. I'll see you around."

As she turned to go, he said softly, "That guy's not worth it."

She turned back. Stan's eyes were glowing bright green in the moonlight—cat eyes—and they were right on her face now, the look in them anything but blank. "You don't know him," she said.

"I know that he's loaded more than he's sober. I know that he's always hitting up the guys who work here for pills, powders, whatever will turn his brain to mush. He doesn't always have cash handy, either. Likes to buy on credit, then develops a case of Swiss-cheese memory when it comes time to remembering what he owes to who."

"So he's got a drug problem," Charlie said. "I'd think you'd be sympathetic."

"Me sympathize with that snot-nosed poor little rich boy? Now why would you think a crazy thing like that?"

"You're an addict, too." She pointed to his cigarette. "Nicotine is a narcotic."

He snorted. "A legal narcotic. And I'm not addicted. It's been a long night, is all."

She shrugged.

"I know he's bad news in other ways, too."

Charlie sensed she didn't want to know the answer to the question she was about to ask, but she asked it anyway: "Bad in which ways?"

"For one thing, he's sleeping with that blond chick that's so hung up on him, the one I always see you running around with."

Trying to keep her voice cool, free of emotion, Charlie said, "How do you know that? Are you going to his house at night with a pair of binoculars?"

Stan made a scoffing sound.

"Then how?" she pressed.

He paused, watching Charlie, and Charlie could see he was trying to make up his mind about something. He dropped his eyes to the ground. When he raised them, their expression had changed, as if he'd thought it over and come to a decision. "You know about those rooms upstairs at the clubhouse, the ones for husbands in the doghouse, guests who've had one too many, need to sleep it off before they hit the road?"

"Yeah."

"Well, his father pays extra to keep one on hold. Needs a place to stash his girlfriends when he's in town, I guess. But Mr. Devlin, as you've probably noticed, is not in town too much, so that room's free a lot. Not as free maybe as it should be, since his boy Jude gets plenty of use out of it. He and blondie stay there at least once a week. Have been doing it all summer."

It's not as if Charlie didn't know that Jude and Cybill had hooked up in the past, but hearing that they still did, and the extent of it—sleeping together on a regular basis, and she was worried about them going to New York for the night without her, Jesus, what an idiot she was—was painful for her. It hit her like a fist to the gut, knocking the wind right out of her. And while she understood she should have been angry with Jude and Cybill for doing what they did, she was angry with the guy standing in front of her for making her know it.

Charlie was silent for a beat or two, then she took a step toward Stan, moving in so close that their hips and shoulders were almost touching, and she could smell his skin, a mixture of soap and sweat and the coconut candles he must've handled at the luau, could see the pupils expanding in his pure green eyes. "Haven't you ever heard of personal space?" he said, but he liked having her this close to him; it was turning him on. She could tell by the way his mouth clenched, the way the muscles in his neck knotted when he swallowed.

"You're paid to work here, aren't you, Stan?"

This wasn't what he was expecting her to say. He blinked, confused. "What?" he said. Then, "Yeah."

"Well, maybe that's what you should stick to doing. Quit getting involved in your employers' private lives. Because that's what we are to you—employers. That's what Jude is to you, that's what Cybill is to you, that's what *I* am to you. It's creepy. And it's kind of pathetic."

He stared at her, mute and unmoving, as she plucked the cigarette from between his fingers, took a deep drag on it, then flicked it to the grass. Letting it smolder there, she turned around, continued on her way to the beach.

Chapter
• FOURTEEN •

Alice entered the dining room for breakfast the next morning a few minutes early. She was surprised to find her sister
already there. The two girls sat across from each other at the table,
slumped low in their chairs, not talking, waiting for Richard and
Maggie to come downstairs. Luz bustled in and out, carrying the
basket of zucchini-pear muffins that Richard had become so addicted to lately, was eating instead of brioche, a little bowl of ketchup for
Charlie and Maggie to smother their eggs in, a box of Grape-Nuts
for Alice, and a small bowl of blueberries.

Alice looked at the cereal, looked away, not sure how she was
going to manage to swallow even a mouthful. She felt sapped of
energy, way down in the dumps on top of seriously sleep deprived.
She'd snuck out of the house last night after Maggie and Richard
had gone to bed, walked down to the bonfire pit at the beach. No
Tommy. She'd sat there, waited around for two hours. Still no Tommy. No call or text either. He must've made a night of it with the
cute redhead from Harvard, she thought bitterly. They probably

taught each other the lyrics to "Onward Crimson," made snickery comments about Yale. For a guy who bitched about his dad so much, he sure was eager to do his bidding.

Alice watched Charlie pour a bit of salt from the shaker onto the tabletop, trace a giant *C* in it with the tip of her index finger. "I'm homesick," Alice announced suddenly.

"Oh yeah?" Charlie said, running her hand over the salt, blotting out the letter, making Alice think of that toy they used to fight over in the old days, Etch A Sketch. "Well, I'm homesicker."

Alice must've looked as surprised as she felt, because Charlie said, "What? I'm not allowed to be homesick, too?"

"No, you're allowed to be. Of course you're allowed to be. I just didn't think you did that emotion, didn't think that it was, like, in your repertoire. Plus, I was under the impression that you loved it here so much."

"I do, I do. I really like it here but . . ." trailing off, shrugging. "You know."

Alice nodded that she did.

"The worst part is," Charlie continued, "that there's no home to be sick for anymore."

"I'm sure Mr. D'Espo has rented out our duplex back in Cambridge."

"Gem that it was."

"It wasn't so bad."

"No," Charlie agreed, with a sigh, "it wasn't."

"And dad's somewhere in Japan. A relatively small country, but still. And impossible to reach."

"With nothing but his horn, a copy of *The Greening of America*, and, like, one change of underwear."

"Our friends are still back home," Alice pointed out.

"Yeah, but they've probably already forgotten us by now. We didn't remember them for too long, did we?"

Or our nice, uncomplicated boyfriends, Alice thought, but didn't say.

"Nope," Charlie said, answering her own question. "We traded them in for a couple of spoiled-rotten richies."

Alice nodded, eager to encourage any signs of de-infatuation with Jude on her sister's part. But then, feeling guilty, she added, "Cybill's not so bad."

Charlie snorted but otherwise let that one go, and they were both silent for a while.

"Hey," Alice said, "how about we spend the morning together? I was thinking about driving into town, going to the library."

"I can't go to the library with you. I have to read."

"Ha ha. Very funny."

"I'm not kidding. I've been hauling around *Tess of the Douchevilles* for more than a week now. I've yet to get through the first chapter. I have to just sit down today in my bedroom and start powering through. Plus, I'm thinking it might be a good idea for me to take a break from the club, give it a rest for a day or two."

"All right, but if you change your mind, just let me know. I'm not planning on leaving for a bit."

"I will," Charlie said, "but I won't. You know libraries give me the creeps."

"You want to go the library, Alice?"

Alice turned, saw Richard striding through the door, Maggie right beside him. Unlike her and Charlie, with their drawn faces and shadowed eyes and lo-fi energy, her mom and stepdad radiated health and vigor, the clear complexions and bright eyes of a good night's sleep.

Alice nodded at him and then looked down, afraid that her thoughts were showing on her face, that he'd know just by looking at her *why* she wanted to go to the library.

"How are you going to get there?" he said.

"I was going to ask to borrow the car if it wouldn't screw up your plans."

"I think that would be all right if you promise to be careful."

"I will be. What time do you need it back by?"

"I'm going to be in the office until lunch. Your mom promised she'd keep me company, help me work the fax machine." He pulled out Maggie's chair, smiled at her as she sat down in it. "It only listens to her."

"Thanks," said Alice, when he handed her the keys. "I'll just be gone a couple hours."

At that moment, Alice's cell vibrated beside her plate. She almost always kept her phone in her bag, tucked out of sight. Couldn't stand people who were constantly looking to see if someone was trying to reach them. But she'd been hoping to hear from Tommy, a call or a text with an explanation as to why he'd ditched her last night. Or, at the very least, with an apology. Kept pulling it out to check. Finally she decided to just leave it on the table. Glancing down at the screen, she was disappointed to see Angela's name flashing across it, not Tommy's.

"Let me guess," Charlie said, smirking at her. "Patrick? Boy, that guy will not give up. He calls and calls."

"It's not Patrick."

"But you're letting it go to voice mail."

Dropping her cell in her bag, Alice said, "Patrick's not the only person I'm avoiding these days. Besides, he actually did give up. A few days ago."

"Finally took the hint, huh?"

"I guess."

"Or got tired of your shit."

Alice laughed. "More that."

Charlie helped herself to a handful of Alice's blueberries. "So why are you ducking Angela?" she said, popping one blueberry, then another in her mouth. "Thought she was your bestie? Hey . . ."

Alice's stomach seized as she saw a thought enter Charlie's eyes. Trying to ward it off, or at least distract her from it, she said, "Will you stop two-fisting my blueberries? There won't be any left for my cereal."

But Charlie wouldn't be distracted. Shoving the blueberry bowl to the other side of the table, she said, "Wait, weren't you supposed to go down to see Angela yesterday?" Snapping her fingers. "Yeah, yeah, you were. You were going to go with her to that Occupy Boston thing, right?"

Alice snuck a quick glance at Richard. He was sitting in his chair, very still, posture ramrod straight, jaw set, face so expressionless it was like a mask. The knife in his hand was suspended midway between the jar of marmalade and the halved muffin on his plate. "I decided to skip it," she said to Charlie quickly, hoping that would shut the subject down.

It didn't.

"But you were so into the whole Occupy Whatever movement," Charlie said. "You chewed my ear off about it. You even made me read that article in *Mother Jones* a couple months ago."

Alice felt a smile breaking across her face in spite of the tension. "*Tried* to make you read it."

Charlie shrugged, like same difference.

"The timing wasn't good, okay?"

"Are there going to be any more?"

Alice snuck another glance at Richard. The muscles in his jaw were so bunched up now they looked like they were about to pop out of his skin. "Yeah," she said, "I'm sure there'll be plenty more. It's a big movement."

"You should take me with you when you go. When the cops come up, try to mess with you, I'll pull up my shirt, flash them. And while they're totally, totally mesmerized, you and Angela can escape. And I'll—"

Richard slammed his knife down on the table, sending bits of marmalade flying.

All three females' heads snapped in his direction.

"You're not going, either of you. First of all, I won't have you allying yourself with crybabies and crybaby causes. It's bad psychologically, bad for the character. Second of all, I won't have you getting thrown into the back of a police cruiser, your mug shots taken. I only have a verbal contract for the Boston Art Institute job. I haven't signed anything yet. Pollard and the rest could still take it away from me, give it to someone else."

Maggie and Charlie looked too taken aback to speak. But Alice wasn't. She'd heard this rant, at least part of it, before. Had seen her stepfather's face go all red and veiny, had seen his lips get all twisty and flecked with spit. "Me and Charlie don't have the same last name as you, Richard," she said calmly. "Who's going to know we're connected? Believe me, it's not something I'm eager for people to find out. So if you're worried about me telling, don't be."

"*I'll* know we're connected. And you're living under my roof, which means you're my responsibility. Besides, you're a senior this year. What college is going to be interested in a student with a criminal record? No decent one."

"You think any art school cares if I attend a political protest?"

Richard pulled his head back, as if recoiling in disgust. "Art school? You want to go to art school? Jesus."

"You have a problem with art school? But you're an architect."

"So?"

"So that's artistic."

"No, it's a trade. I went to school to learn it. Not to get a meaningless degree in arty-fartiness."

"Okay," Alice said, throwing up her hands. "Any kind of school then. I'm pretty sure most colleges look favorably on students with a proven sense of social justice."

"You don't know the meaning of the word *justice*."

"Funny, I was thinking the same thing about you. In fact, you took the words right out of my mouth."

He glared at her, those hard gray-blue eyes glaring away, but he didn't say anything back.

"Look," Alice said, speaking when it was clear he wasn't going to, "I'm really sorry this isn't working out for you."

"What isn't working out for me?"

"This whole replacement-family thing. Well, I mean mostly it's working out. Mom and Charlie are doing just great, performing up to task, all you could ask for. Most people would be happy with that, with two out of three, count themselves lucky. But you're a perfectionist, aren't you, Richard? Well, what can I tell you? We're a package deal, take one, you've got to take us all. And as much as you'd like to bring me back to the store, demand a refund or a replacement daughter for your replacement daughter, you can't." Alice was still running on anger, but she knew that tears weren't far behind, could feel them burning in her sinuses, at the back of her throat. In a rush to beat them, she talked faster: "So maybe it would be best for all concerned if you just gave up the idea that I'm going to measure up to Camilla in any way, shape, or form. It's not going to happen. And I think the sooner you accept that, the happier we'll all be. Just let me have my loser causes, the loser people I associate with. Just let me alone."

A silence followed Alice's speech, a silence so deep it filled her ears, took up all her hearing.

And then Richard broke it, saying, "I'm not letting you alone, Alice."

His voice was rough, and at first she thought it was anger giving it that hoarse, gravely quality. Quickly, though, she realized it was tenderness. But it was already too late. The words were out of her mouth before she could stop them: "God, no wonder Camilla killed herself. Anything to get away from you."

Every face in the room, including that of Luz, who was standing in the doorway, a steaming platter of scrambled egg whites in her hand, was turned to her and openmouthed with shock. Alice, car keys thankfully already in hand, stood up from the table. She ran out of the room, then out of the house altogether, the tears she'd been in a race against bursting from her eyes as soon as she crossed the threshold. She jumped into the Mercedes SUV, jammed the key in the ignition. She didn't think she breathed until she crossed Greeves Bridge and town was in sight.

Alice entered the Serenity Point Public Library, a pretty red brick building to the left of the park, one of the few that was not an expensive clothing or knickknack shop or a simple, unassuming little restaurant that charged twenty bucks for a hamburger, gave you garlic aioli to dip your fries in instead of ketchup. The librarian, a small white-haired lady, sat behind the circulation desk. Alice explained that she was looking for issues of the local newspaper from spring of the previous year. The librarian told Alice that the library had a subscription to the *Serenity Point Citizen* and that normally she'd be able to do a simple Internet search to find what she needed. Unfortunately, the library only had two computers and both were currently in use. She led Alice to the periodicals room instead, pulled every issue of the *Serenity Point Citizen* for the four-week window that Alice requested.

As soon as she was alone, Alice began combing through them. The Floods were an important local family, so the death received a fair amount of coverage. Alice read every single article. All of them said essentially the same thing, rehashed the same basic set of information: Martha Flood, forty-one, had died after a long struggle with cancer. She'd been diagnosed with breast cancer several years before. Radiation and chemotherapy appeared to put the cancer in remission. But it came back, malignant and in an advanced stage. She died in her home attended by her personal physician. She was survived by a husband, Richard, and a daughter, Camilla.

For a long time Alice stared at the photograph of the first Mrs. Flood on the obit page of the *Serenity Point Citizen*. Camilla certainly didn't get her looks from her mom. Not that Martha was ugly or anything. Her features were nice enough, but she had worried eyes and a pinched look to her, especially around the mouth, all of her held in tight. She seemed hounded, hassled. The opposite of sexy. Finally, Alice let the paper fall to the table. If a doctor had been present at Martha's death, a medical professional and disinterested third party, the likelihood of foul play being a factor in it took a serious nosedive. Like a nosedive straight into the ground.

So Richard wasn't a killer. Alice didn't know if she felt disappointed by this discovery or relieved. Probably a little of both. Mostly what she felt was dumb. What was she thinking, that her life had suddenly turned into a Hollywood suspense melodrama? That she was the plucky girl detective star out to gather clues, to crack the big case? Expose the rich, handsome smoothie who'd charmed her mother into marriage as the murderous, monstrous, possibly psychotic villain she and only she knew him to be? Jesus.

What she needed to do now was drop the Nancy Drew fantasy routine, have a straightforward talk with her mom. What she needed to do now was get the real story behind the affair with Richard. All these secrets were unhealthy, caused suspicions and distrust to fester, made the wildest and most far-fetched scenarios seem not just possible but likely. To understand how true this statement was, all she had to do was look at herself, see how far and fast she'd spun out. After little more than two weeks of living like this, she was prepared to believe all manner of lurid, unwholesome things. The truth—or what seemed to be the truth at this point—was, of course, much simpler, and, in a certain way, much sadder, too: Martha had been felled by a disease so powerful and ruthless it needed no help from an unfaithful husband to do her in.

Alice was wrapped up in these thoughts and others like them as she exited the periodicals room. She was about to exit the library altogether when a voice said, "Excuse me, young lady. You can't leave just yet."

Alice turned around. It was the librarian with the snow-white hair, holding out a pen to her. "Would you please sign this first?" The librarian indicated a ledger-type book on the desk in front of her.

Alice walked over. "But I didn't check anything out."

"I know," said the librarian, "but you used the periodicals room. It's just for our records. Records of what, I couldn't tell you. Maybe it's to prove that people still do use the periodicals room. So many newspapers and magazines are available online now."

"Oh," Alice said, taking the pen, "sure. No problem."

As Alice wrote down the date, the time she entered the room, the time she left it, she automatically scanned the page. The librarian wasn't kidding about the room not seeing much action lately. The first entry was nearly three years ago. Her eye continued to move casually down the page, then stopped cold. Camilla Flood, fourth name in. She stared at it so long, at the tall sloping letters, the *C* in

Camilla slightly larger than the *F* in Flood, the dot on the *i* so high it was almost off the page, that her eyes started to swim. The date next to it was a week before the death of Martha Flood.

"Is everything all right, dear?"

Alice looked up, startled. "What?"

"It's just you went sort of pale there for a moment," the librarian said, with a little laugh. "I was afraid I was going to have to break out the smelling salts."

Alice tried to laugh back. "Sorry, low blood sugar," she said. Then she hastily scrawled her name across the line marked GUEST, pushed the ledger back toward the librarian.

"Thank you, Miss"—looking down at the page—"Flood."

Alice, about to turn toward the door, halted. "What did you just call me?"

"Flood. Did I misread? I'm sorry. My vision isn't what it used to be." The librarian adjusted her spectacles, squinted down at the page. "No. It looks to me like you wrote Alice Flood."

Alice glanced at where the librarian was pointing. "You're right," she said, embarrassed. "It does look like that's what I wrote. My handwriting's so bad. Alice Flaherty is what it's supposed to read." She picked up the pen again, scratched out *Flood*, wrote *Flaherty* above it in careful block print.

"It's a strange mistake for you to have made," the librarian said, accepting the pen. "Well, not strange. Uncanny rather."

"Why's that?"

"Because I was thinking when you walked in that you look rather like a member of that family."

Alice tried to shrug, but her muscles clenched up, so that she made a turtle gesture instead, neck stuck inside her shoulders. "Everyone looks like someone."

The librarian gave her a queer look. "Yes, I suppose that's true."

"Take care," Alice said, slipping on her sunglasses, then slipping out the door.

Alice stood on the front steps of the library. It was a bright day, the sun hot and glaring, and it had been so cool and dim in the library. Her eyes needed time to adjust. A voice called out her name, and from the tone of it, she knew it had been doing so for a while. She looked. It was Tommy, about twenty yards ahead of her on the sidewalk, waving. He was wearing one of those muscle T-shirts, no sleeves, cut off at the shoulder. His arms were well-defined and muscular, ropy with veins and smooth-skinned. He must've been out for a run because a pair of headphones was looped around his neck and he had on black Nikes with a white swoosh, mesh shorts. His face was glowing with perspiration.

Having caught her attention, he smiled, flashing those cute, slightly overlapping front teeth of his. "Your mom told me I might find you here," he said as he jogged over to her.

"She did?" Alice said, still a little dazed and blinky.

"I texted you a couple times but you weren't answering, so I swung by the house."

"I didn't get the texts. I turned off my phone when I went into the library. They have those signs with the red line through a cell phone posted all over, so . . ."

"I figured you forgot to take it with you. That's what I did last night. Left it on the table next to my bed." He took another step toward her, shrinking the gap between them. Suddenly she was inhaling his scent, a sweaty, musky, purely male smell that moved right through her, pulled her in. "I'm glad to see you," he said in a soft voice, intimate.

"Me too," she murmured, her mouth moving in close to his.

"I'm really sorry I didn't show last night."

And then she remembered: she was supposed to be mad at him. She stiffened, leaned back. "Yeah. What happened? I was waiting for kind of a while."

"Mr. Mulvey—that's the guy my dad's hoping will hire him— wanted to show us the boat he just bought."

"You went sailing at night?"

"Not sailing. Just took a little cruise around the harbor."

"Okay, so you went cruising at night," she said, put off by his casual attitude, feeling herself getting madder and madder. "Nice. Did the daughter go with you?"

"Sloane?"

"That would be her name."

Tommy looked at Alice, and she could see that it was dawning on him that she planned to be difficult. She also could see him making a plan of his own in response: to be patient with her difficultness. "Would be and is," he said, as he reached into his pocket, took out a Clif Bar. Peanut Toffee Buzz. He unwrapped it.

"What's she like?"

Biting off an inch of bar, "Like?" he said.

"Yeah, you know, as a person. Is she into Dungeons and Dragons? Long walks in the rain? Leather-vested bikers?"

"Well," said Tommy pleasantly, "I don't know about any of that, but I do know she grew up in Scarsdale, went to Scarsdale Academy, an all-girls school. I know she's torn between majoring in history and majoring in psychology. I know she plays soccer, not well enough to get recruited but is hoping to make the team as a walk-on. And I know she's nervous about having a roommate because she's a very light sleeper and has never had to share a room before. Oh, also, I know she and her dad, who's just split up with her mom, are in town for the next ten days for a little father-daughter, precollege bonding. They're staying at the Serenity Point Inn, which is just"—pointing to a pretty, cozy-looking little building across the square—"over there. Now you know everything I know."

"Wow," Alice said, maximum snotty. "Sounds like you two got pretty chummy."

He shrugged. "I guess."

"Well, you have a lot in common. Harvard-bound, love to work up a sweat."

Tommy stopped chewing for a long moment, stared at her. Good. She was starting to get to him. "Not really," he said, swallowing. "Look, I'm not interested in her, if that's what you're thinking."

"No, of course not. I stay out the whole night with people I'm not interested in all the time."

"First of all, I didn't stay out the whole night with her. Second of all, I wasn't with her. I was with her and her dad and my dad. Third of all, I'm just playing along, trying to help my dad out."

"She's interested in you, though, right? Are you two going to hang out today?"

"We might meet for coffee this afternoon," he said, openly

annoyed now. "It doesn't matter. There's nothing going on between us. She's just bored. She doesn't know anyone here and needs someone to show her around."

"I'll bet she does."

Tommy turned to throw his half-eaten Clif Bar in the trash. Then he turned back to her, hands on his hips, eyes snapping, full-on mad. "Alice, I don't know what's making you think you can't trust me all of a sudden. I explained to you last night why I'd prefer to lie low for a little while as a couple. It seemed like that was okay with you. But now you're acting like it's not okay, and I don't understand why."

Alice didn't understand either. Maybe it was connected to finding out that her mother had likely been sneaking around with Richard for years, been a person he kept hidden and lied about like he was ashamed of her and their relationship. Not that Alice could explain any of this to Tommy. Or that the comparison between her and her mom, him and Richard, was apt or even fair. Taking a deep breath, slowly letting it out, she said, "Lying low is fine. I just don't particularly like the idea of you seeing someone else at the same time."

He threw up his hands. "I'm not seeing Sloane. I swear."

"Okay," she said after a beat. "I believe you."

"Good. You should."

"Well, good, because I do."

They locked gazes, matching each other glare for glare, and then, suddenly, they started laughing, the ridiculousness of the situation striking them both at the same time. The tension broken, Alice said, "You want a ride home? I've got Richard's car," using her chin to point to the SUV parked a block up.

"Yeah, sure, that'd be great."

They'd just started walking toward it when he jerked on her arm, pulled her into a little alleyway between the Serenity Point Bake Shop and Crowninshield's Toggery. Before she could speak, he'd taken her face in his hands, tipped it up. She felt his breath, hot on her skin, as he kissed her eyelids, her throat, and finally her mouth.

When they broke apart, she looked at him, smiled. "That's the first time you've kissed me while the sun's up."

"Let's do more of it."

She laughed. "Sounds good to me."

"How long do you have the car for?"

"As long as I want."

"Then let's spend the day together," he said impulsively. "We'll go to the lighthouse. It's the prettiest spot in Serenity Point and I want to be the one to show it to you."

He grabbed her hand and they half walked, half ran the rest of the way to the car.

Charlie left the house only a few minutes after Alice. Sticking around wasn't really an option. Not after Richard's insane burst of temper and the words that had shot out of Alice's mouth like daggers in response. What was Charlie supposed to do? Eat her eggs amidst all the sprayed blood and torn flesh? Her appetite was totally shot. She waited until she heard the SUV's engine turn, then stood up from the table. She excused herself politely, not that her mom or Richard were able to appreciate her good manners—too shell-shocked—and headed for the kitchen. After snagging a six-pack from the fridge, hoping everyone would be too busy being stunned to notice, she slipped out the back door. As she walked down to the beach, she realized that she'd left *Tess* behind. Oh well. So much for her good bookworm intentions. When she hit the water, she turned right instead of left, the opposite direction of the club.

After about thirty minutes of walking, she reached the harbor, which, amazingly enough, she'd never actually seen before other than to drive past it in the car. She found a bench and lay across it, using her balled-up denim jacket as a pillow. She began watching the boats coming in and out, admiring the turquoise of the sky, the slightly darker turquoise of the water, killing the six-pack, one beer at a time. She felt guilty about Alice's fight with Richard, like she should have stood up for Alice. Not that Alice seemed as if she needed anyone standing up for her, not as if Alice seemed anything less than perfectly capable of fending for herself. The truth was, Charlie was a little bit in awe of her sister. Alice was the quieter of the two, and the shyer. Yet she was also the stronger and the tougher, though Charlie would never have admitted this, not to her or anybody else. But Charlie knew that it was true. Alice wouldn't bend or cater. And in a funny way, this unyielding quality, this refusal to change or adapt, was why she was more suited to Serenity Point than Charlie was: she belonged, whereas Charlie merely fit in.

It had been so go-go-go since she arrived in Serenity Point that Charlie couldn't remember the last time she'd just taken a break, been by herself, alone with her thoughts. She knew why, too. Because so many of her actions lately didn't bear thinking about. Like the way she'd spoken to Stan last night. Hideous, shameful, disgusting, cruel. And all to defend the honor of a guy who had none:

Jude. Nor was Jude her only blind spot. Charlie was starting to come around to Alice's point of view on their stepfather as well. Maybe Richard was a bad guy. Maybe Alice wasn't just being a big fat downer drag, determined to see the dark side of a golden situation. He sure acted sinister at breakfast, one mention of Occupy Boston and he went completely nuts. Like, morphed into the girl from *The Exorcist*, the one who puked green slime and whose head did wheelies on her neck, totally and utterly unhinged. Charlie wondered, uncomfortably, if she was only noticing his borderline-scary qualities now because she was less invested in Jude and thus less invested in life in Serenity Point, in general. Probably. It was kind of depressing how self-serving she was turning out to be: only when it wasn't contrary to her own interests was she willing to hear the truth. Make it to Labor Day? At the rate she was going, she'd be lucky to make it to Fourth of July weekend.

No doubt about it, she'd behaved badly. Maybe, though, there was a way she could make it up to Alice, at least a little bit, by tracking down their dad. He was hard to reach, but not impossible. Before he'd taken off, he'd left Charlie the number of the answering service he was switching to, had slipped it under her pillow. (She'd assumed he'd done the same for Alice, but obviously not.) Though she'd been so angry with him for leaving, she'd kept the piece of paper, stuffed it first in her wallet, then in one of the drawers of the desk in her bedroom. Then she'd forgotten about it. Until now. She'd call it when she got home.

She was thinking about heading back there now, when a voice said, "You going to hog the whole bench or can I sit on it, too?"

The sun was directly overhead, so Charlie couldn't see more than a dark, human-shaped form looming above her when she looked up. She brought her hand to her forehead, made a visor of it. Jude. He was wearing a T-shirt, madras shorts, and boat shoes. For once, he was without his shades. Of course he was. With satisfaction she recalled the sensation of the lens shattering under her heel, the torque of her wrist as she sent the glasses sailing into the bushes. "Sure, it's a free country," she said, swinging her feet to the ground, sitting up. "In fact, the bench is all yours. I was just leaving."

He put a hand on her shoulder. "Don't go."

She knocked his hand away, continued to rise.

"Please," he said.

Something in his voice, a tremor, caught her attention. "Why shouldn't I?" she said, but she was already starting to sit back down. "You didn't seem too eager to have me around last night."

He dropped down beside her. She moved so their hips weren't touching. "Yeah, about last night. Sorry. It was a bad time for me."

Charlie snorted. "Not bad enough."

"You'll be glad to know I'm paying for it today."

She took a closer look at him. His skin was tan, but underneath the layer of brown he was pale. His hands, she noticed, too, were trembling. She felt a pang of sympathy for him, and then, remembering what Stan had told her about him and Cybill, remembering how she'd treated Stan after he'd told her, felt the sympathy harden into anger. "What happened?" she said, sarcastic. "Cybill not up for licking your wounds last night?"

"No. Cybill took care of me like she always does."

The affection in his tone when he said Cybill's name further stoked Charlie's anger. "I'll bet she did. I'll bet you two have all kinds of balms and ointments and lotions up there in your little love nest."

A beat of silence. And then Jude said, "So you know about the room in the clubhouse?"

"Last one to know, apparently."

"It's not what you think."

Jude's manner was so different today than it usually was that she was feeling thrown. And when she said, "Then what is it?" in response, her voice caught, making the question sound sincere rather than flip, as she'd intended.

"I've got a drinking issue and a drug problem." He let out a sad little laugh. "Or maybe it's the other way around. Whatever. Safe to say, I'm not on good terms with mind-altering substances these days. That's not exactly a news flash, I realize."

"No," she agreed flatly, "it's not."

He nodded, rubbed his eyes with the tips of his fingers. After a long pause, he went on with difficulty: "I know it looks like I live on my own, no parents or guardian types around, but actually there's a lot of staff in the house. Staff that reports to my dad. Spies, basically. Last year, when it got bad, he sent me to dry out at a treatment program for troubled youth in Arizona, one of those places where they practice tough love. Really tough. It was awful, Charlie, like the military. I got my hair shaved off, was woken up at four A.M. for six-mile runs in combat boots, cleaned toilets with toothbrushes, the whole boot-camp nine yards. Worse stuff happened there, too, but we'll save that for the next therapy session." Jude let out that sad little laugh again. He was quiet for a while before resuming. "My dad doesn't want scandal touching our family. It could ruin his political career, which is what he cares about more than anything else, more than me or my mom by a long shot. If he thinks my using has gotten out of control again, he'll have me back in rehab so fast it'll make my head spin. And not spin in the way I like." He stopped and shook his head, then said, "I don't know if I could make it through another thirty-day stint at Progressive Valley. Cybill doesn't know either. So, when I get . . . incapacitated, she takes me up to that room in the clubhouse, stays with me for the night. Better people think we're a couple than know what a screwed-up mess I am."

Charlie looked at him, straight into his eyes. "So you and Cybill are not sleeping together?"

"No. We have in the past, but not anymore. Physicality is not what she's looking for. At least not from me. And I didn't sleep with Lucy either. I just—we were getting so close, you and me, I mean. I felt so, like, exposed the night before last. It's not a feeling I'm used to."

She started to laugh but was so enraged it came out a bark. "*You* felt exposed? I've never been that naked in front of anybody. Ever. And then you acted like you thought it was nothing. And the crazy thing is, technically it was nothing. You touched my fucking stupid trashy tattoo. Big deal. But somehow it *was* a big deal."

"I didn't think it was nothing," he said quietly.

Trying to keep emotion from making her voice crack, failing, "Why did you do it to me then? I mean, if you knew, why would you want to put me through that?"

"I was getting back at you."

She considered this for a while, trying her best to understand, but came up empty. "For what?" she said, mystified.

"For lying. I knew you overheard me sniveling on the phone with my dad's aide."

"You weren't sniveling. You were upset." The rage coming back, "What did you think I was going to do? Out you? Tell people that Jude Devlin actually has emotions?"

"I don't know what I thought. I wasn't thinking. I guess I wanted to even the score."

"Even the score?"

"It was dumb. It was fucked up. *I'm* fucked up. Things that have happened to me in the past have made me this way. But I'm trying to get un–fucked up, okay?"

Still fuming, Charlie said, "What you did with the tattoo should've put us back on equal terms. But equal wasn't good enough for you. You had to pile it on with the other girl, get the advantage."

"I'm sorry," he said softly.

"And it wasn't on purpose, by the way, my overhearing. I wasn't trying to eavesdrop. So you punished me for something I did accidentally, just so you know."

"I'm sorry," he said again, and as he did, he took her hand in his. She let him.

They sat together in silence for a while, enjoying the sensation of the sun on their skin. And then he said, "You want to go for a ride with me? My dad keeps a boat here."

She turned, stared out at the water, as she tried to decide whether to accept his offer or not. Then, after a minute or so, she nodded. They didn't break hands as they stood up, walked toward the docks.

• • •

Charlie was assuming Jude's boat would be a sailboat—the only type she'd seen in Serenity Point, the only type she thought *existed* in Serenity Point—something staid and uppercrust-y. But it wasn't. It was a cigarette boat, as debonair and stylish as its name suggested.

They spent the afternoon tooling around the harbor, the water going from a brackish blue to a translucent turquoise-green as they moved away from the docks, and, looking over the side, Charlie could see tendrils of seaweed extending up toward the sun and small schools of fish darting through the tendrils, like gold and silver coins flung into the water, sparkling, falling behind, dropping from sight. She and Jude passed the time talking, relaxing, throwing bits of stale bread to swooping seagulls. Every so often, a sailboat would pass them and they would hear the crack and creak of riggings, the slaps of waves against a hull. Charlie had left the remainder of the six-pack under the bench by the docks, so they'd done no drinking. Had smoked no pot either. It was a first for them, she realized, hanging out with no chemicals of any kind. It could have been awkward, shown them how little they knew each other, maybe even how little they actually liked each other. But it wasn't. It was nice. Like being together, with no one else around, no stimulants buzzing through their systems, was a snap, a totally easy and natural thing.

When they got hungry, Jude maneuvered Charlie in front of him, wrapped her hands around the steering wheel. Said, "Hold it steady. I'll be right back. I'm going to see if I can scare up something to eat besides a month-old loaf of sourdough."

As Jude disappeared, a wave rose up to meet the boat. The deck seemed to jump beneath Charlie's feet, shuddering as it met the groundswell. In panic and fear, she gripped the wheel tightly, braced herself. Suddenly her face was wet, a fresh sharp wind alive in her lungs. The wave had passed, she realized. The boat heeled, spray covering the deck. Jude was standing in front of her, as soaked as she was, grinning, and Charlie couldn't help grinning back.

He was holding two jars, one filled with cocktail peanuts, the other with maraschino cherries. "Sodium, high fructose corn syrup, preservatives, and red dye number forty," he said, unscrewing the caps.

"The four basic food groups."

They devoured both jars, wordlessly passing them back and forth, Jude even drinking the lurid neon juice when all the cherries were gone. Before long, afternoon drifted into evening, the lazy hours unfolding, and a soft languor came over their bodies. Serenity Point was in the distance, the not-very-distant distance, but somehow it seemed far away. Everything did.

When the last light fell, the sun sinking below the horizon for the day, Jude got a sudden burst of energy.

"Come here," he said to Charlie as he moved behind the wheel. "I'm going to give you your first boat-driving lesson."

As she stepped inside the circle of his arms, she said, "Wait, is this the rich-person version of the boy taking the girl to the scary movie so he has an excuse to put his arm around her?"

"Yes. And later I'm going cut a hole out of the bottom of a caviar jar."

She laughed. "Like I'd fall for that old trick."

He spent a little time showing her the basics. Soon, though, he took over, becoming more daredevil in his antics, driving a bit too fast, edging a bit too close to the other vessels. He was razzing a large single-masted sailboat with a black stripe on its hull, invading its personal space, when Charlie turned, looked up. He appeared so beautiful standing above her, sharp-cheeked and pouty-lipped with windblown hair, white teeth flashing. She stood suddenly on tiptoe, brought her mouth to his. It was an impulsive kiss, and meant to be fast, but he leaned into it, then twisted her hair into a rope so he could tug her head back, kiss her more deeply.

Suddenly he swore and jerked away from her, yanked hard on the wheel. Charlie spun around, realized that they'd come within a hair's breadth of slamming into the hull of the sailboat, named, she saw now that they were closer, the *Mmm Mmm Good*. Charlie and Jude stared at each other, eyes wide, hearts pounding. When the guy on the deck of the sailboat, middle-aged and wearing some dumb captain's hat and white pants that were too tight, began shaking his fist at them, they both started laughing like it was the funniest thing they'd ever seen.

That's when the marine officer—who knew there even was such a thing?—picked them up, hauled them into the Serenity Point police station. "Reckless operation" was the charge.

"I've been accused of worse," Jude said, which made Charlie laugh even harder, which made the marine officer even madder.

After a heavy-duty lecture and a light fine, Jude, eighteen, was free to leave. But Charlie, sixteen and a minor, had to wait to be released into her mom's custody. He stayed with her, bought her a Coke from the vending machine, and sat beside her, his arm around her shoulder.

The manic mood had passed and Charlie was suddenly nervous about seeing her mom. She didn't regret any of what she'd done, though, not even the tangle with local law enforcement. It had been the best day of the summer so far, maybe one of the best days of her life. And the best part of the best day was happening now: the way she was slumped against Jude's side, his arm slung around her shoulder, a gesture of casual possession that she loved. So what if he was doing it a few feet away from the drunk tank?

Charlie kept her composure, remained sanguine (SAT word: "confidently optimistic, cheerful") when her mom, tight-mouthed and flinty eyed, strode through the door. It was only when she saw the steel-gray head of Richard behind her that her stomach began doing the slow roll of dread. *Shit*. It didn't occur to her that Maggie would bring him with her. She figured her mom would want to deal with her shame, a daughter outfitted in striped pajamas—well, nearly—in private first. Charlie flashed back to breakfast that morning, the spit flying from Richard's lips as he talked about mug shots and police cruisers, the way his hand had slammed down on the tabletop, rattling all the dishes, and a few hours later, here he was, collecting her from the station, his greatest fears realized.

Without looking at her, her mom approached the desk. Spoke in low, urgent tones to the female officer behind it.

When she saw her mom's attention was engaged, Charlie turned to Jude. His eyes were closed, and he was leaning the back of his head against the wall. She could see the chapped skin on his full bottom lip, violet shadows in the hollows under his eyes. He looked like a movie star, the kind that played a soulful vampire or an assassin with a conscience, someone beautiful but deadly. "You'd better go," she whispered to him.

Eyes still closed, he said, "You think I'm afraid of a little parental reaming? Honestly, it happens so often, I'm immune. Bring it on."

"That's sweet, Jude, but—"

"I'm not going to leave you to deal with them on your own."

"I actually think it would be better for me, though, if I dealt with them on my own."

He opened his eyes, looked deep into hers. "Really?"

"Really. Go home. It'll be fine. I'll text you later tonight, okay?"

"Fine, but only if you're sure."

She nodded that she was. He stood, leaning over casually to brush her cheek with his lips, then walked coolly out of the station. Watching him go, she admired the way he wore his clothes—even a dirty T-shirt and a ratty pair of shorts looked elegant on him—as her mom walked up to her.

"Come on," her mom said, in a tight voice, breathing through her nose the way she did when she was angry but controlling it.

"Thanks for getting me, mom. I—"

"I don't want to hear it. And I don't want to be in here for one more second than I have to. Let's go."

"Okay. But I am sorry," Charlie mumbled, as she got to her feet.

"You aren't now, but you're going to be. This is so goddamned embarrassing. Getting phoned by the police to hear that my youngest daughter is out acting like a juvenile delinquent. What's gotten into you? I can't imagine . . ."

As her mother whisper-yelled at her, Charlie, head hung low, walked toward the door where Richard was standing, arms folded across his chest. Heart going like crazy, she took a frightened peek at his face as she passed him. He gave her a wink, a little smile—quick, so her mother wouldn't catch it—before making his expression stern again. The relief she felt was so great she stopped hearing her mom's sotto voce threats, was so great she didn't even notice that she was getting into the backseat of a cab, not Richard's SUV. It was going to be okay, she told herself. He wasn't going to freak out. And her heart, still pounding in her ears, beat out the same message over and over: *he isn't mad, he isn't mad, he isn't mad.*

Charlie headed up to her room before nine P.M., something she hadn't done since she was a little girl. She did it partly to appease her mom. (Charlie was a dyed-in-the-wool night owl. An early bedtime seemed like a self-inflicted punishment.) She did it mostly, though, because she was genuinely exhausted. She'd slept barely at all the night before, and today had been such an emotional roller coaster.

Charlie had escaped serious reprimand. At first her mom had been so angry, her eyes flat, her mouth spitting out words. She'd wanted to lock Charlie in her room for the rest of the summer, throw away the key, let her out for meals and to use the toilet, that's it. Richard, though, had quietly but effectively argued on her behalf: "Come on, sweetheart," he'd said to Maggie softly, in a voice made to soothe flared tempers, jangled nerves. "Technically nothing happened. Sure, Charlie got picked up by the marine police, but no charge was actually brought against her, just against Jude, and a minor one at that. A piffling fine."

Maggie snorted at this.

Richard slipped an arm around her shoulders. "Yes, of course, Charlie will have to be more careful in the future, but she's new to the ways of boating, so allowances should be made. I'll even take her out on my boat sometime, show her the ropes. Would you like that, Charlie?"

Charlie nodded so long and so hard she felt like one of those bobblehead dolls.

"I'll teach her the right way to pull off a crime spree," he said. "How to commit illegal acts and not get caught."

No, no, Charlie thought desperately, it was too soon for jokes. He'd misjudged the situation. She quickly looked over at Maggie, was surprised to see the anger in her mom's face tighten, then drain suddenly away. Her body loosened and her expression went soft, and she laughed, actually laughed, though she assured Charlie she was still very, very mad. But she wasn't, not truly. And the scene was pretty much over at that point. Basically, thanks to her stepdad, Charlie got off with a paltry warning.

Richard really was a good guy, Charlie thought to herself, as she trudged up the staircase, yawning. Not unreasonable in the least. Alice must've brought out the unreasonable in him.

After sending Jude a text letting him know everything was okay, that she wasn't getting shipped off to a convent or anything dire, Charlie crawled into bed with all her clothes still on. Just before she drifted off, she remembered there was something she was supposed to do for Alice. But what? Something about a phone number . . . and an answering service . . . a piece of paper in the back of her desk. . . . Too late. She was asleep.

Alice pulled into the driveway at a little past ten. After parking, she took her time putting her cell in her bag, tidying up gum wrappers, applying a layer of Chapstick to her lips. The time she'd spent with

Tommy was already receding, turning into a beautiful, faintly dim memory. The prospect of seeing Richard had her stomach squeezed as tight as a fist. Not with fear. Or not *just* with fear, anyway. Remorse was mixed up in there, too—she never should have said what she said about Camilla, shoving it in his face that his daughter had committed suicide; if he was in denial it wasn't her job to pull him out of it—and anger. After all, Richard and Maggie had deceived her and Charlie about their relationship.

Alice entered the house, listened carefully. Quiet, the loudest sound the ticktock of the grandfather clock in the living room. She climbed the stairs. A lemony glow showed under Richard and Maggie's bedroom door. She'd been hoping they'd be up and about. At least the lights were still on, which meant they weren't doing lights-off stuff, so there was that piece of good luck. And, besides, holding off on the conversation until tomorrow wasn't really an option, only meant another night of no sleep, which she didn't think her body could take at this point. Gathering together all her courage, she raised her fist, rapped her knuckles lightly against the wood.

"Come in," her mother said.

Alice opened the door, stepped inside. Maggie was propped up in the enormous bed with a pillow behind her back, a book open in her hands.

"Where's Richard?" Alice said, surprised to find her mother alone.

"He's in the office, working. Too riled up to sleep, he said."

Alice nodded, slowly walking up to the bed, sitting at the foot of it. She looked at Maggie. Her mother was wearing reading glasses Alice recognized but a nightgown that was new. The near black hair pressed against the pillow was familiar, but the style it was cut in wasn't. It was like the woman in front of her was her mother and a stranger at the same time.

"Riled up?" Alice said. "You mean mad at me?"

Maggie dog-eared the page she was on, placed the book on the side table. "He's not mad at you, sweetheart. More hurt. So am I, for that matter. You want to tell me what's going on with you?"

Alice took a deep breath, told her. Not all of it, nothing about Tommy or her worries about Charlie and Jude.

Everything, though, about Richard.

At the end, she cast an anxious glance at Maggie's face. The expression on it was suspended somewhere between shock and amusement. "You thought Richard *murdered* Martha?" Maggie said. "That he was some kind of Bluebeard?" She started laughing.

Annoyed at her mother's lightheartedness, she said, "Some kind of what beard?"

"Never mind. Oh, honey, he can't even flush a spider down the toilet, he makes me do it for him. Though I am flattered that you thought someone would kill for me."

Alice shrugged, looked down. "But the rest of it's true, right?" she said, picking at a loose thread on the bedspread. "You two were involved while you were still married to dad?"

Her mom's voice got serious. "I wish I could tell you it wasn't, that we waited, got together in a wholly honorable way, but sometimes feelings are stronger than honor. You'll find that out as you get older. I'm sorry for what I did to your dad, hurting him. He was a good husband and a good father, but it was just never there between us. Not on my side, at least."

Alice waited for her mother to say more. But she didn't, just looked at Alice, her gaze candid and clear. A feeling of disappointment, obscure but somehow acute at the same time, descended on Alice. Trying to shake it off, she stood, moved up the bed. She sat beside Maggie so that her head rested on Maggie's shoulder. Maggie's hand lifted automatically, began stroking her hair. She knew, though, from Maggie's touch that if she hadn't pushed herself on her, Maggie would never have taken her in her arms.

"If it makes you feel any better," Maggie said, "Martha was in remission when Richard's and my affair started."

"It does, actually," Alice said, with a small smile.

"I'm glad."

There seemed to be nothing more to say after that. Alice stood. She was happy that she and Maggie had talked, but still, couldn't help feeling oddly unsatisfied. Yet she wasn't sure why. It was like Maggie had said all the right words, but they were just that—words. Like the emotion behind them was wrong somehow. No, not wrong exactly. More too little. Or maybe that wasn't it at all. Maybe Alice had this flat, muted feeling because she'd guessed at so much of the truth already, was only having these guesses confirmed, no new information or twists. Or maybe because she'd been expecting some big cathartic moment, a mother-daughter hugging-and-crying scene, and there hadn't been one. Or maybe it was just because she was too keyed up from an overly exciting day and everything seemed anticlimactic now. That was probably it. She leaned over, kissed her mom's cheek.

She was just at the threshold, about to cross it, when she remembered Camilla's name in the ledger book at the library, the date beside it preceding Martha's death by a mere week. She turned around, about to ask her mom what she made of that weird little detail, then thought better of it. This was real life, so there were bound to be loose ends. Why stir the pot? She had all the answers she needed.

"What is it, honey?" her mom said.

"Nothing. Just wanted to say good night one more time."

"Good night, baby. Sweet dreams."

"You too."

The dream Alice had that night was anything but sweet.

She was roused from sleep by a scratching noise. It was late, though she didn't know how late exactly because her clock was facing away from her. She sat up in her bed, rubbed her eyes, looked around. Sitting at her desk under the window was a girl, pen in hand, face bent close to the page she was writing on, blond hair glossy in the low lamplight. At first Alice was confused, thought it was herself she was observing, only looking better than she'd ever looked. Then, with a gasp, she realized her mistake.

It was Camilla.

Her dead stepsister was wearing the same outfit she wore in the photo with Tommy in the clubhouse: collared shirt, tennis skirt, sneakers, hair in a high ponytail. The only weird part—well, the whole thing was weird part, the weird*est* part—was that Camilla was in black and white, just like she was in the picture. Everything else in the room was in color.

Alice slid out of bed, walked over to Camilla, quietly, slowly, not wanting to spook her, send her running. When she got close, Camilla looked up at her, not in the least surprised by her presence.

The expression on Camilla's face was troubled. She tapped the end of her pen against her front tooth. "Something's not adding up. I'm trying to balance the figures, but they won't balance," she said, then returned her attention to the piece of paper.

Alice glanced at it. It wasn't numbers that the paper was covered in, though, it was letters: letters forming Camilla's name. She was writing it over and over again, working her way down the page, covering every line, every bit of blank space with black flowing script. Alice had seen the signature only once before but would have recognized it anywhere, the large *C* and *F*, the *C* slightly larger; the letters tall and slim and well-formed, angled to the left; the *i* with that careless, high-flying dot. The signature had force, conveyed a personality: bold and regal and wild, full of easy confidence.

"What does it mean?" Alice said to Camilla.

Camilla kept writing, didn't so much as lift her head, like the words had taken a detour between Alice's lips and her ears, gotten lost. As Alice watched her hand move fluidly across the page, a single drop of blood hit the white paper. Then another. Then another. The drops started to flow together, form a trickle, then a stream. Alice looked up. The blood, a vivid scarlet, was pouring from Camilla's black-and-white nose, cascading down her black-and-white chin. "I have to hurry," she said. But there was no hurry in her voice. No sense of urgency either. Just an absolute calm. "I have to warn little sister that she's in danger."

"Charlie? In danger? What kind of danger?"

"I'm almost too late."

"Too late for what?" Alice said, but as she said it, she looked down at her feet. They were immersed in water, and the water was

rising fast. Where was it coming from? She looked around franti-
cally, but could find no source. Still, it was filling the room, was up
to her knees, then her waist, then her chest.

Camilla was no longer sitting at the desk. She was standing in
front of it, the blood still gushing from her nose. She and Alice were
exactly the same height, stood eye to eye. Alice had never before
been this close to something so beautiful. Looking at Camilla, Alice
could understand how she ruined males, left them half-crazy with
grief, a hole gouged out of their lives so big no girlfriend or daughter could ever fill it: she did it to her father, to Jude, even to Tommy.
Suddenly Camilla stepped forward, then paused. She was so near to
touching Alice that Alice could feel the sweep of her lashes when she
blinked, could smell the blood on her skin, thick and wet and sickly
sweet, warmed by the heat inside her body. Her lips, Richard's lips,
only much fuller so that their down-turned corners made them look
sexy-moody rather than bad-tempered, parted, and she leaned in
even closer, so close that for a second Alice thought she was going
to kiss her. Then she reached out, cat quick, grabbed Alice's wrist.
Her grip was like iron.

"I'm doing everything I can on my end," she said, "but I can
only do so much. The rest is up to you."

The water was still rising, and fast. Alice felt it hit her chin. A
panic unleashed inside her. "The rest of what?" she said. And when
Camilla turned, gave her her profile, "Camilla, the rest of what?
What's going to happen to Charlie? What's the danger I have to
warn her about?"

"You need to leave now. The situation is getting dire."

"Then let me go."

Camilla looked down at Alice's wrist, up at Alice's eyes, as if surprised she was the one holding Alice back. Then a smile crept across her face, the blood from her nose running into her mouth, staining her white teeth red. Slowly she shook her head back and forth.

"Camilla, let go of me—" and on the word *please*, water gushed inside Alice's mouth, shot up her nostrils. She couldn't breathe. She thrashed in Camilla's grip until her lungs were about to burst, and her head felt huge, her eyeballs like they were going to pop out of her sockets, every molecule of her being screaming out for oxygen. Camilla's eyes never let hers go and her smile never wavered, not once.

Just as she was on the point of passing out, Alice woke up, gasping.

Chapter
• FIFTEEN •

*T*hree days later, Alice and Charlie were in the Mercedes SUV, tooling along the scenic Connecticut coastline. They were headed to Darien, the town Richard's mother lived in, a forty-five-minute drive from Serenity Point. Mrs. Flood, who'd been in Europe at the time of Richard and Maggie's wedding and thus unable to attend, had called several times since Alice and Charlie had arrived in Serenity Point, trying to coax the girls down to her house for lunch. Alice had been wanting to pay her stepgrandmother a visit, grill her a little bit about Camilla, but only without Richard around, as his presence would act as an inhibitor. So she'd waited to accept the invitation, cooling her heels until she heard he and Maggie would be in Boston for the day condo hunting.

Alice knew Charlie would balk when she asked her to come along, but she needed Charlie—it would look weird, wouldn't it, like suspicious, if she showed up at Mrs. Flood's all by herself?—so she got bossy about it. Charlie, as anticipated, balked, looked at her like she was out of her mind. Who voluntarily spent time with her own grandmother, never mind someone else's? Then Alice reminded her that they'd be passing an outlet mall in Westbrook, promised to stop at it if Charlie agreed to keep her company. Charlie had regarded Alice through narrowed eyes, then said, "Okay, but I'm only agreeing because you blackmailed me, not because I want to go shopping."

As she drove, Alice snuck glances at her sister out of the tail of her eye. Charlie was looking out the window, bundled up inside her hoodie sweatshirt as she blasted the air-conditioning, probing the nearly invisible blond down on her upper lip with the tip of her tongue. She seemed different lately in a way that was hard for Alice to put her finger on: quieter, calmer, more preoccupied, as if her mind was always someplace else. The manic running around with Jude and Cybill had stopped. Who knew how she spent her time now? It was almost like, Alice thought, she had a secret. Not that Alice could ask what it was. Not when she was keeping so many of her own. Okay, maybe she was being a bit tough on herself with the *so many*. After all, she had shared with Charlie most of her suspicions about Richard and their mom. She'd just never bothered telling Charlie that they'd officially been confirmed. The impression she got was that Charlie didn't want to hear it, anyway. And the stuff about Jude being Camilla's on-the-sly guy didn't really count either since she wasn't at liberty to discuss it, as Tommy had told her in strictest confidence. Thankfully, Jude seemed to be in the rearview mirror as far as Charlie was concerned, so Alice didn't have to feel too guilty on that score. And, finally, if she was acting hush-hush about her relationship with Tommy, well, that couldn't be helped either. Again, he had his reasons for insisting on discretion that she felt she had to respect even if she wasn't entirely clear on what exactly those reasons were.

A sign welcomed them to Darien. Alice didn't have faith in the map application on Charlie's iPhone, so she'd printed out directions from randmcnally.com before they'd left. Fortunately, Mrs. Flood's house was easy to find, just past town center, a great big sprawling Victorian on a street full of great big sprawling Victorians. Alice parked at the foot of the driveway, and she and Charlie walked across the lush green lawn, past the brightly colored flower beds, and up to the door. As Alice leaned forward to ring the bell, Charlie said under her breath, "Remind me, why are we doing this again?"

Alice didn't give Charlie an answer because she didn't have one, not a specific one, at least. *To learn more about Camilla*, was the big-picture answer. But what exactly she was hoping to learn, she had no idea. All her questions should have been laid to rest after her late-night conversation with her mother.

Only they weren't.

She had this nagging sense that she was missing something, that some key piece of information was eluding her, floating just beyond her grasp. Intuition told her it was connected to Camilla. But Camilla-related information was hard to come by in the circles she traveled in. *Camilla* was the word not spoken in the Flood-Flaherty household. And Camilla was the dark alley off Memory Lane that Tommy preferred to creep past, head down. Alice sensed she needed to come at the problem from a different angle. Hence, the elder Mrs. Flood.

"One hour," Charlie said. "That's all the time I'm giving you to indulge your senior citizen fetish. Use it wisely."

The door swung open. The woman behind it, Mrs. Flood, was a pretty older lady, looked closer to seventy than the eighty Alice knew her to be, fashionably dressed in a crisp white shirt and linen slacks, hair twisted into a chignon. She was tall and had the same high cheekbones as her son, the same thick gray hair and piercing gunmetal-blue eyes. More pierced than piercing, though, when she saw Alice and Charlie standing there. For a second, Alice thought she was going to faint, reached out to catch her.

"Mrs. Flood, are you okay?" Mrs. Flood's arm in her hand was so thin, like a twig. She was far more fragile than she looked, Alice realized, her height and bone structure and steely coloring deceptive.

"Yes, dear," she said, struggling to regain her composure, obviously embarrassed at this display of weakness. "I'm fine. You must be Alice."

Alice confirmed with a nod.

Mrs. Flood kept her gaze on Alice, but addressed Charlie, as if she were afraid she'd lose her balance again if she moved even her eyes: "That would make you Charlie?"

"It would," Charlie said. "Nice to meet you."

"I was waiting for the bell to ring. I must've stood up too quickly and . . ." shaking her head, like she was trying to shake off the wooziness. "Come in, girls, come in."

Charlie raised her eyebrows at Alice before following Mrs. Flood inside.

She led them into a dining room that was bright and high-ceilinged, elegant-looking without being fussy-looking. The table was set beautifully, fresh flowers in a tall, oblong vase, hand-painted Italian plates, goblety-type glasses that were probably made of crystal or something even fancier. Mrs. Flood said she'd be right back with lunch, waved off Alice and Charlie's offers of help.

Once she disappeared through the door, Charlie turned to Alice and said, "Jesus, I hope she doesn't have a heart attack in there. I call dibs on not doing mouth-to-mouth."

Refusing to dignify that with a response, Alice rose from her seat, began looking around the room. If she'd been starving for pictures of Camilla in Richard's house, she could eat to her heart's content in Mrs. Flood's, could just pig out, gorge herself to the point of bursting. Camilla's image was everywhere, on every available inch of wall space, on every available flat surface. Alice felt overwhelmed by possibility, didn't know where to begin. With Camilla as a fat-kneed toddler, pink and dimply, as adorable as a kid in any ad? With Camilla as a gap-toothed grade-schooler dressed as a cowgirl for Halloween, gun belt around her waist, ten-gallon hat on her head, hand on an out-thrust hip, pretend sexy? With Camilla as a *Teen Vogue* teen, vamping for the camera in a polka-dot bikini and heart-shaped Lolita sunglasses, all arms and legs and attitude, sexy for real? Wherever she looked, Camilla, Camilla, Camilla. There was even a framed copy of Camilla's birth certificate above one of the Tiffany lamps on the end table. She walked over to it. March 28. Camilla was born two months to the day before she was.

At that moment, Mrs. Flood returned to the dining room carrying a tray loaded with crustless triangle-shaped sandwiches and fruit plates and cornichon pickles, tall glasses of lemonade, tinkly with ice cubes. Alice quickly stepped away from the birth certificate and picked up a photo from the windowsill. It was of Camilla, about age fourteen, and Mrs. Flood. (It somehow seemed more polite to Alice to be caught gawking at a photo that the hostess was actually *in*.) They were in an outdoor setting of some kind, and Mrs. Flood was pulling Camilla to her. Camilla was laughing, the sun glinting off her teeth. "Where was this taken, Mrs. Flood?"

"Please, dear, call me Katherine," Mrs. Flood said, as she carefully set down the tray on the table, walked over to where Alice was standing. "You can even call me Nana if you like," she said, smiling shyly.

Alice smiled back.

"Now let me see." Mrs. Flood took the photo from Alice's hands, held it up almost reverently. "At a handcraft fair in Mystic I took Camilla to a few years ago. Such a wonderful day. I bought her those wind chimes. They were made out of sand dollars. I thought they were tacky little things, but Camilla said, 'Nana, I like the sound they make.'"

Alice squinted. "Oh yeah. You know, those wind chimes are still hanging on the back porch of the house."

A cloud passed over Mrs. Flood's face. "Are they? Richard got rid of so much, almost everything Camilla or Martha ever touched, it seemed like. The wind chimes must've somehow escaped the purge." She gave Alice a pained smile, then said, "Let's go eat. Can't have those cold cuts getting cold."

Charlie was the only one at lunch who exhibited much of an appetite. She ate a roast beef sandwich, half of a ham and cheese, all the fruit salad except for the melon balls, and she picked off the cornichons one by one. Alice and Mrs. Flood just sipped at their lemonades, exchanged more shy smiles. She must be lonely, Alice thought. Husband dead. Granddaughter, as well. Son too busy with his career and his new wife to pay her much attention.

"I was so sorry not to have been at the wedding," Mrs. Flood said after a long silence. "Richard invited me, but I was in Nice. I couldn't just up and leave. I'd rented a house there for the month. Maybe I could have arranged something if I'd been given a bit more notice . . ."

"You didn't miss much," Charlie said. Then, off the look Alice shot her, "What? She didn't."

Alice shook her head at her sister's lack of tact, then turned to Mrs. Flood. "Charlie's right, actually. It was pretty low-key. Just at City Hall. Since it was the second marriage for both, they didn't feel like making a big production out of it."

Mrs. Flood nodded. "Oh, yes, I understand. They wanted to keep it understated, no hoopla." But in a smaller voice, she added, "Still, I would have liked to have been there."

Alice cast around her brain for a change of subject. Finally, she settled on: "Have you met our mom yet?"

"I have," Mrs. Flood said, but didn't say anything after that, which said everything, really. Richard must've introduced them at some point during the courtship. Obviously she wasn't a fan. Or maybe it was the affair preceding the marriage that she wasn't a fan of. Funny, Alice thought to herself, that she'd go out of her way for the kids of a woman she didn't much like. Family must be very important to her.

After clearing the dishes, again refusing Alice and Charlie's offers of assistance, Mrs. Flood brought out the tray again, this time with a beautiful five-piece silver coffee set on it. She placed it on the table, then picked up the pot, pouring the dark, steaming liquid into a delicate white cup. She stirred three spoonfuls of sugar into it before handing it to Alice.

Surprised, Alice looked down at it.

Mrs. Flood, coloring, said, "My goodness, I'm so sorry. I didn't even ask you if like sugar with your coffee. And I gave you so much."

"Don't worry about it," Alice said. "I do like sugar with my coffee. Love it, in fact. As far as I'm concerned, there's no such thing as too much."

Mrs. Flood poured a cup of coffee for Charlie, then herself, then sat down. She still seemed embarrassed, and Alice couldn't think of a way of relieving her of that embarrassment. Was she self-conscious about her memory? Afraid that they'd report back to Richard that his mom was losing it? When the silence went on for a while, Mrs. Flood stood up again. "Excuse me, girls, I forgot the cookies. Stay where you are. I'll be right back."

As soon as Mrs. Flood was out of earshot, Charlie leaned across the table and said, "Better get those cookies to go. I've had about enough of this. And we've been here now for"—checking the clock on her iPhone—"fifty-seven minutes. You have three minutes to wrap this up."

"Or what? You'll turn into a pumpkin?"

"Not a pumpkin, a punk," Charlie said, clearly pleased with her phrasing. "As in a very rude person."

Alice made sad clown face at Charlie.

"I'm serious, Allie. Ticktock, ticktock."

"First of all, you've been kind of rude all lunch."

"And that was without trying. Imagine how rude I can be if I put my mind to it."

"Second of all, we can't just run off, leave her with a bunch of dirty dishes. Clearly she doesn't get too many visitors."

Charlie shrugged. "Not my problem. It's spooky here. Like being in a haunted house."

Alice stood, stepped away from the table, her eye caught by a photograph on the mantel. Camilla, fifteen or sixteen, on her stomach reading a book. She was in Alice's room, or rather, in her room that was now Alice's. (Alice recognized the headboard on the bed Camilla was lying across.) So Richard *did* give Alice his daughter's old room. She knew it. "Oh really?" Alice said distractedly to Charlie. "Because I don't see any ghosts."

"That's because you're not looking in the mirror."

Alice put down the photo, turned to her sister. "What's that supposed to mean?"

"That you are the ghost." A beat, while Alice stared. "Isn't it obvious?" Charlie said. "She thinks you're Camilla."

Alice was about to tell Charlie to quit being dumb when she realized that she was the one being dumb, that Charlie was, in fact, being perceptive: Mrs. Flood's near faint; the three sugars; the *call me Nana*. Alice felt guilty. As if she'd been manipulating the older woman, toying with her emotions, haunting her basically, even though it had been her intention to do none of these things. It was still so strange for Alice to think that people could mistake her for Camilla, a response she found both deeply eerie and deeply flattering. On the inside she couldn't have felt *less* like Camilla, who was so dynamic, so sexually powerful, so morally complex. Whereas she, Alice, was so dull, so virginal, so "what-you-see-is-what-you-get." She assumed that their internal differences would be reflected on their external selves, but evidently they were not. Evidently she could pass for Camilla. And the fact that she could thrilled her. It disgusted her that it thrilled her, but, still, it thrilled her.

Thirty seconds later, Mrs. Flood returned with a plate piled high with oatmeal-raisin cookies. Alice and Charlie stayed the bare minimum required by politeness, then hurried off to the car.

Alice dropped Charlie off at the house, then continued over Greeves Bridge and into town. The trip to Darien had been an out-and-out bust. She'd learned nothing except that Camilla had been a cute baby (no surprise, irrelevant), was fond of artsy-craftsy decorative-type objects that produced a pleasing jangling sound when the wind blew (sort of a surprise, even more irrelevant), and had occupied in the past the room that Alice occupied in the present (a definite surprise, but most irrelevant of all since it was Richard who was responsible for room assignments, not Camilla). She decided to stop by the library.

The sight of Camilla's name in that ledger—it bugged her. It was a detail her brain couldn't seem to process, went over again and again, snagging on it every time. She couldn't explain it away no matter how hard she tried. What did it mean? Why had Camilla visited the periodicals room of the Serenity Point Public Library a week before her mother's death? If she'd wanted to locate something in the archives of a newspaper or a magazine, why didn't she just do an online search in the comfort of her own home? Because, like Alice, she'd been afraid her Internet activities at the house were being monitored, wanted the assurance of total privacy? That was the only reason Alice could think of. Still, even if by some miracle she was right and had correctly guessed at Camilla's motive, Alice didn't see how that helped her. After all, it didn't tell her what Camilla had been looking for, just why she'd been looking where she'd been looking. Nor would a visit to the library tell her what Camilla had been looking for since recorded in the ledger were only a name and a date, and yet she was about to make one anyway. Maybe the librarian could tell her something. Alice laughed at the thought almost as soon as she had it. Yeah, sure, maybe the librarian, assuming the same one even still worked there, retained a crystal-clear memory of a visit made by a girl more than a year ago. Jesus Christ. Alice rubbed her face, sighed. Whatever. It was a long shot, but she had to take it since at this point it was her only shot.

She found a spot for the car, fed the meter, then jogged across the park and over to the library's entrance. As before, the white-haired librarian was sitting behind the circulation desk. She recognized Alice, greeting her with a wave. "You'll have the periodicals room all to yourself again, Alice," she said, smiling. "Both computers, too. We're a bit of ghost town around here today, I'm afraid."

Alice took a quick glance at the nameplate on the edge of the desk. Hildi Snowden.

"I actually didn't come here to use the periodicals room today, Mrs. Snowden."

"No?"

"No. I came to talk to you."

Mrs. Snowden looked surprised but pleased. Folding her hands pleasantly in front of her, she said, "Oh, all right. What do you want to talk to me about?"

"It's the ledger you had me sign. There was another name in

it. Camilla Flood. She's what I want to talk to you about, her visit to the periodicals room." Trying to jog Mrs. Snowden's memory, "The last time I was here, you seemed familiar with the family. In fact, you thought I looked like I was part of it. Actually, I am. I'm a cousin."

"Why didn't you say so before?"

Alice shrugged. "A pretty distant cousin. Anyway, this visit I want to ask you about, unfortunately I can't give you much to go on. It was made last spring, more than a year ago, by Camilla, who would've been about sixteen at the time. I was wondering if you could tell me—if you even know—why she visited." Alice paused, daring to look at Mrs. Snowden's face. What she saw was not encouraging: an expression of bewildered puzzlement. Alice squeezed her eyes shut as she continued, just wanting to get to the end of the clearly doomed pitch now so she could go. "I realize this is an insane request, that there's almost no way you're going to remember an encounter from so far back, an encounter that probably seemed extremely trivial to you at the time, but I had to ask and—"

"I do remember, actually."

Alice's eyes snapped open. "What?"

"I said, I do remember."

"You do?"

"Normally, of course, there'd be no way. The errand this girl—your cousin, Camilla—was on, though, was so sweet. She was planning on throwing an anniversary party for her parents, but was less than fully confident that she had the date right. Told me she didn't want to look it up on her home computer for fear that her parents would figure out what she was up to. It was important to her that the party be a complete surprise. That's why she came to the library. A good thing she did, too. She couldn't have looked up the wedding announcement online, at least not in the *Serenity Point Citizen*. The year 2000 is as far back as their online archives go."

"That's amazing. I mean, that you remember."

"Well, the truth is, I might have forgotten if I didn't know how sick Mrs. Flood was at the time, how unlikely it was that she'd make it to another anniversary. And of course she died so soon after Camilla came in . . ." Mrs. Snowden trailed off. "Well," she said, smiling sadly at Alice, "that really sealed the event in my memory."

"Did she have it right?"

Mrs. Snowden cocked her head at Alice, not following.

"The date of the anniversary, I mean."

"She did. It was the year she had wrong. Her parents were married one year after she thought they were. It could have been embarrassing, I suppose, if she wrote the date on the invitations or the cake or something. Not really, but she might have thought so." With a smile, Mrs. Snowden said, "You young people can be so intense."

For a while Alice and Mrs. Snowden were both silent. And then Alice said, "So you helped her find the wedding announcement?"

"Yes, that's right."

"Do you think you could help me find it, too?"

Looking surprised, Mrs. Snowden said, "I think so. I'm almost sure I remember which issue I pulled. Have a seat. I'll be back."

Alice sat on a red stool sized for a child in the far corner, her mind curiously blank while she waited. She didn't know how much time had passed—one minute or thirty—before Mrs. Snowden returned, bearing a single sheet of paper.

"It was on microfiche," Mrs. Snowden said. "I made a copy for you. It's fifty cents. I supposed I should've asked before I—"

"No, no," Alice said, fumbling around the bottom of her bag for loose change, "I'm glad you did. Thank you."

At last she came up with two lint-covered quarters, handed them to Mrs. Snowden. She looked down at the sheet and began to read. The announcement of the marriage of Richard Bowdoin Flood III to Martha Barrett Briggs on October 20 appeared pretty standard to her eye: age, educational background, and career aspirations of bride and groom; location of ceremony; name of officiant; a few ancestor-worship facts; etc., etc. She scanned it twice to see if any detail leapt out at her. None did. It had to be the date, then, that was significant, specifically the year. So, Richard and Martha had led Camilla to believe that they'd wed one year earlier than they in fact did. Now why would they do that? To what end? And then Alice remembered the framed birth certificate hanging in Mrs. Flood's living room. Camilla was born on March 28 of the following year, the same year she, Alice, was born, which meant that Martha was already pregnant with Camilla when she walked down the aisle with Richard.

So it was a shotgun wedding.

That was the big secret, the big scandal—that Martha had let herself get knocked up slightly ahead of schedule? So what? Alice had done the math; her parents' wedding was shotgun, too. This wasn't the eighteen hundreds. Plenty of couples had families without even bothering to tie the knot, ever. Did anyone care, even in prim-and-proper WASP land, that the bride and groom had seen each other naked before the ceremony? Or, an alternative theory suddenly presenting itself to her, did Richard and Martha fudge the date not to protect themselves but to protect Camilla? Were they afraid she'd be hurt to discover that she was an accident, that she'd feel unwanted or, worse, guilty, like her arrival had forced them into entering a union that they otherwise might not have? But not only couldn't Alice imagine Camilla ever being so fragile, or prone to such woe-is-me thinking, Alice couldn't imagine anyone, Camilla's parents especially, ever perceiving her as such. Maybe, then, the date wasn't what Camilla was looking for after all. Maybe that was simply what she told Mrs. Snowden, a cover for something else.

Or maybe, Alice thought with a sigh, *I'm just on a wild-goose chase*.

Frustrated that her big break had turned into a big nothing, Alice folded the wedding announcement, dropped it carelessly into her bag, and stood up. She thanked Mrs. Snowden for her help and headed back to her car.

Chapter
• SIXTEEN •

*A*lice lay in bed that night, tossing and turning. Her mind wouldn't shut off. She knew Charlie was still awake, too. She'd seen the light under her sister's door when she got up to pee a few minutes ago. Normally she'd just stroll right on in, jump in Charlie's bed, and they'd talk until they both fell asleep. But it hadn't been normal between them for days now. Alice couldn't speak about what was actually preoccupying her. So what would be the point of conversation? Not that she was capable of having a coherent conversation. Or of even having a coherent thought. Her brain was starting to feel to her like a hamster on a wheel, expending energy furiously, getting nowhere. And she hadn't taken out her sketch pad in nearly two weeks. With a wince of guilt she remembered her dad telling her that if you wanted to become an artist, you had to perform your craft every single day, even if it was only for half an hour. Remembered, too, the sound of him practicing his scales in his and Maggie's bedroom every morning at seven A.M. sharp, the sessions more reliable than any alarm clock, the sessions so reliable she used them *as* an alarm clock, interrupted briefly by the seven-fifteen commuter train out of Porter Square, then resuming until seven thirty. She was starting to look forward to the prospect of school starting in eight weeks, new kid on the block or not. Anything to take her mind off Camilla. Camilla, who dogged her every step. Camilla, who occupied her every thought. Camilla, who obsessed her and haunted her and would not leave her alone, who followed her even into her dreams.

Alice's clock was digital but she swore she could hear it ticking, counting off the seconds, then the minutes, then the hours. At last, she sat up. She would read, she decided. Only she had no book. Once she'd finished *The Omnivore's Dilemma*, she'd never quite gotten around to picking up a replacement. Then she remembered the copy of *The Magus*, the reading assigned to her by Wolcott, in the library downstairs. She moved from her bed to the door. Hand on the knob, she strained to hear. Nothing, just a dead silent house in the dead middle of night. Taking a deep breath, she opened the door, ran down the staircase and into the library as fast as she could, head lowered so as to avoid contact with any of the many pairs of painted eyes watching her. After pulling the book from the shelf, she ran out of the room, once more past the staring portraits— inside each frame a different face, though really all the same face, all variations of Richard's face—up the staircase and into her room. She closed the door behind her, turned the lock, and jumped into bed.

As she hauled the book onto her lap, she was almost grateful for its thickness and heft. Even if she read straight through 'til morning, there was no way she'd finish it, be left alone with nothing to do, nothing to occupy her mind but her jittery, fragmented thoughts endlessly chasing their own tails. She fell into the book immediately. Before she knew it, she'd read fifty pages, then a hundred. The young hero, Nicholas, had just completed a miserable week teaching English to schoolboys on the Greek island of Phraxos, was about to return to the magical estate of a wealthy recluse, Maurice Conchis. Alice eagerly flipped the page to return with him when a piece of paper fluttered out of the book, landing on her blanket-covered knee.

Probably a makeshift bookmark, Alice thought, and nearly brushed it to the floor, annoyed at the interruption. Then she noticed that the paper was folded. Curious, she unfolded it.

When Alice saw her name at the top in that handwriting she knew as well as her own, she thought for a second she was in one of those dreams where she couldn't figure out what was real and what wasn't. But, no, as improbable, as *impossible*, as it seemed, this was actually happening. Her brain began working, scrambling to cobble together a reasonable explanation. Yet there were no reasonable explanations to be cobbled, just unreasonable ones: Camilla had either written her a letter before she knew she existed—or Camilla had written her a letter from beyond the grave. Those were the only possibilities that existed, her mind was telling her. And then, there was an instant in which she experienced a flash of understanding:

She'd been tormenting Camilla every bit as much as Camilla had been tormenting her.

She was living in Camilla's house, kissing Camilla's boyfriend, eating breakfast with Camilla's dad. Camilla had every reason in the world to hate her. And the realization that she could inspire a passionate emotion in Camilla, even if it was negative, was beyond thrilling to her. It meant they were on intimate terms. As intimate as sworn enemies. As intimate as people in love. As intimate as family. *More* intimate than family. The truth was, she felt closer to Camilla than she did to anybody else these days, her mother and sister included.

When Alice calmed down enough for her eyes to focus, she began to read:

Dear Alice,

This probably seems bizarre to you, a girl you don't know writing you a letter out of the blue telling you we need to talk, but we do. There's something I need to tell you about. Warn you about might be a better way of putting it. It concerns our parents. I'd prefer to have the conversation in person. I know that you live in the Boston area and I go to school in Connecticut, the part that's closer to New York than Massachusetts. There's an Amtrak station near me. Maybe we could meet at a halfway point? New London or Westerly? The sooner the better.

Sorry to be so mysterious. But you'll understand why it was necessary after we get together, which by the way I'm really looking forward to in spite of the cloak-and-dagger circumstances. Oh, and I Googled you yesterday. Saw that you'd won some big art prize. Congratulations. There was a picture of you. The jeans you were wearing, I have a pair just like them. Crazy world.

Here's my cell phone number: (203) 655-2701. Call anytime.

~~Sincerely~~ Warmly,
Camilla Flood

P.S. Oh, and you should probably trash this letter after you read it. (Just so you know, I do realize how paranoid weirdo this sounds. Still, you probably should.)

Thoughts immediately began to pinball around Alice's skull. Obviously Camilla had cottoned on to Richard and Maggie's affair. She must've wanted to warn Alice that her life as she knew it was about to end. But why had she wanted to warn only Alice? Why not Alice and Charlie? Camilla and Charlie would have had just as much in common as Camilla and Alice. It seemed strange that she'd singled Alice out, decided she connected more with her than Charlie without having actually met either girl. Especially considering the dig she got in about Alice's jeans. (Okay, so they were sort of momish, but Maggie had sent in an old photo to the *Globe* from freshman year, and Alice had long since gotten rid of them.) Or maybe she was going to write Charlie separately and just hadn't gotten around to it yet. Alice was, after all, the older sister, and so was first on the list. Why, though, had the letter never been mailed? Camilla must've meant to mail it, otherwise why preserve it? Why not just throw it out? And when was it written? There was a date, Alice saw, at the top of the page. She gasped a little when she squinted, made out the numbers:

The day Camilla visited the Serenity Point Public Library, a week before Martha died.

Alice leaned her back against the headboard, waited as her brain connected the dots. So what must've gone down was something like this: the trip to the periodicals room confirmed something for Camilla. Maybe Alice was wrong about Camilla's not being prone to woe-is-me thinking. Maybe learning that Richard and Martha's wedding had been the result of a birth control mishap told her that they'd never truly been in love, which explained how her father came to be involved with another woman. (Camilla was, by all accounts, a sophisticated, wised-up girl, but even the sophisticated can be sentimental when it comes to their parents' relationship.) In any case, it confirmed something for her. She was now certain that the affair she'd somehow managed to uncover wasn't just a fling, that Richard and Maggie were a couple for the long haul. She started to contact Alice to give her a heads-up. But then, the next day, her mom's health, which seemed to be improving, took a sudden turn for the worse—and a turn for the way worse a week after that. Maybe once her mom died she was too distracted and grief-stricken to deal with envelopes and zip codes and stamps and all that. Or maybe once her mom died she regarded warning Alice as pointless, a marriage between Richard and Maggie inevitable, a foregone conclusion, so she shoved the letter in one of her schoolbooks, forgot about it. Alice let out a frustrated sigh. Maybe this, maybe that. Maybe, maybe, maybe—she was drowning in a sea of them.

She stuck the piece of paper back in the book, dropped the book to the floor. Listening to it land with a thud, she thought bitterly, another close-but-no-cigar clue, one that led to more questions and no answers, that appeared promising initially but ultimately failed to pan out. Suddenly exhausted, she reached for the cord on her lamp. When she pulled it, though, the room didn't plunge into darkness. Surprised, she looked out the window. Saw that the sky was already turning a pale, streaky pink, the sun rising up out of the ocean. Morning, she realized. It was a sickening sight.

●   ●   ●

Alice was present at family breakfast that day in body only, eating little, talking less. Charlie, who seemed pretty distracted herself, only noticed how out of it Alice was when Alice was slow to respond to a request to pass the almond milk, shooting her a what's-up-with-you? look. Alice mouthed the word *cramps*, and Charlie, who got terrible ones when she had her period, winced sympathetically, nodded, like "say no more." As soon as Luz began clearing the plates, Alice returned to her room, changed into a miniskirt and tank top, her bathing suit underneath. After dousing herself in spray-on sunblock with a triple-digit SPF, she slipped out the back door without anyone observing her.

She was supposed to meet Tommy at this little dive-type restaurant by the docks. It was unlikely that they'd run into anyone they knew there. After a quick cup of coffee, they'd head down to the beach, some spot that was technically public but as good as private, Tommy claimed, because nobody but locals was aware of its existence.

Alice was walking quickly, afraid she'd be late. Walking quickly, too, because she was nervous. She and Tommy had to have a talk. She still didn't know where they stood as a couple, if they even *were* a couple. In so many ways they felt like one. They saw each other nearly every day, and when they were together they were constantly touching, like one part of his body had to be in contact with one part of hers at all times, even if it was just linked fingers. And the secrecy of the relationship, the way it was conducted mostly at night or in out-of-the-way spots, the fact that they were forbidden to get involved with each other if not explicitly than implicitly because of his past association with Camilla—all these things made their romance feel, well, more romantic. To Alice, anyway.

But there were things about the relationship that made her doubt its legitimacy, primary among them the fact that they hadn't ever done more than kiss. Tommy wasn't pressuring her, which was nice. She sometimes wondered, though, if he wasn't pressuring her because he was trying to avoid feeling guilty about not making her his girlfriend, like if held back physically, he didn't owe her anything, didn't have to commit himself, which wasn't so nice. Also, if she was honest with herself, she wanted him to pressure her, wanted him to pressure her because she wanted him to want her. She wanted him. (*Two weeks.* She'd known Tommy for *two weeks.* She almost couldn't believe the period had been so brief. She'd been with Patrick for *two years* and had felt none of this urgency. It was just different with Tommy.) But she didn't think it was her place to initiate. Or, if she did have to initiate, she didn't want it, if that made any sense. The lack of intimacy with him played on all her insecurities, too. She bet he and Camilla didn't wait. Bet he *couldn't* wait with Camilla, couldn't hold himself back. Was he only interested in her, Alice wondered, because he could be relaxed around her? Would feel no uncomfortable heat or passion, no desires that his will couldn't easily overmatch? That must've been it. She was restful for him, and after Camilla he needed a rest. Like, he didn't have to worry that Alice would cheat on him or deceive him, and, since he had all the power, she couldn't really hurt him either. No, she was more of a companion than a girlfriend. And at the word *companion*, her stomach began to heave, her palms to sweat.

Even though she was in the weaker position, however, she wasn't prepared to be passive forever. This very morning, in fact, she was planning on asking Tommy straight out what his intentions toward her were. (She made a mental note to use a less Jane Austenish term than *intentions* when she asked the question out loud.) Basically, did he want to be her boyfriend or not? And if he did want to, then they had to become official. Slinking around couldn't be their permanent state. She wasn't okay with that. Or, rather, she was okay with that—dangerously close to okay, anyway—and she wasn't okay with that. The way she felt about Tommy, she could understand how her mother had fallen into the situation with Richard: being so much in love that you were willing to do anything to stay together, lie to everyone close to you, betray them, sacrifice your own self-respect, waiting and waiting and waiting until he was finally ready for you not to be his dirty little secret anymore. But if you waited like that, you always kind of would be.

At last Alice reached the docks. She stepped inside Redbone's Café, the bell above the door making a little jingling sound. Tommy was sitting at a booth in the back. He was wearing swimming trunks and a plaid shirt, misbuttoned and slightly skewed, rolled up to his elbows, the muscles in his forearms playing delicately under the skin while he flipped the pages of the menu back and forth.

Alice slid into the bench across from him. He looked up at her and smiled. As he inserted one of his legs between both of hers, he said, "I can't decide if I'm hungry or not. I think maybe I'm just going to get a juice and a coffee, then when we come back at lunch, I'll order something big."

"Okay," she said.

He held up a wait-a-second finger, consulted the menu again. "Well, maybe I'll get an English muffin, too. And a side order of bacon. I don't want to lose energy when we're swimming."

"Whatever you want. I'm in no hurry."

He craned his neck, scanning the room for the waitress.

"Um, Tommy, I'd actually hold off for a bit before ordering if I were you. There's something I want to say that might kill your appetite."

He turned to her, concerned. "What is it?"

Looking at the chipped Formica tabletop because she was too embarrassed to look at his face, she said, "I want to ask you what we are to each other. Technically speaking, I mean." She laughed nervously, as if she'd said something funny, then frowned. "I hate being so literal-minded or humorless or whatever, but I kind of need to know."

A moment of silence followed, and then Tommy cleared his throat. She steeled herself for the gentle but firm turndown. "Alice," he said softly, "the reason I never said I wanted to be your guy was because I just assumed I was."

The relief she felt hearing these words was so strong, her whole body just sagged. It was like she momentarily lost control of her spine. "Yeah?"

"Yeah. This is the happiest I've been in a really long time."

"That's good," she said. "That's great. I mean, not that you were unhappy before, but that you're happy now."

He smiled at her, flashing that ever so slightly crooked front tooth. "And I'll be even happier when I order." He began craning his neck again. "I don't see the waitress, do you? Where do you think she disappeared to? I went from kind of hungry to starving."

"So, we'll go together this weekend, then?"

Turning to her, cocking his head. "Go where?"

"The Fourth of July party at the club."

There was a one-second pause, and in that second Alice's relief turned into disappointment: nothing between them had really changed.

"I don't think that's such a good idea."

"Why not?" she demanded.

"I'd prefer for you and me to just stay, you know, you and me." Her feelings must've shown on her face, because he reached suddenly for her hand, began talking fast: "Look, not for forever, just for now."

"I was joking a couple days ago about the secret-shame thing, but are you ashamed of me?" she said, trying to control the wobble in her voice, and failing.

"God, no. Of course not. This has nothing to do with you. It's"—looking at her, looking away—"it's my family."

"Your family? Why would your family care if we were dating?" she said, really trying to understand him, understand where he was coming from.

"They've just been through a lot lately. The divorce, the trial, my dad losing his medical license."

"Yeah, but it's like a fake divorce, right? And things are looking up for your dad. I thought it seemed like he was going to get that job with the hedge fund guy, Sloane's father."

"Actually, he got the offer just before I left the house to meet you."

"That's good news," she said. And then, noticing the troubled look on Tommy's face. "I mean, isn't it?"

He shifted uncomfortably in his seat. "No, it is good news. Beyond good news, in fact."

"Then I don't understand what the problem is."

A beat passed, and then Tommy said, "I wasn't being totally honest with you a minute ago."

Alice withdrew her hand from his, folded her arms across her chest. "Okay," she said, her voice cool.

"It isn't for my family's sake that I want us to be secret. It's for mine. Actually it's for yours."

"You're going to have to explain that."

"Look, I like you, really like you. And I want to be with you and only you." She melted a little when she heard those words. But then she froze up again when he went on to say, "It's just, I need for us to keep our relationship private. Just for a little while longer."

"Private? You mean, something you lie about."

"Why would you say that, Alice? Since when do the words *private* and *lie* mean the same thing?"

"Since you decided I'm some kind of circus freak you can't be seen with in public," she said, worn out from trying to be rational and logical, giving in to wild emotion.

"What?"

"Yeah, apparently I'm some mutant monster you can only show affection to when there are no witnesses present."

"What you're saying is so ridiculous I'm not even going to justify it with a response."

"Right. I'm the ridiculous one."

"Why is it so important to you that we be Serenity Point's golden couple, junior division, anyway?" He paused, looking at her desperately. "What's your obsession with everybody knowing about us?"

The question brought Alice up short. She was stumped as to

how to respond to it. Answering it honestly, opening up to him about her mom and Richard, was a risk, not just a personal risk, as in it was embarrassing for her; it was a risk for her family, as well: it would ruin her mother's reputation if word got out, Richard's too—cheating on a terminally ill woman is almost unforgivable—and could also affect Richard professionally, keep him from getting jobs. But if she wanted to make her case with Tommy, she felt she had to be truthful. Felt she had to tell him that Maggie was Richard's mistress, his secret girlfriend, before she was his wife. Otherwise how could Tommy understand why the idea of being his secret girlfriend was so unbearable to Alice? "If you really want to know, I'll tell you," she said. And then she did.

When she was finished, she looked at him. His eyes were on her, the expression on his face pained. "I'm sorry," he said.

Just hearing those two simple words, she started to come undone, a lump forming in her throat, tears suddenly clouding her vision. She blinked them back furiously. Shrugging, trying to sound breezy, she said, "Now you get why it's so important to me that we not hide this."

"I do get it," he said, the expression on his face moving from pained to agonized. "And I hate to say this, but it doesn't change things for me. And don't ask me why it doesn't because I can't tell you."

"I just told you something I didn't want to tell you."

"It's too risky."

Really mad now, hurt as well, Alice said, "And I didn't take a risk?"

"Alice, you're not understanding me. It's not that I don't want to tell you, it's that I *can't* tell you. You have to believe me, I would if I could."

There was a pleading note in his voice, and hearing it caused the anger she was feeling toward him to vanish. "Tommy," she said softly, "what is it? What's going on here?"

He turned his eyes away from her, took a second to compose himself. When he turned them back, they were glassy, slightly red, but his voice was calmer, slower: "I know this is hard for you. I know you want to be in a normal, out-in-the-open relationship, not hiding in the shadows, but believe me when I tell you, the shadows are where we belong right now. It's where we're safe."

"Safe from what? I haven't noticed any menacing forces around me lately. I mean, apart from Mrs. Buckley."

He gave her a weak smile. "That's because you're still new in town. You don't know how to look." He shook his head, sighed. "I should probably let you break up with me like you want to."

She let out a cheerless laugh. "I don't want to break up with you, Tommy. In fact, it's pretty much the last thing I want to do."

As if he didn't hear her, "I should let you because I'm trouble. I'm bad news, Alice. That night, when Camilla died—"

At the mention of her dead stepsister's name, Alice's heart leapt, began beating wildly in her throat. "Yes?" she said breathlessly.

"It didn't happen like everybody thinks it did."

"What do you mean?"

His voice sinking to a miserable whisper, "I've already said too much. Please don't make me say any more."

The silence between them stretched. At last she said, "Okay. I won't."

He looked up at her, surprised, grateful. "You won't?"

"No."

"Why the change of heart?"

"Because I trust you," she said, though she might have said, *Because I love you*, since it was at that exact moment that she realized she did.

Chapter
• SEVENTEEN •

*I*n what felt like no time but in reality was probably fifteen or twenty minutes, Alice was back at the house. She felt as if her body had made the decision to leave Redbone's and go to Richard's without her, as if it understood that her brain was too consumed by thoughts that were like pieces of a jigsaw puzzle she was trying to put together, failing to put together, to work out even the simplest of logistics, as if some emergency system had kicked in, taken a quick inventory of options, settled on the least troublesome one. As she climbed the steps leading to the deck, she looked up, saw Richard in the window of his second-floor office. A telephone was cradled between his jaw and his shoulder, and his mouth was moving. Good. He was occupied.

She entered the kitchen. Luz was unloading the dishwasher, listening to her iPod. The music leaking out of her tiny earbud speakers had a salsa-type beat. "Have you seen my mom?" Alice said. When Luz didn't turn around, continued transferring handfuls of knives and forks and spoons into the silverware drawer, gently shaking her hips, Alice tapped her on the shoulder.

Luz jumped three feet in the air. Hand to heart, she said, "Oh, Alice, you frightened me. You shouldn't sneak up on people like that."

Alice apologized, asked her question again.

"Your mom?" Luz said, closing the dishwasher door with a neat kick of her sneakered foot. "Outside somewhere, I think. The garden maybe?"

"The garden," Alice repeated, then headed there. She walked quickly, past the hedges and the rhododendrons, the vine-covered pergolas hugging the high walls of the house. She turned the corner, and suddenly there she was: Maggie. Maggie was wearing a sleeveless summer dress with polka dots on it and a floppy brimmed hat. A large wicker basket dangled from her wrist. She had shears in her gloved hand, was snipping small white roses from their stalks, beheading them. She was alone, which was what Alice had been hoping for.

As if sensing someone was watching her, Maggie looked up. Seeing Alice, she smiled. "I think I'm going to try floating blossoms in a bowl filled with water. I read about it in *Better Homes and Gardens*. It sounded pretty. Honey," she said, holding out the basket, "can you take this for a second? There's one flower up high, and I want to try and reach it. Or maybe you could since you're taller."

Alice stared at her mother. She was struck anew by how much Maggie and Charlie resembled one another: the features, the bodies, the coloring.

The smile fell off Maggie's face. "What is it? Alice, honey, you're scaring me. Why do you look like that? What's wrong?"

"Something's not adding up." It was only as the words left

Alice's mouth that she realized they were Dream Camilla's. "I've been holding off on this second talk, this second confrontation, because I've been looking for evidence. I know it sounds ridiculous, but that's what I've been doing. Trying to prove that there's weirdness afoot, or rottenness or badness, or whatever name you want to give it. Then I realized that I don't need evidence. My intuition is my evidence. Something isn't right. You're not telling me something. And it's about you and Richard and your relationship, and I want to know what it is."

Alice watched Maggie's face carefully as she spoke. Saw Maggie's expression change to no expression at all, drawing completely inward, her face turning as blank and rigid as a mask, as if she'd retreated behind it.

When Maggie continued to stare off into space, not saying anything, Alice snapped her fingers a couple times. Said, "Mom."

Maggie shook her head, like she was shaking off her stupor. Then said, "I didn't lie to you, you know. In that first conversation, I mean."

"No, I don't think you did lie to me. I think you told me the half-truth, and nothing but the half-truth. I want the whole truth now."

Slowly Maggie pulled off her gloves, then rested the gloves, the basket, and the shears on the ground. She opened her arms, held them out to Alice. Alice shook her head. Maggie regarded her for a moment regretfully, then dropped her arms and sat down on one of the granite benches, crossing her pretty, young-looking legs. She gestured for Alice to sit on the other. When Alice again shook her head, Maggie said, "You really just want to get right down to it, don't you?"

"Wouldn't you if you were me?"

"Maybe not. Not if someone who loved me as much as I love you told me to leave it alone."

Alice laughed. "So for my own good I should stay in the dark? That's what I'm hearing?"

Not laughing, deadly serious, Maggie said, "Exactly. Sometimes lies are necessary."

"Like when?"

"Like when the truth is sure to cause pain. Alice, I'm trying to protect you here."

Alice stared at her mother, at this woman she'd known all her life and never really known at all. "I don't want your protection," she said. "Tell me."

Maggie turned away from her, then turned back. There was something in her eyes—a wild look, maybe even a desperate one. "Why are you so fixated on the past anyway?"

"You mean the truth?"

"No, I mean the past. Why do you make such a fetish of it? You can't change it or undo it. It's dead and buried. So why go grave digging?"

"The past is never dead. It's not even past."

"You're quoting William Faulkner to me right now?" Maggie said, letting out an angry little laugh of disbelief.

"Your past is my past, too. I have the right to know," Alice said, and as she did, she held Maggie's gaze with her own, not allowing Maggie to blink or look away. And in Maggie's eyes she finally saw it, the anger and upset draining out, replaced by resignation and defeat, saw that her words had done the job at last, that she'd won. "Tell me," she said again.

Maggie nodded slowly, dragged her hands through her hair. She seemed so tired and done in all of a sudden, so beaten down, her shoulders slumping like all the bones in them had been shattered. Which was why Alice was surprised when all at once she was up, pinning Alice to the trestle, her eyes radiating a manic energy, her voice not dull and toneless, as Alice expected, but harsh and combustive as she said, "Like you don't already know."

"I don't. But I will when you tell me. Which you're going to do right now."

"But you won't understand."

"I don't need to understand. I need to know."

"You want to know so bad? Fine. Richard's your father." Maggie loosened her grip on Alice, sat back down. "He's your dad."

The shock Alice felt on hearing this news was double: first, the shock of the news itself, second, the shock of the news not being quite shocking, the realization that Maggie was right, that some part of her had known already. "Charlie's too?" she said.

"Just yours."

And suddenly everything made sense, the jigsaw pieces all fell into place. That Richard was her dad explained why he was so relaxed with Charlie, so much easier and more natural. He didn't give a shit. Not in a harsh way. He liked Charlie, wished good things for her; she was his wife's daughter after all, but he didn't take her personally. Why should he? She wasn't his. Alice wondered if her dad—no, Phil, not her dad; she'd have to stop thinking of him as her dad, she realized painfully—hated her now. He must. It explained why he hadn't called or written in months. How could he help but hate her after he'd been tricked into loving her and caring for her all those years, thinking of her as a daughter? She'd obtained his affections under false pretenses, even if unknowingly. It felt to Alice almost like he'd died. And, in a sense, he had. To her, he was no longer that person. That person no longer existed.

It was with a start that Alice realized Maggie was telling the story of her romance with Richard, was already a little ways in. Alice did her best to focus, but her hearing went in and out as she listened, so she missed chunks. She got enough of it, though. She got the gist:

Maggie was twenty-three. She was starting at Yale School of Drama in the fall, specializing in set design. She'd received a full scholarship, but there were still living expenses to be met, and she was looking for a way to make cash fast. Word was there was a rich beach community called Serenity Point not too far from New Haven, plenty of money to be made off tourists in the summer. She went and got herself a job as a waitress at one of the Point's more popular watering holes. The bartender was a twenty-six-year-old in between his first and second year at Harvard Graduate School of Design, Richard Flood. Richard and Maggie fell in love, only it was complicated. They were from different backgrounds: his fancy, hers not. Richard was home for the summer, helping his mom take care of his dad, in the advanced stages of Parkinson's. Bartending was a slumming job for him, one he was doing more to get out of the house than to generate income. He was also seeing another girl, Martha Briggs. She was the daughter of his parents' friends. It was a casual thing for him. He liked Martha well enough, and she sure liked him, and it made his mom happy. But it didn't make Maggie happy. And once Richard proved unwilling to commit to her, be exclusive, she said yes to Phil, the horn player in the cover band that played in the bar on Friday and Saturday nights, who'd been asking her out all summer. It wasn't just a revenge move. She genuinely liked Phil. They had a lot in common. Not only did he want to be an artist, but he was as politically engaged as she was as well. In fact, their first date was going to a NAFTA protest in Bridgeport. Richard, on the other hand, was totally apathetic as far as politics and human rights issues were concerned. And he was more than apathetic when it came to Phil, was downright hostile, referring to him as "that hippie," which he wasn't, and making fun of his Birkenstocks, which he didn't wear. Still, Richard was the one Maggie was in love with, as much as they fought, as little as they saw eye to eye. And, slowly but surely, they were starting to work things out, figure out a way to be together. And then, Martha came into the bar one night waving around one of those pee-stick thingies. She was pregnant. She said it was an accident, though Maggie had her doubts. When Martha refused to even consider an abortion, Richard did the honorable thing and married her.

"Not that it wasn't agonizing for him," Maggie concluded. "We both cried and cried and cried. His dad was dying, though, and his mom was in too delicate a state to accept a bastard grandchild. So." She shrugged. "We parted ways. But I never forgot him."

"But you ended up getting your prince and your happily ever after," Alice said. "That's what's really important, right?"

Maggie smiled a self-pleased smile, nodded.

"All you had to do was wait a few years and for a few bodies to fall. No biggie."

Maggie's smile quickly reversed into a frown. "That's not a very nice thing to say."

Alice let out a short, snorting laugh, but otherwise refrained from comment. For a long time she was silent, her brain straining to process certain details. For example, Maggie's passion for set design. Since when? Since where? And she wasn't just passionate about set design; she was gifted at it, too, had to be if she was accepted by Yale and on scholarship. So that's where Alice got her artistic talent from, not from Phil, like she'd always thought. And now she understood the origins of Richard's irrational hatred of stick-it-to-the-Man politics, as well. It was rooted in jealousy of Phil. No wonder he had fits over Alice's interest in the Occupy Wall Street movement. He perceived it as a threat to him, a direct challenge. And then there was the peculiar matter of her bedroom, Richard's giving her Camilla's when there were other free rooms in the house. Again, his behavior made complete sense now that she knew the backstory. Why wouldn't he think it perfectly natural for his two daughters to share a room?

The biggest details to process concerned Camilla's letter. Camilla had known that she and Alice were sisters. That's why she'd written only to Alice, not Alice and Charlie. And that weird jab about Alice's jeans—"I have a pair just like them"—wasn't a jab at all. She was teasing Alice rather than insulting her. She really did have those jeans, too, *jeans* as in *genes.* They shared DNA.

At last Alice regained her bearings enough to speak. "When did you find out you were pregnant with me?"

"About a month after Richard and I broke up," Maggie said. "It could've been Richard's or Phil's. I chose to believe it was Phil's."

"Yes, I suppose he was the more convenient option at the time, the other one basically being off the table."

If Maggie registered the sarcasm in Alice's voice, she didn't show it. "I called Phil. Told him I was going to have a baby. He immediately proposed. I dropped out of Yale. Not that *dropped out* was the term I used. A *voluntary leave of absence*, I believe, is what I went with—less permanent-sounding—but even at the time I knew it was for good. Get off the grad school train, it's hard to get back on. I married Phil and moved into his one-bedroom apartment in Medford. He was beginning to get sideman work in Boston and Cambridge, I earned extra cash waitressing at a bar in Beacon Hill, and our life just started to take shape."

"You didn't tell Richard you were pregnant?"

"Not until years later. As you grew up, you looked more and more like him. That blond hair—his was as blond as yours when he was young—the shape of your eyes, even certain inflections in your speech, ways of standing. And the mouth, my goodness, it's his, identical down to the last contour, though fuller, of course. You were his. When you were around fourteen, I contacted him. It was just to tell him about you, show him pictures. I asked him if he'd be willing to take a paternity test. Not because I wanted anything from him, money or any of that, but just to know. He did, happily. And the answer was what we expected it would be, what we hoped it would be. Seeing each other again, it was like no time at all had passed. We were as in love as ever, more." Maggie's eyes went misty, lost in the past, lost in memories.

"Hey," Alice said, getting in Maggie's face. "Earth to mom."

Maggie blinked, returned to the present. Focusing her gaze on Alice, she said, "And the rest you know. It's what I told you a couple days ago in my bedroom."

"Did Martha know about you two, that you'd resumed your affair?"

"No. Though I suspect she knew he was seeing someone. She watched him so closely," Maggie said, allowing a note of contempt to enter her voice. "I suppose that's because she never really had him."

"Then how did Camilla find out?"

A vertical line appeared between Maggie's brows. "About me and Richard? I don't think she ever did." Thinking about it, shrugging. "Maybe after Martha died? You'd have to ask your dad."

Alice flinched.

Maggie, not noticing, added, "He and I were steering clear of each other during that period for obvious reasons."

Testing Maggie, watching her face for any telltale signs of deception, Alice said, "So, as far as you know, Camilla wasn't aware of you two, that there even was a you two."

"As far as I know, no."

Alice could tell from the way Maggie was looking at her that she thought it strange Alice was persisting in this line of questioning. Maggie wasn't lying. She really didn't know. Wow, so Alice was in possession of a piece of information that Maggie didn't have. First time in a while, maybe ever. It felt good, and Alice decided to keep feeling good a little longer, decided not to share with Maggie. "What about da—Phil?" she said. "Did he know whose daughter I was?"

"Not until I told him I was leaving him for Richard. He never knew Richard and I were a couple. I mean, he didn't really work at the bar, was just in and out a couple nights a week, so . . ." She let her voice trail off.

"So he was a perfect sucker," Alice finished for her.

Maggie shrugged, nodded. "The truth was, he wasn't as good a father as you thought. He never really earned a dime, could hardly support us. And you girls were going to be heading off to college soon. Richard could provide you with so much."

"Right, because money's the only thing a father can give his child."

"It's not the only thing, but it's a big thing."

Alice looked over at Maggie. Her mouth was curling up into that self-pleased smile again. Seeing it, Alice felt a dull, deep rage burning inside her. Without another word, she turned, began walking out of the garden.

Maggie's voice stopped her: "You're not going to tell Charlie, are you?"

"Of course I am," Alice said, although she hadn't thought about it until that second.

"I'm asking you not to."

"Why? So you can play her for the fool even longer?"

"So I can tell her myself." There was a throb of silence, and then Maggie said, "Please, sweetheart, let me be the one to tell her."

Alice heard the begging note in her mother's voice, and when she did, she understood that her mother was at her mercy. Alice liked that idea. The tables were finally turning. "No," she said simply.

"It would be cruel."

Alice snorted. "You'd know all about that. Not too eager for a taste of your own medicine, I see."

The smile was gone from Maggie's face now, and tears were in her eyes as she reached out a hand to touch Alice's cheek. "Cruel not just to me, to Charlie as well."

It *would* be cruel to Charlie, Alice realized, hearing that she was the odd man out in the family she loved so much. Alice suddenly felt like crying, too, but she wouldn't let herself. This scene between her and her mother was almost over. Whatever she'd thought knowing the truth would do for her, it hadn't. And she wanted to hurt her mother the way she'd been hurt. It was the last bit—the only bit—of real power she had, and she'd use it, even if it meant hurting Charlie, even if it meant hurting herself. She brushed Maggie's hand away, more roughly than necessary. Said, "No," again.

As Alice walked into the house, she could hear the sounds of Maggie's sobs behind her. She kept walking.

Stepping into the entrance hall, Alice was confronted by one of the many portraits that lined the downstairs walls: a Flood girl in a gilt frame. Staring at the face that was staring back at her, Alice could see the resemblance, not just to Richard, but, for the first time, to Camilla, as well. And to herself. Then she blinked, saw that it wasn't a portrait she was looking at—it was a mirror, the tall cloudy one, the glass inside it not gilt-framed, but gilt-edged. It seemed to Alice, as she stood there, peering at her own reflection, pale against the house's dim interior, so dim you couldn't distinguish floor from wall from ceiling, everything an amorphous dark, that she was standing at the edge of the world, and if she didn't tread carefully, took one false step, she'd fall off it into black nothing.

After a minute or so, Alice walked out the door she'd just walked through, went around to the back.

As Alice climbed the steps to the deck for the second time that day, she wondered how Camilla had found out they were sisters if not from her mother, wondered what had tipped her off. Had she somehow stumbled onto the name of the woman Richard was two-timing her mom with, then connected it with the name of an old girlfriend of Richard's that her grandmother had let slip at some time or other? (Connected it by first name since Maggie had taken Phil's last. Even more Sherlock Holmesian of her.) Or had she somehow stumbled onto the name of the woman Richard was two-timing her mom with, then done an Internet search? Maybe when she'd found Maggie, Alice had popped up, too, that old picture in the *Globe*. Maybe Camilla had studied it—crazy to think that Camilla might have looked at a picture of her with the same intensity as she'd looked at that picture of Camilla—and picked up on the likeness.

Alice began moving quicker, climbing the steps two at a time, eager to get into the house and up to her room, shut the door behind her. She wanted very badly to be in a private, secure space where she could be by herself with her thoughts. She'd just reached the deck when she nearly collided with Charlie, moving equally fast in the opposite direction. Charlie was dressed for the beach, bikini top, cutoff shorts, flip-flops. Alice was so happy to see her sister's pretty, suntanned face, smell her clean coconut-y smell, she had to restrain herself from jumping into her arms.

Charlie didn't seem quite as overjoyed at the chance run-in. "Oh," she said, shifting the strap of her bag from her left shoulder to her right, "hi."

"Hi, yourself. Guess you're going to change at the club." Off Charlie's blank look: "Your afternoon tennis clinic. It starts soon, right?"

Charlie blinked, then nodded. "Yeah, really soon. And I'm a little late. Like you said, I still have to change first."

When Charlie started to move past her, Alice said, with a laugh, "Hey, space cadet, you forgot your racquets. Tough to play without those."

"Actually, I'm skipping today. We're focusing on serves and I can practice serves on my own, so . . ." Charlie trailed off, began looking at her nails, her flip-flops, the horizon. Anything to avoid eye contact.

At first Alice just thought that Charlie was being moody and weird, but then she looked at her sister's face, saw the shifty-guilty expression on it, the gaze that didn't want to be pinned down, that kept trying to slip away. Alice turned, spotted Jude and Cybill stretched out on a towel on the beach below. And in that instant Alice understood that Charlie had been lying to her, or at least had been hiding the truth from her—just as bad—that Charlie was still seeing Jude. Suddenly, the anger Alice had been feeling all day and keeping a lid on, through her scene with Tommy at Redbone's, then with her mother in the garden, boiled up, got so intense she started to physically tremble, her breath coming out in little sharp gasps, her brain dizzy. At last she had a target: her sister. And everything she needed to bring that target down: Richard's true identity, *her* true identity, Charlie's outsider status.

What was the matter with Charlie anyway? Wild in all the wrong ways. Not wild like Camilla was wild, out of control but in it at the same time, calling the shots, running the show. Camilla, who only looked proper and pretty and girlish in her immaculate tennis whites and bouncy teen-queen ponytail but was really dark and dangerous and hell-bent, a femme fatale disguised as the all-American girl, her lips shiny with blood not gloss. No, Charlie was dumb wild, obvious wild, wild with no real purpose or to no real end. In fact, what she was doing couldn't even properly be termed being wild. It was misbehaving. And at someone else's command, no less: former Camilla boy toy and weak-link druggie, Jude Devlin.

"You're pathetic, you know that?" Alice said.

Charlie was too stunned to react immediately. She just stared, looking bewildered and victimized, totally unprotected, like she'd been punched in the face for no reason and without warning. All at once the anger drained out of Alice's body, replaced by horror. She wished she could suck the words out Charlie's ears and back into her own mouth, swallow them down into her belly. Because as mad as she was at Charlie, she loved her more and couldn't bear to see her upset or in pain, could bear even less the thought that she was the cause of her upset or pain. But it was too late.

Charlie's face had hardened, eyes flat, lips a straight white line. And then the lips parted. Out came spitting rage: "You hate me because Richard hates you."

"What?" Alice said.

"He can barely stand to be in the same room with you, but he likes me, and it drives you crazy. And you know what? I like him back. He's a better father than our crappy father ever was, and he needs a daughter. Camilla got bored with her life? Didn't want it anymore? Decided to throw it away, drive it off a bridge? Well, okay, I'll take it. Her loss, my gain."

"You don't mean that," Alice said quietly.

Charlie was crying now, hot, angry tears, not bothering to cover her face with her hands. "Don't tell me what I mean and don't mean."

"I'm sorry for what I said. It's just, Jude. He's not good for you."

"Oh, come on, Allie, you don't like anyone."

"He's bad, I'm telling you. A year ago, when Martha died, he—"

"A year ago?" Charlie repeated, like she couldn't believe what she was hearing. "Who the hell cares what happened a year ago? Besides, he told me about all that, the stint in rehab and everything else."

"No, not rehab. I don't care about rehab. It's—"

"Well I don't care about the past, his or anybody else's. I care about now, about the present. Just butt out, okay? You're a loner and a weirdo and you want me to be the same way."

"Charlie, that's not true."

"It is true. You're just jealous because I belong here and you don't."

Alice opened her mouth to reveal the truth about Richard, but no words came out. And in that moment, she realized that she wouldn't be the one telling Charlie. Not out of kindness to Charlie, out of fear for herself. She and Charlie had already moved so far apart since they'd arrived in Serenity Point, and it had only been a few weeks. The bond between them was fragile, and weakening by the day. If Charlie knew how frayed family ties had become, that they weren't even full sisters, that bond might break completely.

Alice closed her mouth. Wanted to close her ears, too, but she couldn't, so she closed her eyes instead. When she opened them,

Charlie was gone, off the deck, already moving down to the beach and over to the towel shared by Jude and Cybill, her back a smooth blank, the tattoo edited out by a Band-Aid. As Alice watched Charlie drop down beside them, accepting their gestures of comfort, a thought occurred to her: she'd gained a dead sister, but lost a living one.

Then a second thought occurred to her, this one causing her stomach to get that weak, fluttery, altitude-displaced feeling it got when she was flying and the plane hit an air pocket:

It had been Camilla's intention from the beginning to separate the girls.

Camilla, she understood, wanted Alice to herself. That had been the plan all along and Alice had fallen victim to it. She'd been played by Camilla as thoroughly as any dumb, hormone-addled boy. The monstrousness of this realization overwhelmed her. She suddenly recalled Cybill's words from that night at the club: *Nobody beats Camilla. She's stronger than anybody, above ground or below it.* Alice leaned on the railing of the deck and looked out.

Charlie, Jude, and Cybill were walking down the beach now, toward the club. A minute later they'd disappeared from view, and Alice wondered if there'd ever been a time when she'd felt so alone. She knew it was weird—beyond weird, sick, really—to blame a dead girl for her troubles, but she couldn't help herself. This was all Camilla's fault. Camilla, no longer living and yet the most alive person she knew. The most powerful, too. Camilla could come between people even if she wasn't in this world anymore. Could do it easy, without even breaking a sweat. A ghost who taunted as much as she haunted. And it was as Alice was thinking these thoughts that she heard it: the high, silvery tinkling. It might have been the wind chimes hanging above the sliding glass door, reacting to a breeze coming off the ocean. Might have been but wasn't, Alice knew. It was Camilla laughing at her from the other side of death, from beyond the grave.

Alice laid a palm flat on either side of her skull, pressed as hard as she could. Blocking her ears, though, didn't block out the sound. Just made it seem like it was coming from inside her head. *She loved her sister; she hated her sister. Her sister hated her; her sister loved her.* Alice turned and fled, running into the house so big that in it she felt like a doll in a house for humans, through the kitchen, and up the twisting staircase to her bedroom. The laughter followed her every step of the way.

ACKNOWLEDGMENTS

I'd like to bow deeply to my agent, Jennifer Joel. To Jennifer's assistant, Clay Ezell. And to the team at Razorbill, my editor Jocelyn Davies and publisher Ben Schrank. You've all been a pleasure to work with.

And my everlasting gratitude to John Holodnak and Robert Anolik, both of whom have read this book more times than any sinner ought.

A special thanks, too, to Allison Lorentzen, without whom none of this would have been possible.

Keep reading
for a sneak preview of

THIS SIDE
OF JEALOUSY

the second book
in the **INNOCENTS** series!

*T*ommy called Alice just before noon. She was in a bit of a panic because lunchtime was fast approaching and she didn't want to get stuck eating it with her mom and Richard, just the three of them. She'd holed herself in her room after breakfast so as to avoid her mom, in the garden checking roses for black spots, and Richard, in the office bent over his drafting board. Trapped herself in her room, was more like it. If evasion of Maggie and Richard was the goal, the simplest means of achieving it would have been to go somewhere they *weren't*. Only she had no car (Richard, after the fate that befell Camilla, was understandably wary of mixing adolescent girls and motor vehicles), and the club was off limits since Charlie was there and she'd promised to respect Charlie's need for space. Consequently, when Tommy asked her if she felt like going for a drive, she said yes even before the question was all the way out of his mouth. He laughed and told her he'd be right over.

Alice stood with her ear pressed to her door. When the loudest sound she could hear was her own heartbeat, she opened it, started down the wide, turning staircase that led to the first floor. She used to be afraid of the men and women in the portraits lining the walls of the front hall and entranceway. Floods, every last one of them, their dark eyes—watching eyes—following her from inside the heavy gilt frames, tracking her movements, storing up information on her comings and goings to report back to Richard. His informers. His *spies*. She was one of them now, though. Blood. They wouldn't dare tattle.

Keeping what Jane Austen would call her countenance, what Charlie would call her shit together, Alice walked out the front door, calmly returning any gaze she happened to meet on the way, maintaining an even, unhurried pace. At last she was in the sunshine. She knew Tommy wouldn't want to run into anyone from her family. Nor would she for that matter. So she decided to intercept him at the top of the driveway.

As she walked, she threw a quick glance over her shoulder. At a distance—up close, too—Richard's house appeared jaw-droppingly, eye-poppingly, heart-stoppingly grand. When she'd first seen it, she'd thought it looked like a castle in a fairy tale, beautiful but forbidding at the same time, the people inside it leading charmed lives that had been cursed. She was one of the people inside it now, and a cursed charmed life sounded about as accurate an assessment of her situation as she could imagine: it turns out she was really of noble birth, a princess disguised as a peasant girl, but with a father who may or may not have been an evil king; and though her mother was still her mother it was possible she was also a wicked witch, too; and as for the handsome prince who'd come to rescue her, well, he was still handsome and still princely, only he seemed in need of rescuing himself.

Speaking of which, here he was, on his white horse. Or, rather, in his cream-colored Volvo.

And it was as he was pulling up to her that it occurred to her wonder: should she tell him that she and Camilla were half sisters or not? Until this moment, she'd just assumed she would. After all, she'd been honest with him about everything else, even the ugly, shameful stuff like Maggie and Richard's affair, which had been going on while Martha Flood was dying of stage four breast cancer. Alice had put her trust totally in Tommy. And it wasn't a lack of trust that made her hesitate now. It was a fear of rejection. His feelings toward Camilla, his ex-girlfriend—his *dead* ex-girlfriend—were so powerful and so, largely, negative. What if the thought of being with someone who was so intimately connected to her, shared blood with her, turned him off? Like, what if he found himself repelled by Alice in ways that were instinctive and involuntary and thus un-get-over-able? That would be it for their romance. And Alice loved Tommy. She hadn't told him yet, had only just figured it out herself, but she did. The thought of losing him was painful to her to a degree that was almost unbearable.

So, for the second time that day, Alice decided to keep someone she was close to in the dark because she was afraid honesty would exact too high a price. It was a despicable move, she knew, craven and cowardly. But the truth of the matter was, she didn't think she could handle any more change or loss in her life. At the moment she was at her limit. It occurred to her that from another perspective she was only evening the score between them. After all, Tommy was keeping a secret from her, too. A big one. And one that also concerned Camilla. The other day at Redbone's Café, he'd said to her of Camilla's death, *it didn't happen like everybody thinks it did.* When she'd pushed him for more information, he'd started talking very quickly and very urgently about how Serenity Point was more dangerous than she realized. He had insisted that her ignorance was for her own good, that to be in possession of certain knowledge would put her in harm's way, and that he was just trying to protect her. Well, it could be argued that his ignorance was for his own good, that the possession of certain knowledge would put them in harm's way as a couple, and that she was just trying to protect the two of them. Okay, maybe she was reaching a little, pushing the comparison a bit hard to justify her own questionable actions. At least Tommy was being open about what he was concealing. She, on the other hand, was being flat-out deceptive.

Alice pushed these thoughts from her mind, resolving to sort them out later, as Tommy applied the brakes and rolled down the window, turned his face to her. She loved looking at him. He was handsome in the cleanest, most straightforward way imaginable: light brown hair and even features, long, lanky body, muscular from all the crew—he was set to row for the team at Harvard in the fall—strong, white teeth, the front two slightly overlapping. His beauty was of a totally different order than, say, Jude's. There was nothing decadent or androgynous about his appearance. He was what you envisioned when you were a little girl dreaming of your first boyfriend.

"Hop in," he said, and when she did, kissed her twice, the first kiss soft, the second hungrier.

She reached for her seatbelt. "We going anywhere in particular?"

"I told my mom I was taking the car to get a jump-start on

picking up college supplies. That's the only way she'd let me borrow it."

"This is your mom's? I just assumed you had your own car."

"I did. But we're down to two now. My dad had to trade in the Lexus."

Tommy's dad, Dr. van Stratten, had recently been sued for malpractice after a patient had almost died from a medication he'd prescribed. While Dr. van Stratten had managed to evade a prison sentence—it was touch-and-go there for a while—his medical license had been revoked. And when the wife of this patient had announced that she'd also be seeking damages, and thus potentially bankrupting him, Mrs. van Stratten had filed for divorce. (Though Tommy had told Alice that his parents weren't really splitting, that the divorce was a loophole thing, a way of protecting the family's assets, and that Mrs. van Stratten had to be pushed to do it.) Light, however, seemed to be shining at the end of the tunnel for Dr. van Stratten. He'd just been offered a position at a hedge fund in Stamford. Had, in fact, used Tommy—much to Alice's annoyance and dismay—to woo the daughter of the man who ran it.

"Sorry," Alice said.

Tommy shrugged. "It wasn't only about the money. We needed to get rid of one of the cars anyway since I'll be heading off to college in the fall."

"Yeah, it's not like you're going to be doing much driving in Harvard Square."

"Nope. What is it you have down there? The T?"

"That's right. The Massachusetts Bay Transportation Authority, referred to by the natives as the T. I can help you buy a metro card, tell you which stops and stations to avoid, which lines break down the oftenest—all that."

"My own private tour guide," Tommy said, with a tender smile.

Suddenly shy, Alice broke off eye contact. "So, shopping for school supplies. Okay, I'm up for it even though it's barely July. What should we buy first? Dry erase boards? Laundry bags? Ethernet cords? I guess I'm going to be needing that stuff, too, for Wolcott."

Alice and Charlie would not be graduating from Rindge and Latin, nicknamed *Sy*rindge and Latin because of its druggy rep, the public high school in Cambridge where the sisters had begun their academic careers. Instead, this fall they'd be transferring to Wolcott Academy, a boarding school located on thirty rolling acres just outside of Montpelier, Vermont, and known for its elevated scholastic standards as well as its low student-teacher ratio; Alice as a senior, Charlie as a junior.

"No, no," Tommy said, "that was just a line to get my mom to hand over the keys to the Volvo. I'll do that boring stuff with her, not you."

"All right. But I really don't mind."

"How about I show you around Serenity Point?"

"You do realize I've been living here for almost a month now."

"Yeah, but how much of Serenity Point have you really seen? The club? A little bit of the harbor? The downtown area? A private beach or two?"

"I thought that was all there is."

"Oh, no. That's only *mostly* all there is."

Alice laughed. "Then by all means, show me the rest."

• • •

The rest turned out to be the Serenity Point lighthouse, just across the bay on the western bluff. (Tommy had actually taken Alice once before. Had tried to, anyway. They'd driven to the lighthouse, parked in front of the lighthouse, but never quite made it out of the car and inside the lighthouse.) The lighthouse, Tommy informed her, was one of the oldest in the country, built out of wood in 1777, rebuilt out of stone in 1812 after a fire—a suspected, though never proven, case of arson—had destroyed the original. The spot was a lovely one, so private and unspoiled it must've looked much as it had a hundred years ago, Alice thought, no, *two* hundred years ago, when it was constructed for the second time.

"So you like it?" Tommy asked, after they climbed to the top of the lighthouse tower, climbed back down, explored the old keeper's house next door.

"I love it."

He looked hard at her face, like he was trying to gauge the truthfulness of her statement. "Really?"

"Really," she said gently, reaching for his hand, squeezing it. "It's the best thing I've seen in Serenity Point. Looking at it makes me feel lonesome but in a way I like, the same way I get when I'm standing in front of an Edward Hopper painting."

His voice happy, "You should paint it."

"Somebody should."

"Why not you? I thought you loved to paint."

"Well, I brought my sketch pad and pencils from home. They're sitting on my desk in my room at Richard's. And I know I brought my acrylics, too. But I can't find the box I packed them in. They must've gotten lost in the move. I'll just have to get another set, I suppose. It's just, I hate to spend money on something that still might turn up. Richard didn't want Charlie or I to get jobs this summer, which means I'd have to ask him for the cash. Oh well"— shaking her head at herself, smiling—"it'll teach me not to be so casual about labeling."

"Just the paints?"

"Unfortunately, no. Brushes, canvases, easel, palette. All of it, pretty much. Everything was packed in the same box, you know?"

He nodded. "Sure. Well, that explains why I've never seen you paint."

It did and it didn't. While a lack of supplies was part of the reason Alice hadn't been painting, it wasn't the whole reason. She also connected the activity with her father, or the man she used to think was her father, Phil. Phil was a trumpeter, jazz by training and inclination, but often taking jobs with rock bands to pay the bills. He was in Japan right now, doing sideman work for a pianoless quartet, and had been out of contact with the family since he and Maggie split at Christmas. He and Alice had always been close, their shared artistic interests a strong bond between them. Picking up a paintbrush or a sketching pencil now only reminded her of him, of all she'd lost in learning the secret of her paternity.

"I've got something for you," Tommy said. "Well, for us. Wait here."

He disappeared, and a minute later she heard the slam of a trunk. When he reappeared, he had a blanket draped over his shoulder, a couple of plastic bags dangling from his wrist.

"You brought lunch?" Alice said, delighted.

"I wasn't sure what kind of sandwiches you liked so I got a few—tuna salad, ham and swiss, roast beef. There's a vegetarian option in there, too. Avocado and cheddar, I think. Take whichever you want. I like them all equally. And there's fruit salad and soda, diet and regular, and chocolate chip cookies for dessert."

"Oh, Tommy," she said, throwing her arms around his neck, "you went to so much trouble."

"It was no trouble," he said, blushing. "I mean, I wanted to do it."

There were a scattered tables and benches around the base of the lighthouse. Alice and Tommy, though, chose to have their picnic on a shady spot a couple hundred yards away from the area designated for the public, just on the other side of a swell in the land and so out of sight. They spread the blanket on a bit of ground that was half grass, half sand, laid out the food and drinks.

After they'd finished eating, Alice curled up next to Tommy, settling her head in the crook of his arm. It was a warm day rather than a hot one, a soft breeze passing over her, working its way into her clothes. As she stared at the sky above, watching a fat white cloud blow across the sun, momentarily eclipsing it, she realized that she hadn't thought about her mom or Richard or her fight with Charlie in almost an hour, and it was because of Tommy and the perfect afternoon he'd arranged. She stretched her neck up, pressing her lips to the underside of his jaw. He laughed and told her she was tickling him, then leaned over and kissed her for real.

They kissed and talked, talked and kissed. And in such a pleasant manner, the day began to pass. After a while, though, the kissing and the talking tapered off, and they fell into a drowsy half sleep.

"Did I travel from Hanover in a time machine or a car?" a voice said.

Alice surfaced from the dream she was having and looked up. The sudden glare of sunlight after the dimness of her closed eyelids made it difficult for her to see the figure standing above her as anything but a tall, dark shape. After a moment, though, her vision adjusted and details emerged: the figure belonged to a man, young, in a suit and tie, sunglasses. Alice supposed she should be frightened, a male stranger coming up to a sleeping teenage couple in an out of the way spot. If this guy was an ax murderer, though, he was a well-dressed one. A chatty one, too.

"You tell us," she said, smoothing down her shirt, making sure all the buttons were fastened.

The young man made a disappointed face. "A car. You're not who I thought you were."

"Sorry."

Not registering the sarcasm of her tone, or pretending not to, the young man said, "Oh, don't be. It's just, you look like someone I used to know."

Alice tried to see the eyes behind the dark, reflective lenses. She couldn't, though. All she could see was herself. Herselves, rather. Two of them, shrunk down and slightly warped. "Let me guess," she said, "a girl who you used to know but don't know anymore because she died."

"You must get that a lot around here."

"You have no idea."

The young man laughed, clapped Tommy on the shoulder.

There was something off about his manner, Alice thought. It was odd, a little too intimate.

"So, did you grow up around here?" she asked.

"Yes, but not in the way you mean," the young man said to Alice. And then to Tommy, "Well, I think it's safe to say you have a definite type, kiddo."

Alice looked over at Tommy in surprise. Tommy was sitting up, perfectly still, staring at the young man. Obviously, Tommy knew him. Equally obviously, Tommy didn't like him.

"You going to introduce me to your little friend here?" the young man asked.

"Hey, you stole my line," Alice said, confused, a touch angry, as well. She didn't appreciate being referred to as a *little* anything, not in this context, not by this guy.

"Alice Flaherty, Nick Chillingworth," Tommy said, his eyes never leaving Nick's face.

"Nice to know you, Alice."

"Nick used to work for my dad."

Nick shoved his hands in his pockets, rocked back on his heels. "How is the old man, anyway? I was sorry to hear about his troubles. The bad news traveled all the way up to New Hampshire." Nick's words were the proper ones, polite and sympathetic, yet somehow his tone negated that politeness and sympathy. Changed the words' meaning, made them nasty and jeering.

"My dad's fine," Tommy said, a defensive note entering his voice. "Better than fine, actually. He's about to start working as a consultant on the pharmaceutical industry for a hedge fund."

"Glad to hear it. Not that it's a surprise. Your dad's a survivor.

I always tell people, bet on Dr. van Stratten. He'll come through. No matter how dire the circumstances, he'll figure out a way to save himself."

Again Nick had said the right words, the words any courteous person would say in such a situation, but in a way that subverted their meaning, somehow turning a generic compliment into the most pointed of insults.

Tommy nodded once, tightly, clearly wishing to close the subject.

Nick, though, kept going: "Even if everybody around him is drowning, he'll find the one life preserver. Tear it out of the hands of an infant if he has to." This last line got a laugh from the speaker himself. "So, Tommy, I was thinking about swinging by your parents' house later today, saying hello. Think I should?"

"I think you should do whatever you want."

"I was planning on talking to your dad. Telling him I'll be interning this summer at Dr. Rose's office. Do you know Dr. Rose?"

Another tight nod from Tommy. His skin was pale. Alice saw a little vein in his forehead begin to throb.

"Of course you do," Nick said smoothly. "Serenity Point is a small town. Not too many concierge doctors in it."

"No there aren't," Tommy agreed.

"I just interviewed with Dr. Rose at the club over lunch."

"You must've really wowed him if he offered you the position right then and there."

"Oh, he didn't offer it to me. Not yet. But he will. I understand he's the primary beneficiary of your father's misfortune. A lot of new clients—excuse me, patients—have been coming his way in the last few months. Can't imagine him turning down an extra pair of hands. Especially an experienced pair like mine."

When Tommy said nothing in response, and the silence started to grow into an awkward one, Alice stepped in. "So where are you staying, Nick? Do you have family in town?"

Nick turned to Alice, taking off his sunglasses. For the first time, she got a real look at his face. It was thin-lipped, sharp-nosed, keen-eyed—the face of an animal known for its cunning, a fox maybe or a wolf. Also, it was younger than she initially thought it was. Much younger. He was probably only a year or two older than Tommy, two or three years older than she.

"Serenity Point's a little rich for my family's blood," he said. "I'm staying at a rooming house one town over."

"How did you find out about it?"

"Dr. Rose's secretary is friends with the woman who runs it. She got me a good deal."

Alice was racking her brain for another neutral topic, when Nick abruptly straightened. "Enjoy the rest of this beautiful afternoon, you two. A pleasure meeting you, Alice. Tommy, I'll be seeing you around."

As he sauntered off, his movements loose-limbed and springy, Alice thought to herself that maybe Nick wasn't an ax murderer, but he was violent, the violence in him coiled up and controlled. And all the more deadly for it.

The spell of the day was broken, no mending it. In silence, Alice and Tommy stood, began gathering together the trash, repacking the uneaten food, shaking out and folding up the blanket. They then started walking, Tommy carrying the bags back to the car as if they were full of something heavy, though they were much lighter than when he carried them from the car, Alice trying to restrain her curiosity until they were strapped in their seats, the engine humming, definitively out of earshot of Nick and anyone else, but wanting answers so badly she thought she'd burst with all the questions she had.

Relief, however, was not forthcoming. Alice made several attempts to start a conversation, ask more about the young man they'd just encountered: Who was he besides Dr. van Stratten's former assistant? Where did he come from, if not Serenity Point? How had Dr. van Stratten happened to hire him, under what circumstances? But Tommy's responses, when he responded at all, were one-worded. Grunts, basically. Alice would've gotten angry, only she noticed the pained, almost pleading look in his eye. His reluctance to speak obviously had something to do with Camilla—didn't *every*thing have something to do with Camilla where Tommy was concerned?—and thus something to do with his desire to protect Alice. (Nick knew Camilla, had to have if he mistook Alice for her. The question was, how well did he know her? What was the nature of their relationship?) Clearly Tommy wouldn't be providing Alice with any of these answers even though he had them. Alice was starting to get this itchy sensation, like when she got a scratch at the back of her throat and no amount of coughing or rasping would relieve her of it. Only now the itchy sensation was in her brain. She wanted to cry out in frustration.

To distract herself, Alice turned her attention to her window, letting the scenery slide past her eyes and into her brain. And it was as they crossed Greeves Bridge, the site of Camilla's grand exit, the repairs in the section of the barrier that she had rammed her car through—or so the official story went—still visible, that it occurred to Alice to wonder: was her relationship with Tommy damned, doomed from the start, the secrets between them too many and adding by the day, piling up, higher and higher, creating a wall so tall and so thick that soon they wouldn't be able to see each other over it, feel each other through it?

Tommy dropped Alice off at the top of Richard's driveway. His kiss was quick, closed-lipped, perfunctory, and he drove away fast. In the falling light, she began the long trek to the house, her movements as heavy as his had been back at the lighthouse. At last she reached the front door. Just as she was opening it, her cell phone, an old model and not a nice one even when it was new—unlike Charlie, she'd refused to let Richard buy her an iPhone—buzzed. A text message. Alice looked down eagerly, hoping it was Tommy, as unhappy with how they left things as she was, wanting to say goodbye properly. But it wasn't. It was Patrick.

Thinking of you

For the first time since she'd arrived in Serenity Point, certainly for the first time since she'd met Tommy, Alice was tempted to return one of Patrick's text messages, maybe even give him a call. It was funny. She wanted to talk to the boyfriend who was still not officially her ex to discuss the boyfriend that was not officially her boyfriend. Funny in a way that made her want to cry rather than laugh.

No, Alice decided, calling Patrick was not an option. She did her best to quell the surge of affection rising up in her. It wasn't easy, though. (Patrick, so unfettered! So uncomplicated! So what-you-see-is-what-you-get! And with a back story she knew by heart!) But if she did call him, she'd just be giving him false hope, especially since she couldn't mention Tommy. He'd just hear the sadness in her voice, and, not knowing the cause, think she needed him. And she couldn't mess with his emotions that way. He was too nice a guy.